A LEGACY FORGED

BLOODLINES LEGACY
BOOK THREE

USA TODAY BESTELLING AUTHOR
ROSE GARCIA

A Legacy Forged © 2026 ROSE GARCIA

Published by Pluma Publishing, LLC and Rose Garcia Books
Cover Concept by Get Covers Designs
Cover by Steven Novak
Editing by Karen Meeus
Map Illustration by Cartographybird
Map Additions by Cait Marie
Formatting by Cait Marie
ASL Consultation and Review by Kyle Shimpock

DEDICATION

For those who keep choosing hope even when the world is falling apart.

The dawn always comes.

TO THE FAR NORTH

THE EVENING SEA

THE
SUBLAND

SUMMIT
RANGE
WEST

QUIETUS
VALLEY

HIGH
MEADOW

MAJESTIC
CHASM

CUESTA

THE
SOUTH

THE FAE REALM OF
FAEVENLY

TORCH
LAKE

STRONG
HAVEN RUINS

MOTHER OF RIVERS

THE MORNING SEA

SUMMIT
RANGE

GREEN
FALLS

SAND
BLUFF

THE
GREAT
COVE

PROLOGUE

Before House Strong abolished the seasonal courts, before humans crossed into the fae realm, and before Princess Celyse uttered the prophecy, Lady Sonia received a message.

Lady Sonia jolted upright, breath ragged, her night-clothes drenched in cold sweat. "Sun, Moon, and Stars," she whispered. "What was that?" She pressed her hand to her chest, willing her heart to slow, flashes from her dream swirling in her mind.

The vision clung to her like a shroud. Mist black as ink oozed over valleys and fields, dirt and sand choked rivers and brooks, forests and their inhabitants disappeared into shadow. Even the Green Falls had been reduced to nothing but a glimmer of its once roaring power. The worst were the dragons. Once proud and mighty, she saw them writhing mid-flight and crumbling into ash, their wings dissolving like dust on a breeze.

1

Faevenly would topple into eerie silence. So slowly no one would notice until it was too late.

As she watched the vision's terror unfold, a single phrase echoed in her mind. A call. A plea. Impossible to ignore. *Protect the North.*

Her hands shook as she smoothed her long dark hair away from her face and sprang from bed, every muscle tight with urgency. No time to hesitate. No time to question. The message needed action. She dressed with speed, then slipped out of her bedchamber, her pace swift down the corridor. Drawing her cloak around her shoulders, she stepped into the crisp night air.

"Lady Sonia?"

She spun around to find Draven, the boy she and her coven sisters had rescued from an overturned carriage two years earlier. An uneasiness stirred within her whenever she met his ever-growing distrustful gaze. She would come to regret saving his life; she knew it in her bones, but now was not the time to dwell on it. The Sun, Moon, and Stars must have had a purpose for him. Besides, what was done was done.

She placed her hand on his slim shoulder. "What are you doing outside at this hour?"

He moved out from under her touch, as if she were a curse he feared would stick. His gaze stayed on the ground. "I like it out here."

She lowered her head, wishing she could help him. Perhaps later. "Please, Draven. Go inside and get some rest. I will return in a few days."

With a flick of her cloak, she rushed to her steed and mounted quickly, spurring the beast into action. She rode for days, stopping only for short breaks. Finally, the lush landscape morphed from green and vibrant to icy and cold. How long would it take for the Valians to meet her? Not long, knowing the dragonfolk. Sonia was sure they had sensed her presence the moment she entered their land.

Her horse slowed as a brood of dragons soared across the skies, their multicolored scales sparkling in the sunlight. And on land, a single rider approached.

"Here we go," she muttered, patting the horse's neck. "Stay sharp, my girl."

The Valian closed in like a storm sweeping across the frost. Closer now, Sonia recognized Zalarae, the young leader of the dragonfolk. Why would she approach alone?

Zalarae's silver steed circled hers, prancing in a show of superiority before coming to a complete stop. She nodded. "Lady Sonia."

"Zalarae." She nodded back. "I take it my arrival is no surprise?"

"It is not. We received a vision and knew you would be coming. Please, follow me."

Spurring her horse forward, she followed Zalarae over a frosty field, through snow-laden pines, until they reached a clearing where a shimmering dragon with hues of blue, purple, and pink waited. Sonia reined in, her gaze caught by the sight. She had never seen such a magical beast up close.

"This is *Izel*." Zalarae dismounted in one fluid motion. "She knows what must be done to protect the North."

Good. Sonia knew something needed to be done, but she had no idea what. With a slight bow, she said to the dragon, "I am Lady Sonia. I am honored to be of service." She held her position for a few seconds before straightening. "But pray tell, what does the Wild North need protection from?"

Though Sonia aimed the question at *Izel*, Zalarae answered. The silver-haired frost fae moved in front of the dragon. With flared nostrils, she jutted her chin, the clean, sharp scent of snowmelt and wild pine carrying with her. "From you, the Faevenly fae." She narrowed her eyes at Sonia. "And humanfolk. They are coming."

Sonia had dreamed of humans crossing into the realm. She saw death and destruction, but also beauty and life. Should she argue for things to unfold as they would? To let the natural order proceed? She knew Zalarae well enough to know she would not listen. Besides, the message Sonia had received rang clear.

Whatever the reason, whatever was coming, the North needed protecting. "How may I be of assistance?" Sonia asked.

The dragon stirred. With a low rumbling breath, the creature lifted her head. Her wings unfurled, graceful and wide, sending ripples of cool air through Sonia's long hair. With the quiet dignity of an ancient queen, *Izel* moved forward with elegance, talons crunching softly in the frost. Her bright, intelligent eyes met Sonia's with a keen, assessing gaze.

"*Together, we will fashion a veiled boundary.*" She crouched low. "*Climb onto my back, and I will show you, lady,*" the dragon said inside her mind.

Sonia's heart beat with a wild rhythm. Magic whispered through the clearing, old and sacred. But what if she misread the vision? What if this dragon turned on her midair? Cast her down like ash on the wind?

Her palms tingled. Her muscles tensed. She had always trusted her power, but this felt like stepping into the unknown with nothing but faith to carry her. Should she risk it? Still, the vision's message echoed. *Protect the North.*

With the scents of frost and pine filling her lungs, Sonia set her fear aside. She studied *Izel's* eyes, which now shone brighter, radiating with an ancient warmth. The Sun, Moon, and Stars had never led her astray. Surely, they would not do so now.

Pulling her shoulders back, Sonia stepped forward and climbed *Izel's* wing. Maneuvering around the spines, she found a spot along the base of the neck to sit. She held on to the thick ridge there.

"*I am in place,*" Sonia thought.

Izel shifted, muscles rippling under Sonia like waves beneath a mighty ship. Then, with a great thrust of her wings, they launched.

Wind roared past Sonia's ears, and her breath caught in her throat as the ground fell away. The pine trees shrank, the frost-laced clearing became a blur, and the sky opened wide all around her like a vast, pale ocean.

She clutched *Izel's* ridge and tightened her legs, heart pounding, not from fear now but from excitement. Below them, the Wild North stretched endlessly with snowy ridges and rivers winding like silver veins. Beyond it all, the jagged mountain peaks clawed at the sky.

The wind slowed as *Izel* circled lower, wings dipping as they neared the eastern edge of the North. *"It is time, lady."* She hovered midair, like a creature carved from sky and ice.

Sonia stayed still. *"What will you have me do?"*

"Lean forward," Izel instructed. *"Place your hands on the scales near my throat. Lend me your magic so that my fire may become more than flame."*

With a nod and a swallow, Sonia stretched out her arms. Her palms hovered over the scales at *Izel's* neck. She hesitated for only a moment before pressing her hands down. She held steady, the dragon's pulse beating against her skin like a living drum. The powerful hum filled her chest, resonating with the magic curling in her bones. She focused on her power, drawing it forward with her will, then began chanting out loud as the words rose to her lips. A spell, ancient and instinctive. It poured from her like a prayer.

Veil of frost, veil of flame,
Keep the wild, protect the name.
Mist and fire, sky and stone,
Let the North stand safe, alone.

She repeated the spell over and over, the words braiding into her thoughts as *Izel* surged forward. They flew steady and low while Sonia kept her hands pressed down and her eyes shut. Her magic flowed into the dragon, weaving into the force she could feel bubbling in *Izel's* throat.

And then—*Izel* released it.

Sonia's eyes snapped open as a column of flame erupted from the dragon's jaws, not orange and red, but silver and blue. The blast danced and rippled, like ice and moonlight made one. With her spell still repeating, Sonia shifted and peered downward. Wherever the fire touched, the land shimmered like a curtain of glassy silk. From its edges, mist began to rise. Not smoke, but a thin, nearly invisible barrier. It bent the air and shimmered with light, forming a line like a seam between worlds.

They soared along the Wild North's border, coast to coast, sky to stone, marking the land with fire, spell, and will. When the work was done, they circled back to where they had started and touched down near the barely visible glow.

Sonia sagged, breathless, her hands still resting against *Izel's* warm scales. "Is it done?" she asked, her voice in a whisper, hoarse from magic and wonder.

"It is," *Izel* replied out loud. "Now, lady, before you dismount, take one of my scales. Keep it in memory of what we shared here today."

Sonia blinked, stunned, her breath catching in her throat. A dragon's scale. One of *Izel's* own. The offering felt impossibly sacred, heavier than any crown or blade. "I am honored," she said.

Her hands trembled as she reached out. She brushed her fingertips over the dragon's smooth scales, resting on the curved edge of one near her throat. It hummed like a pulse of living magic. With care and reverence, Sonia slipped her fingers beneath the scale's edge, easing it free from where it nestled between larger plates. It gave way with a soft pop, releasing a tuft of warmth, as if *Izel* herself had exhaled in approval.

Sonia lifted it to her chest, pressing the scale over her

heart. For a moment, she closed her eyes, breathing in the curious, metallic scent—something like rain on stone mixed with smoke and salt.

Bowing her head, she spoke in a soft but resolute voice. "I vow to keep it well."

Izel's voice rumbled low and ancient, tinged with wind and wisdom. "When the way is lost, and your heart is heavy with doubt, remember this moment. Remember the fire we shared. The scale will answer when it is time."

A shiver ran through Sonia—not from cold, but from the weight of the words. "I will remember." She slipped the scale into the inner pocket of her cloak. "Thank you, *Izel*."

Zalarae approached, her steps quick and hurried as she joined them. She kept her gaze on the newly created boundary. "Will it hold?"

"Yes," *Izel* answered as a tuft of smoke puffed into the air. "The magic will hold as long as the North's guardians remain."

"The North will never fail," Zalarae declared.

Prying her stiff legs from her perch, Sonia dismounted with a shaky step. She stamped her feet against the ground to steady herself, then approached the magical border. Her fingertips grazed the surface, a quiet power vibrating against her skin. "What will happen to those who venture here? The Faevenly fae?"

"They will know the border magic when they are here; they will forget it when they leave," *Izel* answered. Her gaze roamed from Sonia to Zalarae. "Any who cross into the Wild North will lose their memories and be claimed by the land forever."

Sonia's hand dropped. The implications swirled around her like smoke, impossible to ignore. *Claimed by the land forever.* It sounded like being held prisoner.

She loved her realm—its beauty, its wild, untamed magic. She would protect it with everything she had. Though she had aligned with the Valians, she would stand against them if need be. Would it come to that?

A heaviness settled in her heart, deeper than duty, like the echo of a future already written. She saw it in the shadows of her vision—the fall of Faevenly, the price she would pay. Losing many along this now chosen path.

She offered Zalarae and *Izel* a silent nod. She did not know when, or even why, but she would be back. With a final glance at the boundary, Sonia turned and mounted her steed. Cloak drawn tight, she rode into the thinning light. The path she had chosen would not spare her.

Still, it might just save them all.

CHAPTER ONE

Avalynn plunged toward her death. Eyes squeezed shut. Heart shattering. Mateo did it. He let her go. Cold air sliced across her skin, wild and biting, as she fell faster and faster. How could he?

Tears streaked across her cheeks as the wind roared past her ears, drowning every thought but one—Mateo was lost. After everything they had endured, everything they had shared, she couldn't break through the shadow magic that had consumed him. And now she would die for it.

Or maybe not? *Izel* could save her.

Her gaze flicked about. The sky above was awash in purples and grays, swallowing the last streaks of amber and pink like ink poured into water. But where was the dragon?

A tug pulled at her back. She looked behind her. Her sword! It slipped free from its scabbard, twisting in the air beside her. She lunged for it, fingers brushing the hilt, but it tumbled away, falling faster than she could reach.

No, no, no! Not the sword!

Her pulse surged, panic knotting in her chest like a tangled ball of breeding snakes. That blade was more than steel. It was her legacy, her purpose. It was her father's sword infused with human magic from her mother, Gabriela, and her grandsire, Julio. Without it, she was nothing. Without it, there was no hope.

She clawed at the air, stretching her fingers toward the shrinking glint of the blade as it spun out of sight. Gone. The purple-and-gray sky swallowed it, along with the last remnants of amber and pink.

A lump like ice lodged in her throat while the sun set. When she, Mateo, Lirien, Gareth, and Keeth crossed the magic border into the Wild North, they were told they'd have three days to return to Faevenly or be lost here forever. Not that it mattered now. She wouldn't survive this fall. So much for being the so-called Only One.

Soaring downward, every care was stripped away— her quest, her prophecy, Mateo's face, their fragile hope ... even Keeth, Lirien, Gareth, and the Sublander family who had counted on her to succeed. She had nothing left to hold on to but loss and regret.

The frosty landscape rushed toward her. She would soon be in the Passing Place, surrounded by ... Who would meet her on the other side? Names. She reached for names, even faces, but her mind slipped. Family? Friends? Who would be there?

The question twisted inside her, sharper than the

cold. Who would come for her? Who was she, anyway? Her name ... What was her name?

A roar split the air around her, and a voice pressed into her mind. "*I am coming, Avalynn. Hold on.*"

Avalynn. That's right. Her name was Avalynn.

Her white-streaked hair lashed across her face as memory fragments collided. She had come to this land for Mateo ... Mateo Stromm. She ... she loved him.

But who was speaking to her? Who was coming?

A massive shape loomed above her—wings spread wide, scales gleaming with iridescent flashes of purple and pink. *Dragon!*

Her breath caught. *Sun, Moon, and Stars.* She swallowed the frigid lump. *Please, let it be a friend.*

"*Friend,*" the voice answered in her mind. "*My name is Izel. You are Avalynn, say it.*"

The dragon swooped lower. Thick talons locked around her waist, yanking her from her free fall. Air punched from her lungs as her limbs dangled, hair whipping wildly.

"*I-I-I'm Avalynn.*"

"*Avalynn Strong, from Faevenly. The Only One.*"

Could she trust the dragon? Everything inside her said yes. It was saving her, after all. Or did it simply want her as prey, to carry back to her lair? An evening snack?

With a low snarl, *Izel* commanded again. "*Repeat. So you remember.*"

Fear jolted through her. The sun was setting. She was about to lose everything.

"*I am Avalynn Strong from Faevenly,*" she repeated in her mind as they soared upward. Panic clawed down her spine. *"Avalynn Strong."* She craned her neck toward the last flicker of light on the horizon, a single ember fading into the darkness. *"Avalynn."* The final glimmer disappeared. Stars blinked awake.

"Ava."

Wings beat steadily around her, lifting her higher into the dark sky. The wind whispered cold against her skin as the dragon carried her over a mountain of frost and stone. Far below, a valley opened, a vast, hidden place, draped in mist. Tiny lights flickered there, soft and welcoming, as the dragon's voice, gentle yet firm, curled in her mind one last time. *"You will be safe now."*

She had no idea how the dragon could know that, but she trusted the creature and slid out of her grasp. Her boots planted on the dirt as the dragon rose back up into the night sky with a whoosh.

Ava blinked and studied her surroundings. The air bit sharp and cold but carried a faint warmth, almost magical, like an invisible fire trailing through the haze. Pale golden orbs floated gently over a cluster of huts, their soft glow reflecting off snow-dusted thatched roofs. The huts were arranged in a loose circle around a large central fire, its flickering light dancing against the darkness like fireflies caught in a jar.

Beyond the village, towering pine trees enclosed the clearing, their branches dusted with snow. A jagged mountain rose in the distance, like the profile of a face forever watching the sky. A silver mist rolled from its slopes and spilled into the Vale, hugging protectively around the village below. The place sang to her like a beautiful, ancient melody. One she knew but had forgotten. She shook her head. No way. She'd remember a place like this.

She wrapped her arms around herself. Not from cold, but from uncertainty mixed with fear. Would the fae living here accept her? *I am Ava*, she told herself firmly, as if that name alone could anchor her here. *Ava.* That much she knew.

Scanning the surroundings, she began to make out the forms of villagers dressed in green. They made no move to approach, their gazes calm but steady, as if they were statues come to life beneath the glow of the orbs. How long had they been standing there?

Two figures stepped forward. The first stood tall and muscular, with ruddy skin, sharply pointed ears, and long dark hair flowing down his back. The other was a pale-skinned lady with pointed ears and silver hair and eyes. Her tall and elegant stature suggested royalty.

Ava touched her own ears. They, too, were pointed, but not as sharply.

The lady smiled gently. "You are here."

What a strange greeting. But somehow, it felt right. Appropriate, even. "Yes, I am here. My name is Ava."

Closer now, she saw dragon-scale markings on their faces and hands. She lifted her hands to eye level. Her sun-kissed skin bore no designs. No marking whatsoever. She knew it. She didn't belong here but desperately longed to. Would they accept her? A girl from the sky brought to them by a dragon? She glanced up at the night sky, the bright stars blinking awake. She had been brought here by a dragon, right? Suddenly, everything about arriving here clouded over.

"I am Zalarae," the lady said. "This is Dorn." Zalarae turned to the villagers who had gathered close. They, too, bore the same dragon markings. "This is Ava. Brought to us by divine purpose. She is now one of us." Facing Ava again, she added, "You are meant to be here. A Valian of the Frost Vale. A keeper of the mountain and her dragons."

Ava gulped. The pronouncement carried a certain weight, as if she had stepped into a great and mighty role. She looked around nervously, then bowed her head. Pride budded within her, like a hearth newly lit after a long winter. She didn't understand it, only that it felt like home. "I am honored."

Two villagers stepped out from the back of the group, and a soft gasp escaped Ava's lips. They were dressed like her in black and brown travel clothing. One stood tall and lean, with long silver hair and lavender eyes. The other was a short, thick dwarf with full blond hair and a bushy, braided beard.

Zalarae gestured toward them. "These two are newcomers like yourself. They belong here too. This is Axe," she said, nodding toward the dwarf. "And this is Rien." She gestured to the other.

They were new here, too? She pulled her chin in. Such a strange coincidence. "They have just arrived?" She clasped her hands together in front of her. Questions burned on the tip of her tongue, but the words escaped her.

"They have, along with another who remains in our healing lodge," Zalarae answered.

Healing? Flashes of blood, swords, and birds streaked

through her mind. She shook her head, the images vanishing before she could grasp them. She caught her breath. "Will he recover?"

"Most assuredly." Dorn nodded. "And in plenty of time for us to prepare."

Murmurs rippled through the other Valians. The kind that suggested excitement and eagerness. "Prepare for what?" Ava asked.

"War," Dorn said flatly. "From Faevenly, the land to the south across the border." His eyes hardened into a deadly stare. "A dark prince rises there. Magic bleeds from him like poison. We must be ready for him."

"Oh," she whispered. "A dark prince ..."

Her fingers twitched at her sides as an ache bloomed in her chest, followed by a hollow feeling, as if some half-remembered name lingered just out of reach. *A prince.* Why did that title feel sharp and heavy all at once? Why did it stir something deep and distant inside her? She pressed her palm to her chest, willing the ache to fade.

"I will be ready!" Axe, growled, a grin spreading across his face.

"As will I," Rien added.

"We will all be ready," Dorn answered. "But night calls, and now we rest."

"Yes, rest." Zalarae placed a gentle hand on Ava's back. "I will show you to your home."

The elegant lady steered her away from the gathering and along a narrow path that curved toward a small hut at the far edge of the village. As they passed Axe and Rien, a prickle traced the back of her neck, but it faded quickly as a wave of sleepiness dragged at her limbs, heavy as iron chains. By the time Zalarae opened the hut's door and motioned her inside, Ava's mind was unraveling, her thoughts dissolving like fog at sunrise.

A small fire crackled in the corner of the hut, welcoming her like a warm embrace. She turned to thank Zalarae, but the lady had already gone. She stared at the wooden door. "My home," she murmured.

Her gaze roamed the thick clay and stone walls. Rugs of green and brown were layered across the thatched floor. A chair and a table took up one side of the small space. Across from that was a pallet of blankets and pillows. Green attire that matched the Valians hung from a row of hooks nearby.

She glanced down at her travel clothes, suddenly itching to remove the threads that did not belong here. As she reached to take off her tunic, her hand brushed against something at her back. *What?* She pulled off the scabbard and stared at the empty opening. She had a sword?

Her stomach sank. Tears filled her eyes. Where had it gone? But as soon as the emotions surfaced, they faded away. She tucked the scabbard under the thick pallet, then began stripping off her clothes.

Across the small chamber, a basin of water and a folded washcloth caught her eye. She dipped the cloth and ran it over her face, neck, and arms, washing away the grime of travel. The water turned cloudy, the scent of metal and dust lingering. When she finished, she wrung out the cloth, set it aside, and dried her hands on a nearby towel.

Feeling lighter, she donned a simple green gown, its

fabric soft and cool against her clean skin. She tucked away her travel-worn clothes beside the scabbard, the gesture feeling both ordinary and strangely final.

She lay down and pulled the blankets up to her chin. She breathed in the scents of ember and pine, satisfied that this place was hers.

Curled up on her side, her tension melted away, but Dorn's words lingered. A prince with dark magic was coming. He would threaten her new home and her new family. This time, a face rose in her mind's eye—hair black as midnight, steely gray eyes shadowed with calculated menace. A face that felt like a deadly secret barely out of reach.

She was destined to destroy that prince.

CHAPTER TWO

M ateo thumbed through the stack of new threads
Maid Penny had brought him—tunics of black,
silver, red, and green, along with coordinating trousers
and coats. His hands ran across the smooth, rich fabric,
then moved to his chest, where his Stromm pendant
hung. His fingers curled around the gold, his fingertips
brushing the engraved S on one side and the tree on the
other. Satisfaction thrummed deep within him, like a
resounding victory bell. His time as prince had only
begun, and he was ready.

"These will do," he called to Maid Penny, who had
stationed herself against the wall of his bedchamber.

The petite maidservant rushed forward with a bow.
"Yes, my lord prince." She took the stack but kept her
eyes cast down. "Which garments would you like for
today?"

He was due to meet with his mother and father to
discuss the next steps for House Stromm. He would need

a color befitting his new station, something that exuded power. His thoughts went to *Teyocel's* black-hued scales. With the dragon by his side, no one would ever touch him or his family. Everyone needed that reminder.

"Prepare the black. I will wear my new coat as well." The shadowy gray coat had been gifted to him by his mother. The stitching echoed *Teyocel's* scales and shimmered under the light's touch. It marked him exactly as he now was—no longer a mere prince in waiting, but a weapon made visible. "In fact, keep only the black and send for more. The other colors are not needed."

"Yes, my lord." Penny placed the dark tunic and trousers at the foot of his bed. She smoothed them out with her small hands. After everything was in place, she offered a bow, then exited the bedchamber.

Mateo removed his robe and slipped the tunic over his head, then pulled on his trousers. Next, his leather belt and gray boots. With everything on, he studied himself in the mirror. His long dark hair framed a hard-edged face. Steely gray eyes stared back at him. But then, he froze. Fear and guilt struck him like an anvil as visions of a girl with white-streaked hair flooded his mind—kissing, hugging, then plummeting through the skies.

He stumbled back, his mind spinning. *Avalynn?* He looked at himself again, seeing someone he didn't recognize. *Who am I?* His hands shook like a reed in a storm. *What have I done?*

"*My prince.*" *Teyocel* spoke into his mind, each syllable resonating deep within him like a hammer striking stone. "*You are Lord Prince Mateo Stromm of*

21

House Stromm. Future ruler of Faevenly. Conqueror of realms. Protector of your name."

The words landed like a gut punch. He grasped for his pendant as if it were air and he was suffocating. He closed his eyes, the metal pulsing against his skin as his heart slowed and his breathing steadied. A few more breaths and he released the pendant, tucking it under his tunic and pressing it to his skin.

Prince Mateo. Destined to rule as the future high king of Faevenly. He had eliminated Avalynn Strong, the Only One, who threatened his house and his realm. That's who he was. *"Thank you, Teyocel."*

"Of course, my prince. Do you require my assistance today?"

"I will call for you if I do."

"I will be ready."

A knock sounded at his door. "Enter," he called out.

Maid Penny's slippers padded against the polished marble floor. She stopped before him with his coat draped over her slender arms. Bowing low, she extended it without meeting his gaze.

"Your coat, my prince," she murmured. "I have been asked to remind you that weapons are not allowed in the war room."

"Is that so?" he said, his voice cool.

He hadn't planned on carrying any. But now? He crossed to the carved wardrobe nestled in the corner of his chamber and pulled open the lower drawer. He retrieved a sleek obsidian dagger and slid it into the sheath tucked inside his boot.

Let them try to stop him.

He snatched his coat from Penny, slipped it on, then left his bedchamber with long strides. He marched down the corridor and made his way down the stairs. Several maidservants scrambled away when he approached; others froze in place. He commanded their respect and expected nothing less. Now that he had brought glory to House Stromm, everyone needed to remember that. If they forgot, he'd remind them.

Down another long corridor, he stopped at the thick double wooden doors to the war room, where guards flanked each side, rigid and silent. They bowed and pulled the doors open. A wave of lamplight spilled out, casting golden shadows along the stone walls. The air carried oiled leather and melted wax, mingling with the damp of ancient stone. In the center was a worn round table, surrounded by high-backed wooden chairs.

His mother and father sat side by side at its head, regal and powerful, dressed in matching dark purple. To the queen's right, Raelor lingered like a shadow given shape, his diamond eyes striking like a viper.

Mateo's skin crawled. He had expected the witch's presence, but that didn't make it easier. Raelor never blinked. He never looked away, always watching. Mateo didn't trust him. Not with his secrets. Not with his thoughts. Definitely not with his future.

The queen broke the tension, gesturing to the seat next to hers. "My son, please sit."

He took the chair, angling himself toward her and the king. The wooden back pressed cold against his spine. A guard from inside the room closed the doors and stationed himself at the ready.

The queen's gaze flicked briefly over her shoulder to where the witch stood behind her, tall and still. "Raelor insists we verify a few details before we proceed," she said, her tone clipped. She turned her attention back to Mateo. "Tell me again—the girl is gone? And the sword with her?"

Mateo had told them when he turned from the Wild North. Why did he need to tell them again? He gripped his knees under the table. For a moment, he saw it again— Avalynn's body plummeting through the sky, the sword slipping from her grasp and vanishing into the clouds. He forced the image away. "Like I said, she is gone, as is her sword." The edge in his voice cut sharply. He leaned forward, his glare locking on the witch standing behind his mother. "Got it, witch?"

"Fine," the queen snapped. "Enough of that. We have much to discuss today." She adjusted her gown and lifted her chin. "We have made progress these last few days. The post of Master of the Blade, left vacant by Keeth's unfortunate disappearance, has been filled."

Mateo's jaw tightened at the name Keeth. Images of the stocky dwarf and the Wild North flashed through his mind. He pressed his palms flat against the armrests, forcing the memories back. The past was weakness. He had no use for it now.

"Who is the replacement?" he asked.

"He is a seasoned warrior from within our own ranks," she went on. "A Stromm loyalist who's trained for years under Master Keeth himself. He is quite skilled." She looked to the king, then back to Mateo. "He is here for a formal introduction."

"He will take on an important role as we reinforce our strongholds in the provinces," the king added. "He has good relations with many of the families."

Mateo straightened in his seat. "He sounds useful."

The queen nodded to the guard. "Show him in."

The guard opened the door, disappeared for a few moments, then returned with a dwarf with long, thick blond hair, a braided beard, and a scar that cut from his forehead across his eye and down to his chin. Mateo did a double-take. The dwarf was the spitting image of Keeth.

"There you are!" The dwarf raised his fists at Mateo. "Where is Keeth? Where is my brother?!"

The king sprang to his feet and pounded his fists on the table. "You will mind yourself, Master Karl! Lest you be removed from this chamber at once."

The dwarf's stare burned into Mateo, his broad chest rising and falling in ragged, shallow breaths. "I want answers," he said, each word slow and tight with restraint. "What happened to my brother?"

"We have told you—" the queen began, but Mateo raised a hand, silencing her.

When the room stilled, Mateo leaned forward, his attention fixed solely on the dwarf. "Master Keeth journeyed with me faithfully to the North." His voice came out even, but low. "We became separated. As for my part, I do not know what has befallen him."

Karl's eyes narrowed to slits. He matched Mateo's posture, voice grating with barely bridled rage. "If I find your words to be untrue, I will—"

"—what?" Mateo cut in, meeting him with a calm,

dangerous smile. "Careful, Master Dwarf. Your threats may cost you more than your temper can afford."

"Enough," the queen said smoothly, resting a hand on Mateo's shoulder before pointing to Karl. "Now sit, Master Karl. Before we think better of offering you Master of the Blade."

Grumbling, Karl stalked to the seat opposite them and dropped into it with a thud. Arms crossed, he muttered, "I have served House Stromm since I was a lad, as did my brother. I remain for him, in hopes of finding him."

Ahh, so this dwarf was more loyal to his brother than the Stromms. Duly noted. Mateo would keep a sharp eye on him.

"Thank you, Master Karl. We recognize your loyalty." The queen threaded her fingers together on top of the table. "Raelor, please begin."

The witch moved out from the shadows. He approached the table and laid out a rolled parchment he'd been holding. A map of Faevenly. "With the traitorous stewards executed, the provinces hang in the balance."

Mateo rose from his seat, hands behind his back.

Raelor pointed to the middle of the map, "High Meadow." His hand went down to the region near the Great Cove, "Sand Bluff," and then rested on the region west of High Meadow, "Cuesta." His fingers tapped the map. "New stewards are needed. Ones loyal to House Stromm."

"Easy." Mateo smirked, lowering himself to his chair.

"I take *Teyocel* and show them our strength. Then we handpick whom we see fit. They will never oppose us."

The queen's lips curled in satisfaction. "Exactly what I was thinking. But before we make any move, we need more information."

"Precisely," Raelor agreed. "We have two merchants joining us here today who deal in information."

He gestured to the guard, and the door opened again. A young lady entered, clad in a simple brown dress. Her silver hair was woven into a loose braid. Her amber eyes swept the room with quiet precision, though they never quite met Mateo's. Behind her, a boy dressed in black trousers and a brown tunic, followed. He had the same silver hair worn loose at his shoulders.

"May I present Kessa and Taren of Quietus Valley," Raelor introduced.

The young lady bowed with grace. "My king, my queen, my prince—thank you for the audience." She placed a hand to her chest. "Like Raelor said, I am Kessa, and this is my brother Taren. We belong to no marked province. Our home is tucked near the edge of Quietus Valley. We are weavers who trade in wool."

"You are welcome here," the queen said. "We thank you both for making the journey. Raelor speaks highly of your skills. He says you are trusted information gatherers."

Mateo leaned forward. At last, someone of value. "How do you gather information if you live near the valley?" he asked. "Isn't the area mostly abandoned?"

Kessa nodded. "It is. But we gather information on

our trade route, which passes through villages in every province. We are friends with everyone. And no one."

The young Taren blurted, "We hear all."

Mateo's brows lifted. *They hear all?* A bold claim—one he wasn't sure he believed. Yet there was something about the girl's confidence. Her sharp yes made him pause. He rested his forearms on the edge of the table. "What kinds of things?"

Taren straightened with a spark of pride, but Kessa answered. "Whispers," she said calmly. "In taverns. Temples. Merchant stalls and border outposts. Elders from every province have begun to meet quietly, discreetly."

Mateo tilted his head, his eyes narrowed, but he kept silent as he waited for her to continue.

"What do they say?" Karl asked in a gruff voice.

"They speak of dissolving the High Court," Kessa went on. "Of overthrowing House Stromm. They believe Faevenly should return to its old ways. With each province ruled by its own court. No high crown."

The air thickened. The oil lamps hanging from the walls dimmed as Mateo's pulse accelerated. The king and queen remained still, yet he could feel an undeniable shift in the room. The threat of something long buried clawing its way back.

The queen narrowed her stare. "Which provinces?"

Kessa swallowed. "All, my queen," she said. "Cuesta, High Meadow, and Sand Bluff."

The king shot to his feet, his face red, his hands curled into fists. "All?!" He eyed the queen. "Do they not know what we can do to them?" He pointed in Mateo's direction. "Do they not care that the prince has a mighty dragon?"

"Please," the young girl said in a quavering voice, the courage she held when she had walked into the room quickly dissolving. "I have shared what we know." Her hand clutched her brother's arm. "May we take our leave?"

"You may," the queen said. "You will be escorted to the guest house. Food and drink and reward for your time will be provided." She smoothed her voice. "Please, rest. You will stay as honored guests here, until you are dismissed."

The siblings paused and glanced at each other, the queen's last words clearly affecting them. They held hands and exited in silence, the thick doors thudding shut behind them.

A stillness followed. Heavy and muffled. The king muttered darkly under his breath. Karl's eyes remained narrowed, teeth clinched. Mateo's mind churned. Foolish provinces. He could incinerate each one, burn them all to the ground. It would serve them right.

He folded his arms in front of his chest. He was ready to shut them down. He just needed the word. "This requires action."

Queen Lysandra placed her hands atop the table. "It does." She tapped her long silver-painted nails on the wood. "We cannot allow whispers of rebellion to take root." Her gaze swept the room. "If they mean to test our strength, we will remind them who holds the crown."

The king slammed his fist on the table. "Yes, we will."

The queen rose, power radiating from her like a

tempest. "We will go on tour. Province by province. A show of unity, of control, of unshakable reign. We will offer favor to the loyal and make examples of the traitorous." Her lips curled at the edges. "It is time for all of Faevenly to see the power of House Stromm. The power of the prince and his dragon."

Mateo tipped his head. "Nothing would please me more."

His throat burned with the memory of fire—*Teyocel's* fire. The whispers in his mind stirred again, curling like smoke through his thoughts. This was what they wanted of him and what he craved for himself. Destruction in the name of duty. Strength that demanded obedience.

He kept his voice steady, controlled, but inside, something frayed. Was this who he had become? A weapon dressed in royal threads? He could feel the necklace pulsing beneath his tunic as if it, too, was pleased by the plan, satisfied by the blood that would follow.

He should have felt dread. Anticipation coiled inside of him instead.

CHAPTER THREE

Queen Lysandra Stromm paced her private study. Dressed in dark green, her long train swished across the gold and marble floor. Everything should have been falling into place for House Stromm's dominance. Mateo had brought a mighty dragon to the palace. He had eliminated the traitorous stewards. Yet still, the provinces opposed her. Did they not comprehend what could happen to them? Had they not sent them a strong enough warning with the stewards' death?

There was also Avalynn to contend with. Something about Mateo's response gnawed at her. His words had been measured, as if holding something back. What really happened to them in the Wild North?

She rubbed her forehead. Unease took root when a new thought struck her. What if it wasn't only the provinces rising against her? What if Avalynn, the Only One, still lived?

Her gut clenched tight. When Mateo returned from the North, he said Avalynn and her sword would not be seen again. He said the same thing at the meeting. She took that to mean he had ended them. But what if he hadn't? She had sent Verona to bring back Avalynn's body, along with the sword of power if it still existed. She needed to do more. That fool Verona could not be trusted, least of all with someone like Avalynn.

Avalynn... Lysandra smashed her hands together and dug her nails into her skin. The meddling, part-human lowborn had been raised a Stromm but was really the last remaining member of House Strong—the so-called Only One. If anyone could slip past death, it was her. The red-haired madman, Kragar, had trained her too well. There was also the innate energy power she possessed from her human-blooded ancestors. Could House Stromm defeat a magic like that?

She snapped her fingers at Marina, who stood in the corner like a statue. The green-skinned, half-troll had no idea how fortunate she was to have secured a place at Stromm Palace. Found as a young one, she had been left alone after her village flooded. Lysandra was quick to take her in. A troll servant would keep her safer than any guard. She has served Lysandra since.

"Bring me Raelor," she ordered.

"Yes, my queen," Marina said with a bow.

She watched the hulking figure leave, then turned her attention back to her troubles. She stopped in front of the fireplace and gazed at the flames within. She needed assurance that Avalynn was gone. Dead. Sent to the

Passing Place. Only Raelor could help her with that. No one else, and definitely not her mate, the king. He favored brute strength over cunning edge. Right now, his brawn was not needed.

She smoothed her long, dark hair away from her face and drew in a sharp breath. The Stromm tour would cover the provinces, and preparations had begun. But the likes of Avalynn and the people of the North required a strategic mind like hers.

The North. The Valians. Fresh unease crept into her thoughts. Would the frost fae somehow play a role in all things? Did they care about the Only One prophecy? She rubbed her temples, an ache brewing beneath her skin. Would they band together to gain power? Even though the Stromms had a dragon now, they had no other families standing by their side. They had never been more vulnerable.

Her scowl deepened, fingernails pressing harder into her palm. Where was that witch? Her gaze whipped to the door. She needed him. Now!

"My queen," Raelor announced, entering the study with quick strides. He wore silver and gray with his long white hair flowing down his back. He scanned the room, no doubt assessing if she was alone.

"Raelor." She motioned to the velvet chairs in front of the fireplace and watched as he lowered himself on the nearest one. She took the open seat beside him.

He sat back and studied her. "How may I be of service, my queen?"

Where to begin? She sifted through her thoughts,

organizing them in order of importance. All of them were so interconnected that they could have been one. "I have been thinking about Avalynn, her sword, and the Wild North." A wave of fury rose inside her. "We cannot trust Verona to do her job."

Raelor gave a slow, thoughtful nod. "I agree." He leaned forward. "If Avalynn is alive in the North, the Valians would've claimed her. And if she has been claimed..." His voice dropped, taking on an almost sinister tone. "Then she is no longer Avalynn Strong. She is a Valian. One of them. If that is the case, we cannot reach her."

The queen exhaled sharply through her nose, her fingers curling against her dress. It was not the answer she wanted. The Valians were legendary—phantoms of an older time, keepers of dragons. She had never seen one, never spoken to one. She had only heard whispers in the dark. They were said to live beyond the reach of Faevenly's crown, protected by ancient magic. Little was known about them.

If Avalynn truly lived among them, what would become of her? What power would awaken in her veins? Her head spun imagining the possibilities. "There must be something we can do," she said tightly. "Some way to reach her. Some way to see if she still lives, and if so, to end her once and for all."

Raelor dipped his chin, moving in closer. "I have been working on a solution. If she is there, alive, then magic holds her now." His eyes glinted like frozen glass, and a low hum seemed to stir the very air around him. "But dreams are the one place no can hold. I can attempt to send something into her sleep. A whisper of the past carried on the wind. A flicker of memory bent just enough it should lure her southward. She won't question it. Not when it feels like hope."

The queen tilted her head, intrigued. Finally, Raelor offered something promising. "You speak of a spell?"

He smiled faintly. "A spell, yes. Crafted from memory. Woven from what she's lost. I will make her dream of Faevenly, of Mateo. But altered. Twisted enough to make her seek the truth. And in doing so ..." He let the words hang.

"She will seek us out," the queen said, finishing his thought.

"And bring her sword," Raelor added, almost triumphantly.

"And you can penetrate the Wild North's magical boundary?" she asked.

He nodded as he sat back. "I believe so."

The queen's mind turned sharper than a dagger's edge. Yet a flicker of something like fear tightened in her chest. Fae and human magic from Avalynn's bloodline crafted the sword. It pulsed with a power none could mimic, much less withstand.

Worse, it bore the weight of prophecy.

The sword didn't merely represent Avalynn's return. It confirmed her identity. The Only One. The one who could unite the bloodlines. The one who could end the Stromm line. The queen's fingers found the arm of her chair, nails biting into the carved wood. She would never let that happen. That sword was hers.

Her voice dropped to a whisper lined with frost. "Proceed carefully. Mateo must never know."

Raelor nodded, his eyes glowing with quiet menace. "I feel the tether between them. It pulses faintly, but it is present. Even with the pendant around his neck, he cannot be trusted."

"As I said. We keep the plan hidden from him," she demanded. "No matter the cost."

"Indeed," Raelor agreed.

She held up her hand, slowly curling her fingers into a fist. "And if that magic around my son's neck is too weak, strengthen it." She shook her fist at him. "It must be absolute."

"It will be done," he assured.

A new fear washed over her. If Avalynn was indeed a Valian, what role, if any, would the dragons play? *Teyocel's* black scales came to mind, followed by the memory of flames incinerating the stewards in her own hall. Her skin shivered. "And what of the dragons?" she asked in a low whisper.

Raelor's brows tightened. "The dragons have been linked forever with the Valians. If Avalynn is truly one of them, they may rise for her." He paused, eyes distant, almost wary. His voice dropped low. "But my main concern is the prince. *Teyocel* remains close to him. I feel the bond between them. It is strong, but strange. Twisted. I sense it was forged in darkness, in desperation. I do not fully understand it." He let out a soft sigh. "I do not know if it will hold."

He continued, his voice dropping lower. "There is also a chance that *Teyocel* is acting independently, and maybe even against the prince. If that is the case, he has been cast out of the Vale and would be considered an unstable element."

A beat passed, the air tightening. *Teyocel* cast out? And possibly acting against her son? They needed that dragon—its power and its allegiance. "Can you do anything to influence their bond? Make it stronger?"

"I cannot," Raelor admitted. "Their connection is beyond me."

She rose, turning to the hearth, the firelight painting her in gold and shadow. She hadn't thought of *Teyocel* as a manipulator against Mateo. Until now. One deceiver knew another; how had she missed that? She and Raelor were artists at the craft. An ancient dragon would be a master. Yet she had to believe that her son would be up for the challenge. He was a Stromm.

"*Teyocel* and Mateo's bond is out of our hands. Make sure the girl who believes herself a storm comes to us," she said. "And with her, the sword." She stared into the flames. "Let the dragons do what they will." The fire crackled like bones breaking beneath the weight of a heavy stone. "Let Avalynn come." She gritted her teeth. "We will end her once and for all. That is the ultimate goal."

"Yes, my queen." He bowed his head.

She lifted a single finger, halting him mid-breath. "One matter remains unfinished." Her gaze narrowed, sharpened to a blade's edge. "I entrusted you with finding the one who dared steal my son from me, the one who switched him at birth and believed themselves clever enough to escape my reach."

Raelor remained still, though the queen caught the flash of unease in his sparkling eyes. "I have not forgotten," he said carefully. "I am still working to uncover the truth."

"Work faster." Her lips curved, slow and cruel, not a smile. "I do not forgive betrayal. And I do not wait kindly."

CHAPTER FOUR

Darkness haunted Lady Sonia, preventing sleep and tormenting her waking hours. It spoke to her of a lost Avalynn, a corrupted Mateo, and a shadow rising deep within Summit Range, inside the walls of Stromm Palace. Something so significant it could break the land. And she had no idea what to do.

"You have to think of something!" Manny pleaded, his frailness never more evident now that both Mateo and Avalynn were gone. His back hunched deeper, fresh lines carved his tanned face, the potions she had made to stop his aging clearly no longer worked. He ran his fingers through his thick gray hair as he paced. "The stewards of the great houses have been wiped out. Gareth and Lirien are missing. Mateo has secured a dragon, and Avalynn is God knows where."

"She could be dead," Camilla muttered.

Manny spun toward his eldest daughter and wagged his finger at her while his younger daughter, Floriana, clung to his leg. "¡*Mija, no mas*! I did not raise you to speak like that!" He held her in his stare. "She is alive, I can feel it. And Mateo, my boy ..." He pounded his fist against his chest. "We can still save him!" He lowered his hand and raised a pleading brow to Sonia. "Right?" His bottom lip trembled. "Please tell me I'm right."

Her heart ached for him, a human who had left everything behind in his realm to stay in this one. He had sacrificed so much here. When would it end? She placed her hand on his shoulder and squeezed. "There is always hope. As long as we believe."

"Believe?" He laughed as he shook his head. "We need way more than that, and you know it."

Her gaze roamed Manny's humble abode. A row of small windows was set deep within the stone walls, and worn rugs of blue and purple covered the rocky floor. A fire crackled in the stone fireplace, yet Sonia felt no warmth in her chest. Manny was right. Hope needed more than belief. It needed action. Verona had journeyed for answers, though she knew not where. The Sublands had been left in the care of the witch Rhyka and a small group of advisers. And while the number of cases of Dragon's Bellow had improved, the water supply still suffered.

Faevenly was dying, and Sonia had no idea how to save it.

She inhaled deeply, then released it with quiet determination. After all they had endured together, Manny deserved more than her guarded silences. "My friend, let us go for a walk."

They left the house and made their way toward Spirit

Butte. Manny walked in slow, deliberate steps while a hush fell over the dirt path ahead. The wind moved behind them, not as a force, but as a quiet urging—as if the land wanted them to go. As if it sensed they were the ones who could mend what had been broken. If only she had as much faith as the elements.

They stopped before taking the long, narrow path up to the flat-topped hill and sat on a sun-warmed slab of rock cracked with age. The silence stretched between them, not heavy, but expectant. It was as if the rock itself was waiting for them to share their truths. Or at least, her truths. There was much she needed to say.

"Out with it." He folded his arms and leveled her with a stare. "What are you not telling me?"

If it had been any other time, she would've chuckled, leaned her head against his shoulder, and told him whatever it was she had been keeping to herself. The human had a way of sensing when things were wrong. But this was different. Manny loved with his whole heart. Despite everything that had happened, Mateo was still his son. Avalynn was his best friend Julio's granddaughter. Manny would do anything for them. The last thing Sonia wanted was to hurt her dear friend.

She pulled her cloak tight around her shoulders. "Avalynn and Mateo are lost."

"What do you mean, lost?" His brows stitched together.

"My coven sisters and I have been going to great lengths to find them. We have tracked whispers, read the stars, and invoked old blood rites known only to our coven."

Manny's eyes widened as he used the human gesture of his faith, moving his hand from his forehead to his chest and shoulder to shoulder. "And?" he whispered.

"We've discovered that Mateo is under the influence of shadow magic. Likely cast by Raelor at Queen Lysandra's command. We believe it drove him to the dragon, who now shares a dark bond with him."

"Oh no," he said with a gulp, tears forming in his eyes. "My boy."

She paused, her voice dropping low. "As for Avalynn ... she has been claimed by the Valians—the dragon-marked who dwell in the Wild North beyond the magical boundary."

"Claimed?" He blinked, almost looking lost. "What does that mean?"

She paused, her mind drifting to a time long past when she had ridden upon *Izel's* back and helped seal away the Wild North from the rest of the fae realm. She had believed the barrier would protect Faevenly from harm. Now, the magical veil kept Avalynn. The Only One. The last true hope for peace in the realm. Did Zalarae know that would happen? Did *Izel?* Had they used Sonia as a pawn in a quest to destroy Faevenly all those years ago?

A cold wind stirred the edge of her cloak, the skies darkening from a great cloud. "Avalynn, Mateo, Gareth, Lirien, and a dwarf from Stromm Palace crossed into the Wild North. Only Mateo and his dragon got out. We can only assume the others stayed behind. If they stayed, they were claimed." Her voice faltered, weighted with the guilt of a thousand shattered promises. Everything she had done was for the good of Faevenly. Or so she thought. "If the North has truly claimed her, then she is no longer Avalynn. She is something more. Something forged by the Wild North itself."

Manny clutched his knees, his eyes drifting far away. His voice choked up. He brought his closed hand to his lips and cleared his throat. But the crackle remained. "After everything. All the struggles. All the death. All the pain." He glanced at her with wet eyes. "This is how it ends?"

Sonia's chest tightened, the ache blooming behind her ribs like a bruise. So many had fallen. So many had trusted her, believed in the hope she had crafted. And now that hope teetered on the edge of ruin. The boundary she'd helped forge to protect the North held Avalynn captive. The magic meant to save them all might be the very force that broke them. Was it a mistake? She had guided with wisdom, with hope, with belief. But that had never been enough. Not then. Not now. She was foolish to have ever thought otherwise.

Her fingers curled at her sides, and she clenched her jaw as she drew in a slow breath that tasted of sand and wind. *Not again. Not like this.* She turned toward Manny, voice low but steady. "Not if we can help it."

He brought his fingers to the cross necklace he wore around his neck. He held it with resolve, the fight returning to his brown eyes. "Faith is a warrior. And so are we."

Sonia gave a slow nod, more to herself than to Manny. He was right. Her pulse quickened as memories pulled at her—the shimmer of *Izel's* scales beneath the sunlight, the thunder of wings over the frosty North, the ancient words she had once spoken to fuse her magic with *Izel's* flame. She helped create the boundary. She must be the one to cross it, to find Avalynn, to bring her home.

"There is no one else," Sonia whispered.

Manny pulled in his chin. "What?"

She looked him full in the face, her voice steady. "I must go to the Wild North. I must bring Avalynn home."

He knitted his brow. "But I thought you said no one returns once—"

"I did." Her words cut clean. "I have been there. I know the Valians. And I know the dragon, *Izel*. They may still listen to me." She paused. *Please, Sun, Moon, and Stars, let them listen.*

He stared at her, the fear in his gaze giving way to determination. "I'm coming with you."

She'd expected nothing less from her friend. But her heart ached all the same. There was no way he could survive the trip. "Oh, Manny." She took his hands in hers. "If only you could, but you must stay here. The journey will be fraught with dangers. Travel will be difficult." She held his gaze. "You must stay here. Avalynn will need you when she returns."

"Damn my old bones." Manny bowed his head. "I don't like it, not one bit." His eyes filled with unspoken worry. "When will you go?"

"I must return to my coven first, to prepare," she replied. "Then I will head north straightaway."

They sat together in silence. The sunlight from above faded as puffy clouds trailed across the darkening sky.

Sonia's mind drifted beyond the red craggy hills and parched earth of the Sublands, beyond the magical boundary that shimmered between lands. *Zalarae. Izel.* The Wild North had changed since she had last stood upon its soil, and she had changed too. She did not know what awaited her in the frosty region. Only that it called to her now, just as it had then. Once, she had gone as a friend. Now she would return as an adversary to the very thing she had helped create.

She had to be ready.

CHAPTER FIVE

Ava emerged from her hut and stretched her arms wide, a soft yawn escaping her. The village lay quiet in the early morning hush, cloaked in dragon mist that clung to the thatched rooftops and coiled low around the sleeping huts. Frost kissed the grass, and a pale gray light crept over the treetops. A pair of frost sparrows fluttered from nearby branches, their downy white feathers puffed against the cold. They trilled a low, rapid beat as they skimmed across the rooftops and vanished into the morning haze.

The sound followed her longer than it should have, tugging at something beneath her ribs. Mornings were always like this. Peaceful on the surface yet threaded with an ache she couldn't name. She inhaled the cold air, and the calm fractured as the memory of the dream rushed back.

A face slipped into her thoughts. Dark hair. Steely eyes. A shadowed figure standing on the edge of a cliff.

He called to her without words, beckoning her to him. She didn't know who he was or why he haunted her sleep. Only that every time she saw him, her heart ached followed swiftly by fury.

He had to be the dark prince. Ava exhaled sharply, the name settling like frost in her chest. She shoved the image away and straightened her shoulders. *Enough.* Today was not about him. It was about this place. Today marked the beginning of the Frost-Forged Trials. If she passed, she would finally stand before the dragons and claim her place among the Valians. No more being new. No more unanswered questions. As a full-fledged Valian, she would be ready for the rising dark prince. Ready to defend her home.

But first, she and the others had chores.

She marched to the next hut and knocked on the door. Axe jerked it open, a scowl visible beneath his thick, unkempt beard and bushy blond braid. "Get back, now." He shooed her away so he could step out. "No need to crowd my doorway like that."

She crossed her arms with a smirk. "I was not crowding." She took a long step back and motioned him out with a sweeping arm gesture. "I was only knocking, and you know it."

"I know no such thing," he grumbled. "Too early. Too cold. And your footsteps are too loud."

Axe complained about everything. How close she walked beside him. How loudly she chewed. How she breathed as if she owned the air. And Ava loved adding to the list.

She gave his shoulder a playful push. "My footsteps

are too loud? Is that the best you can do?" Before he could reply, she added, "Come on. We've got water to fetch and a fire to build. Let's get Rien. Keep up if you can."

"Keep up?" He harrumphed. "You'd best watch yourself today. I am in no mood."

She flashed him a huge smile. "Are you ever?"

Most days, she clipped her long stride to match Axe's short one, but not today. She reached Rien's quickly. The silver-haired, violet-eyed fae opened his door before her knuckles hit the wood.

He rolled his eyes. "I know how excited you are, but calm down."

She didn't know who was grumpier. Rien or Axe. Not that it mattered. No one could ruin her spirits. She spun on her heels, heading for the path to the small brook. "Water first," she called out behind her. She scooped up her buckets from a stack at the village's edge. "Hurry up."

"You do not need to order us around. You are not an elder," Axe grumbled, fumbling with his own buckets. "We know what we are doing."

Elder? She liked the sound of that. She straightened her shoulders, lifted her chin, and regarded Axe with a raised brow. "You are right, my wise friend. One day I *will* be an elder. Or maybe even a princess." She looked down at him as if he were a servant. "Or better yet, a queen."

Axe stopped in place. "I would no sooner bow to you than kiss a frost toad's behind."

"Thunderation," Rien muttered. "Are you two going to bicker the whole way? It's exhausting."

"I'm not bickering." Ava kept walking, chin held even higher.

The path wound its way through pines and frost-laced brush, the twang of sap burning from a distance in the air. Peaceful silence clung to the forest, broken only by the rhythmic crunch of boots against soil. As they neared the brook, the faint gurgle of water grew louder, gentle and melodic, like a lullaby from the land itself. The brook ran narrow but deep, its icy water gliding over dark stones like liquid glass.

She leaned forward and dipped her buckets into the stream. As she straightened, a flicker of white caught her eye through the trees on the far bank. She stilled. Between the frost-laced trunks stood a horse—tall, luminous, its coat so pale it seemed carved from moonlight. Its mane stirred though there was no wind, silver strands glinting softly in the filtered light. The animal watched her with calm, knowing eyes the color of a winter sky.

Ava's breath caught. Something deep in her chest tightened, warm and aching. She blinked, and the forest was empty.

A sprinkle of water on her face drew her attention. Her gaze snapped to Axe as he dipped his fingers into the river for another dousing. "You dozing off over there?"

"No!" She scooped up her own handful and splashed him.

"Cut it out," Rien snapped.

"Fine," she grumbled.

"You're about as fun as a stale turnip," Axe said with his own flick of water at Rien.

The splashes echoed softly through the trees as Ava worked swiftly, filling her buckets to the brim, the cool water gliding over her hands. Axe grunted beside her. He managed his buckets with a determined scowl while Rien finished first and waited.

"Are we going to talk about today?" Rien asked.

Ava didn't answer at first. Her gaze followed the silver ripple of the brook, but her thoughts raced far beyond it. The Frost-Forged Trials. They began with combat skills where each of them would face off against Dorn, the most skilled fighter amongst the Valians. After that was fire-making. If they proved themselves worthy, then came their formal introduction to the dragons with fire branding, a sacred moment when dragon flame would mark their skin with shimmering scales, a symbol of belonging. Only then could they call themselves Valians, protectors of the Wild North and the dragons who lived there.

"Of course we're going to talk about today," she said finally, standing tall with her buckets in tow.

"Which one of us will go first, then?" Rien asked.

Dorn had said they could choose their order, but so far, no one had claimed a place. Now that the day had arrived, they needed to decide. They set their buckets down.

Ava crossed her arms. "I will," she and Axe said at the same time.

They side-eyed each other. "I said it first," Ava declared.

Axe stomped. "Did not!"

Rien exhaled. "Enough. We throw fingers. On three. One, two, three."

All three shot out their hands. Axe threw a single bent finger. The Talon. Rien flashed two fingers spread wide. Wings. Ava held out three fingers pressed together. Flame.

Axe cursed, kicking at a pile of leaves while Ava smiled and said, "Flame burns Talon. Of course." She narrowed her eyes on Rien. "And Wings beat Flame, so that makes Rien, me, then Axe." Gripping the handles, she lifted her buckets. "I knew I should've thrown Wings."

Behind her, Axe muttered something about toads and unfair wins, while Rien laughed and followed. She ignored them. Who cared about order? She planned to burn through every challenge like fire through dry grass. Besides, it was best she *didn't* go first. That way, she could study Rien's turn. His skills were equal to hers. He would be good to watch.

Buckets sloshing at her sides, Ava crested the rise leading back into the heart of the village but stopped short. The fire at the center of the village crackled with flames, and every Valian in the village had gathered around it.

"That's not supposed to be burning yet," she said in a low voice.

"No, it's not," Rien said.

Axe glanced at Ava. "Something is amiss."

They approached with slow steps, weaving through the silent onlookers. They came to a stop before Dorn, who stood closest to the fire. Zalarae kept her place beside him, her silver braid catching the orange and red light like glass. The sun had barely begun its ascent, and the trials were to begin at the end of the day, yet the fire already roared.

Ava cleared her throat. "The fire is lit."

"It is." Dorn held his hands together in front of him. "The Frost-Forged Trials will begin early. The three of you will deposit your water, then retire to your huts for preparation and return here for the *Tletl Xochitl.*"

The *Tletl Xochitl.* The fire blessing. The ceremony had been explained, but she had never seen it. Fresh excitement sparked within her. Her legs twitched with coiled energy. This was it; the time had come. Who cared why Dorn and Zalarae wanted to start early? Early suited her fine. She was as ready as a storm cloud aching to burst.

Ava, Rien, and Axe strode to the village basin and dumped the water inside. Ava placed her buckets back where they belonged, then shoved Rien and Axe out of the way with a grin. "See you at the fire."

She darted into her hut, heart pounding, legs buzzing with urgency. She tore open the woven chest at the foot of her sleeping pallet and pulled out the fighting clothes the weavers had made for her—sleek green pants lined with silver thread built for speed and a matching long-sleeved tunic threaded thick for protection. She brought the clothing close to her chest like a hug and smiled. She would make herself proud. The village, too.

The rising dark prince would regret *ever* challenging the Valians.

She sat on the edge of the pallet, dressing quickly. With the outfit on, she roped her long hair into a tight braid, one strand over the other, and tied it off with a ribbon. She reached for her boots, then the new laces she had tucked under her pallet, when her fingers brushed against something hard. She stilled. What was under there? She wrapped her fingers around the object and pulled out a scabbard. She sat back, mouth open.

What was this?

Her head swam. Her hands weakened. The scabbard slipped from her grasp and *ka-dunked* onto the ground as images rushed into her mind. Sky above. Hair whipping across her face. Wind screaming past her ears. Then a face. Beautiful and deadly with dark hair and steely gray eyes. The one from her dreams. Another flash. A black onyx sword with blue etching twirling in the air. It floated away like a whisper, disappearing into the clouds.

She fell to her knees, a crushing sensation of loss and despair piercing her heart. Sun, Moon, and Stars. Was this a memory? Or a dream? Her hands shook like a leaf in a storm. Had she fallen from the sky? The dark prince. Was that him? Had he watched her fall? She gaped at the empty scabbard. The sword that fit inside, was it hers? His?

A knock jolted her, and the visions erased like a flame snuffed by wind.

"Ava," Zalarae called out. "May I come in?"

She grabbed the scabbard and stuffed it away, not even knowing why. She pressed her hands on her heart and slowed her breathing, then rose to her feet. "Yes, come in."

The tall and elegant lady stepped into the room. Her gaze roamed the contents before settling on Ava. Was she looking for the scabbard? "I have come to wish you success with the trials."

Ava forced a smile. She also forced her gaze away from the pallet. "I am honored. Thank you, Zalarae."

Silence hovered between them, filled with a dozen unspoken questions and accusations. Did Zalarae feel it? Was it just her? Why was she still in her hut anyway? Surely the village elder had other duties to attend.

"I will leave you to your preparations." Zalarae bowed her head. "Make us proud, Ava."

"I will do my best, my lady."

The door closed, and a heavy breath escaped Ava's lips. The scabbard meant something. So did her visions. Her dreams, too. She flexed her fingers, a faint unease coiling in her chest. She had to tell someone. The only ones she could trust were Rien and Axe. They had arrived when she had. Maybe they were experiencing the same weirdness.

But first, the trials. Ava dropped to her knees and shoved the scabbard deeper beneath her pallet, as if hiding it would quiet the questions clawing at her. Then she rose, squared her shoulders, and brushed off her trousers. Time for the fire blessing.

THE
GATHERING

CHAPTER SIX

Ava made her way to the fire, her steps slow yet steady. The excitement that had raced through her veins was now dampened, replaced by a myriad of emotions she struggled to understand. Duty, responsibility, but mostly fear. Why would she suddenly be afraid of this place? Pinpricks skittered down her spine. Her breath came out short and shallow. She wasn't used to fear. And she didn't like it.

Get it together. Ava clasped her hands together and squeezed. *Focus.* She released her hands and shook them out. *Do well. Let nothing get in the way.* Her nerves settled with each commanding thought. The overriding desire to prove herself and take her place as a Valian had firmly retaken root.

The fire in the village center roared, its flames stretching skyward with eager purpose. The Valians had shed their everyday green cloaks for silver threads, the formal fabric catching the firelight as they moved. Ava's chest ached at the sight. How she longed for her own set of silver—proof she belonged here.

They gathered in a wide circle around the communal blaze. Beyond the shifting bodies, she spotted Axe and Rien dressed as she was, already standing before the fire. Axe lifted a brow in silent question, and she didn't hesitate. She quickened her steps and slipped into place beside him.

"Took your time," Axe mumbled.

She shot him a glare. Before she could snap back, the Valians started humming. Low at first, then the rumble grew deeper and louder. Foot stamping followed, each strike against the cool dirt blended with the hums like an ancient tune filled with divine purpose. The music thrummed in Ava's chest, filling her like water topping a vessel. This. All of this. She had craved this. Had been waiting days for this.

So why did it suddenly feel wrong?

Dorn and Zalarae moved forward. Their steps silenced the song, leaving only the fire's crackling sizzle. Zalarae spoke. "My fellow Valians. Today is the first day of the Frost-Forged Trials. The day in which our friends take the first step to becoming Valians, protectors of the Wild North and keepers of the dragons who roam here. We mark them worthy of their endeavor." Her gaze landed on Rien and Axe before settling firmly on Ava. "May the strength of the Frost Vale be with each of you, and may the wisdom of the dragons guide you well."

Dorn moved closer to the fire, the orange and red flames dancing against his face. He cupped his hands together, then plunged them into the fire. He held them steady, then scooped out handfuls of ash. He moved to Rien and smeared the powdery cinders over the back of his hands. He did the same to Axe, and then finally to Ava.

Zalarae followed with a fine, thin stick. She poked through the black smudging, rubbing the wood over their skin in intricate dragon-scaled patterns. "With this mark, you carry the strength of the Frost Vale. Let your hearts burn bright with courage. May the dragons lend each of you their power and wisdom."

The ash dissipated, leaving only glowing dragon-scale markings. The markings would fade. But when they completed the trials, they'd become permanent when touched by dragon fire. Ava traced the warm lines with her fingertips. She wanted this. Really and truly wanted this. *Right?*

"And now," Dorn said with a raised fist. "To the training circle!"

The Valians began hooting and hollering as Ava, Rien, and Axe followed Dorn and Zalarae to the training circle beyond the village. The crowd closed in fast— voices rising, boots crunching over packed earth, pine and fresh wood thick in the air. Ava's pulse matched the rhythm of their chants, a steady beat beneath the fading morning mist. The Valians lined the edge of the clearing, forming a loose ring around the circle as she and the others stepped into the center, where the ground was bare and waiting.

Ava eyed Rien. His angular features were set. His brows gathered together. Did he have any doubts? "You ready?" she asked.

"Yes." A hard nod. "You?"

"She thinks she is," Axe cut it. "But I see the fear in her eyes." Ava shot him a look as a wicked grin spread across his face. "Got ya!" He chuckled. "Or were you not fearing?"

Ava shoved him as a young Valian maiden entered the circle. The maiden held her arms out with two wood-carved swords and an axe lying across. She placed the weapons in the center of the space, then took her place with the others.

Dorn stepped out next. "New friends," he said with a raised voice. "We now commence with the first part of the trials. Combat!" Everyone cheered, raising their fists high. He strode to the circle's center and picked up one of the swords. He sliced through the air. "These weapons are fashioned from the Wild North's ember bark, a dense wood veined with gold and said to hold the warmth of dragon fire during the coldest night." He lifted the wood to his forehead. "May the wood guide our hands today."

"For the Frost Vale," the others replied.

Dorn lowered the sacred weapon. He faced Ava and the others. "Who goes first?"

The crowd hushed, the air teeming with anticipation. "I go first," Rien announced. He cracked his knuckles and stepped forward, boots crunching against the frost-laced dirt.

Dorn stood opposite him, the sword dangling loosely from one hand. "Whenever you are ready, Rien."

Rien selected his weapon, a sword. He tossed it from one hand to the other, testing its weight. He circled Dorn. Then he pivoted and lunged. His form was clean, practiced. He swept forward with a diagonal strike, which Dorn parried with a quick flick.

"Too rehearsed," Ava muttered to Axe.

"Slower than a slug," Axe replied.

Rien spun, bringing the sword around for another swing, this one lower. Dorn stepped aside as if avoiding a leaf, then countered with a quick jab and a slice that Rien barely deflected.

"Good," Dorn said, shifting from one foot to the other. "But predictable."

Rien gritted his teeth and pushed harder. He moved with precise footwork, sword slicing in sharp, controlled arcs. But Dorn's movements were effortless. Smooth as silk. Where Rien swung with ferocity, Dorn glided with calm. Then, in a flash, Dorn pivoted. He swung the sword sharply, disarming Rien with ease. The wooden blade clunked to the ground.

Rien froze. His breath came out in spurts. He looked down at his empty hands. He hadn't seen it coming. Neither had Ava. She gulped. Did she stand a chance against Dorn?

Axe let out a low whistle. "That's faster than a lightning bug."

"It was." Ava's heart raced from watching the duel. She would have to dig deep to prove herself. She had seen Dorn's moves. Now she knew exactly what she needed to do.

Be unpredictable.

Dorn stepped back from Rien and lowered his sword. "You have strength and speed. But you will never win if your enemy can predict your moves."

"Understood." Rien dipped his head.

Dorn turned to Ava and Axe. "Who's next?"

"I am," Ava said with a swallow, stepping into the circle.

Her breath came fast, and her palms grew slick. She wiped them off on her trousers, then picked the unused wooden sword from the ground. She sliced it back and forth in front of her, a finely carved blade, perfect for proving herself.

Dorn nodded, and the test began.

She moved differently from Rien. Less refined. Less disciplined. Much wilder. She darted in low, feinted right, then twisted into a slash aimed at Dorn's ribs. He blocked it cleanly, but his eyes sharpened.

She smiled. Good. She had his attention.

She pressed the attack, her moves unexpected and unrelenting. She felt like a wild harpy, but she didn't care. She wanted this win. Her blade hummed through the air—left, right, a spin, a sudden drop to the knee. But Dorn was water to her fire.

He flowed with every blow, never rattled, never rushed. She ducked for an upward strike, and his blade came down with a crack, the edge of his wooden sword whacking her knuckles.

She hissed through her teeth, stumbling back several paces and nearly falling over. She took a knee to steady herself as blood welled from a narrow gash across the back of her hand.

Her arm reverberated from her fingertips to her shoulder, like a snapped harp string. Heat bloomed in her palm. Not pain. Something deeper. The air around her hand shimmered, faint and fleeting, like sunlight refracted through water. A soft blue glow pulsed beneath her skin, gone so quickly she wondered if exhaustion had finally captured her.

She shook it off, heart racing. *Focus.* Whatever that was, it didn't matter.

"Get him, Ava!" Rien called.

"Come on, now!" Axe hollered with a clap.

She switched the weapon to her other hand. When her nerves settled, she raised her blade and came at him again. But Dorn stayed one step ahead, predicting her every move. With a swift motion, he swept her sword to the side and caught her arm in a firm grip.

"You fight well," he said, steadying her. "But you lead with your emotions."

Ava swallowed. *Emotions?* She'd show him emotion. She yanked back when a scream shattered the air. Not a scream. A roar. Wordless. Guttural. Wild.

Heads turned. Everyone jumped back.

A figure with wild red hair sprinted from the far side of the circle, coming from the village. He wore a blood-soaked, tattered brown tunic and green trousers. Dark stains like dried blood streaked his pale face and neck. His bare feet pounded the dirt. He clutched a stone-carved dagger in his grip. He ran, not at them. Toward Rien.

"NUUEEAHHNN!" he cried, raw and hoarse. A call. A plea. The word was indecipherable, but shot a warning signal through her body.

Ava darted out of the way as the wild fae barreled past her and Dorn. Rien flinched as he approached. The fae shoved his dagger under his arm, his hands flying with precise and desperate movements. His mouth opened, garbled grunts spilling out, trying to tell Rien something.

"Take him!" Dorn hollered.

The stranger spun around and widened his stance in front of Rien. He held out his dagger. Was he protecting Rien? Ava's eyes locked with the stranger's and a vision hit her. Feathers. Blood. A scream in the dark. Her knees buckled.

"Ava!" Axe grabbed her and held her up.

She could only watch as the stranger waved his dagger back and forth, warding off the approaching Valians.

"Stop!" Rien called out. "Don't hurt him!"

Half a dozen Valians surged and snatched the stranger's dagger. They restrained his arms and legs. He roared and fought back like a feral beast, kicking, twisting, lashing out with maddened strength. It took all of them to wrestle him down.

Her gut clenched, mind reeling. This wasn't right. "No. Wait! You're hurting him!" She stepped forward, but it was too late.

The Valians dragged him away, feet scraping through the dirt, his cries splitting the air. "NUUEEAHHNN!"

Rien stood rigid, breath ragged, hands clenched at his sides. Though he said nothing, Ava saw it in his eyes— that wild stranger had struck something deep within him like in her, too.

She nudged up against Axe and wrapped a hand around his arm. Tears sprang to her eyes. "This isn't right."

Axe looked at her, confusion creasing his brow. "I sense it as well."

Voices murmured as the Valians moved in close. Zalarae approached and stood beside Dorn. "The trials today are canceled while we deal with our intruder," she announced. She motioned with wide arms. "Everyone, please go about your daily tasks."

Ava, Rien, and Axe stayed together while everyone filtered out. Rien touched his chest, his eyes dazed. "I—"

"No," Ava snapped. "Not here. To the river."

They left the circle, then cut through the thinning trees, the murmurs of the Valians fading behind them. The cool air near the river hit Ava's skin like a sobering slap, but it did nothing to calm the storm building in her chest. She'd seen him. The stranger. The fae with the red hair. She had no idea when, or where. But she recognized him—those desperate eyes, the blood on his clothes, the way he'd flung himself in front of Rien like a shield. He hadn't come to harm them. He had come to protect them. He had tried to speak to Rien, maybe even to her and Axe.

Her trembling hand brushed the blood from her knuckles. It lingered on her fingertips where the scabbard had poked her when she reached under her bed pallet earlier. She had no idea where it had come from, but she knew it had held a sword. The same one she'd seen in a vision spiraling through the clouds. Her vision blurred for a moment as blood, feathers, and a face screaming without sound played in her mind. Had that face been the red-headed stranger? Not to mention her dreams of the dark prince. Everything seemed to be crashing down as her mind spun in a million different directions.

Ava didn't realize she'd quickened her pace until she reached the river's edge. She turned sharply but didn't say anything as she caught her breath. "Now," she said. "What in thunderation is happening to us?"

Rien rubbed his head and lowered himself onto a rock near the water. "I-I-I know that fae." He met their stares with a confused look. "I don't know how, but I know him."

"I think I know him too," Ava said, pacing in a circle. "But how?"

"I as well." Axe wrapped his hand around his bushy beard. "He couldn't speak words, but he was trying to say something."

"Nuueeahhnn," Rien muttered. "He said it over and over to me. Like I should've known what it meant. And his hands... He was using them to communicate with me."

"A warning," Ava cut in. "It had to be a warning."

"Of what?" Rien asked.

She slowed her pacing. "I've been seeing things." She stopped in place and faced them, ready to tell them everything. "Like visions, but they all seem so real. At night..." She swallowed and lowered her voice. "I dream of the dark prince. At least, I think it's him." She rubbed her forehead, trying to remember the details. "He calls to me, asking me to find him."

Axe and Rien glanced at each other before looking back at her.

"I'm not having any dreams like that, but I'm seeing things too," Axe admitted. "Red—"

"Feathers," they all said together.

"And blood," Rien finished. "Like the blood on that stranger." His eyes took on a faraway look. "He was so close to me I saw a wound on his neck. A gash, healed over but barely so."

The three moved in close, huddling as if someone might be listening. For all Ava knew, someone was. She, Rien, and Axe were new here. They were still learning much about the Frost Vale. They weren't even Valians.

She blinked, her mind spinning in a new direction now. *They weren't even Valians.* "Hey," she whispered. "Where are we from?" She was certain the confused looks on Rien's and Axe's faces matched hers. "How did we get here?"

Ava loved coming to the river. It soothed her, made her feel safe. But those tranquil effects had long gone. Instead, panic began taking over, creeping across her skin and sending shivers down her arms.

"We were travelers, looking for a home," Axe said, his voice drifting. "And we found this place. They took us in."

"From where?" Ava asked. "Where were we traveling from?" She racked her brain for the answer, tracing every moment in the Frost Vale, but could remember nothing prior to her arrival.

Rien scooped up a rock and chunked it into the river with a splash. "He knows," Rien murmured. "That stranger. He was trying to tell us."

A chill rippled through her. Rien was right. She

didn't know how she knew, but she *knew*. The moment the stranger had charged into the circle, something in her had surged to life. Not fear, not confusion, but a fierce recognition. The way he had looked at them—at Rien especially—like he would tear down the world to reach him. That wasn't madness. That was purpose. That was memory. Maybe not hers, but his.

The stranger knew something.

"We find him," she said. "And discover the truth."

Axe dropped his hand from his beard. "The Valians have him."

The river whispered beside them, its dark surface catching the shreds of daylight. A chill crept through the air, curling around Ava like mist. She glanced downstream, the woods feeling watchful. Something in her chest stirred, faint but fierce, echoing the stranger's cry. Whoever that stranger was, he wasn't merely a Valian captive. He was part of whatever they had forgotten.

A sly smirk spread across Rien's face, breaking the tension like a blade through silk. "They may have him, but not for long."

CHAPTER SEVEN

Mateo drew in a deep breath of crisp mountain air as he soared over the palace grounds. His dark cloak flapped behind him like a banner of strength while *Teyocel's* wings sliced the morning haze. Below, the royal carriages rumbled through the gates, gilded with House Stromm emblems—the great tree and the large S for Stromm.

There was no ceremonial procession. No rose petals strewn about the road. No cheering. The king and queen ordered this conquest tour with a clear mission to restore loyalty, crush dissent, and remind the provinces who ruled. It would be Mateo, crowned prince, conqueror in waiting, who would carry that message like a blade across the land.

His hand moved to his tunic, to the spot where his necklace hung beneath the fabric. Pride filled his chest like a glorious sunrise. Everything he had ever wanted was coming to fruition. Status, power, wealth. "*They will all bow to me.*"

"*They will, my prince.*" Teyocel huffed a tuft of smoke. "*And if they do not, we will make them.*"

Mateo's lips curved into a smile. "*Oh yes, we will.*"

The king and queen remained behind to rule and strategize while Mateo flew the skies with *Teyocel.* His escorts followed below: the ever-cunning Raelor, the newly appointed Master of the Blade, the scar-faced dwarf named Karl, the half-troll maidservant Marina, and a dozen armed riders sworn to House Stromm. They would take the long road by carriage. Mateo would follow from above.

Their first destination lay to the south in Sand Bluff, the province in the southernmost region of Faevenly. The stronghold nestled between rolling hill country and the Great Cove beaches. If even a whisper of rebellion stirred there, Mateo and his forces would root it out and crush it.

The realm needed an example, and Sand Bluff was poised for the role. Selene Baffin, now rotting in the palace dungeon, hailed from there. Her father, the former steward, had been incinerated, reduced to ash and dust. Wherever the Baffins had walked, others like them surely followed.

Mateo gripped the ridge of *Teyocel's* neck. He would make every last Baffin loyalist pay for standing against his house. With Sand Bluff put in place, the other provinces would fall in line. He was sure of it.

They traveled for hours, over terrain that shifted from mountainous peaks to grassy fields, the air growing heavier and thicker the deeper they traveled into Sand

Bluff. When the bright sun began to set, Mateo guided *Teyocel* into a wide arc and skimmed the terrain. He spotted a flat grassy area not far from a trickling stream.

He swept closer to Master Karl, who led the riders. He pointed to the area. "We stop there for the night."

A sharp whistle from Karl, and the caravan moved in the direction he indicated before rolling to a stop. *Teyocel* circled once overhead before landing with a thundering crash.

Mateo dismounted with a hop. "*Stay close.*"

"*Of course, my prince.*"

Karl barked orders to the guards, setting a perimeter watch. Marina directed the traveling maidservants on tent placements and fire positioning. Raelor roamed the grounds, watching. By nightfall, everything had been set up.

After having his fill of food and drink, Mateo kept to himself then retired to his tent. He pulled off his boots and cape, setting his things aside. He rolled his shoulders with a crack, then lay back on the hard pallet.

His thoughts buzzed. The whispers the brother and sister had told them about days earlier swirled in his mind. A rebellion brewing. The provinces uniting against the crown. The weight of the pendant around his neck pressed against his chest, his insides as tight as a pulled bowstring. He rubbed the spot. A breath. He needed a quick breath.

His fingers curled around the chain. Just a tug. That's all it would take. A single pull and he could ease the weight, if only for a short time. No one would know. He tried to free it. The chain refused to yield. Its links held fast, as if fused around his neck. Tingles raced down his back. He pulled harder. The pendant throbbed against his skin, warm and alive, and for a fleeting, horrifying instant, it seemed to beat in time with him. He had to get it off. Now.

A tremor ran through his hand. His grip tightened. He yanked the metal. *Off!*

"*My prince!*" *Teyocel's* voice blasted through his mind like a crack of thunder splitting the sky. "*Let go!*"

He stilled. His shallow and ragged breathing slowed. His hand, clenched around the chain, relaxed. The moment he released it, his pulse calmed. The choking heat behind his eyes dissipated. He gulped air like he'd been suffocating, relief sweeping through him like a gentle breeze.

"Thank you," he whispered aloud, not sure if the words were for *Teyocel* or himself. Maybe both.

"*Of course, my prince.*"

He brought his shaky hand up to his face. A thin red mark like a burn crossed his palm. He brought the mark closer. Had the chain done that to him? Was it even possible? The thought unsettled him. Yet, something about it soothed him too. The chain knew what was best for him. It had saved him from his own weakness. It kept him sharp. Strong. Focused. It understood what was required better than he ever could.

He breathed in, slow and full. The chaos inside him settled, like fire controlled by the rain. The pendant wanted him to rise. To become what he was meant to be. And wasn't that what he wanted too? Greatness? He could be more than an heir—he could be a legend.

71

His fingers brushed the links one final time, like a promise. This wasn't a thing to discard or remove. It was a precious gift, given to him by his mother and father, the high king and high queen of Faevenly. He would wear it like a crown.

"I will never take you off," he promised.

With his muscles relaxed, Mateo lay back down when a holler cascaded through the night. He jolted upright, muscles coiled. Shouts exploded outside the tent, followed by the unmistakable clash of steel. Metal against metal. Screams and snarls.

He sprang to his feet in seconds, sword in hand, storming out into the camp. Firelight flickered wildly, casting erratic shadows as riders, dressed head to toe in black with dark face coverings and hoods, thundered into the clearing. Smoke curled in the air, thick with dust and the scent of blood. Horses reared. Blades sang.

"Teyocel! We are under attack!"

Karl was already in the fray, his great axe whirling with brutal force. He knocked one rider off their steed with a *thwack*, then spun to clash with another barreling straight for him. Nearby, two riders circled Marina. They closed in. She charged, mouth twisted with a bellowing battle cry, her fists hammering with bone-shattering strength. One went down hard. Another staggered back in terror, then bolted for the trees.

Raelor stood still as stone, his staff in hand, releasing waves of raw power that burst from its tip like invisible shockwaves. The blasts struck the attackers with the force of a tempest, sending them tumbling backward, limbs flailing. Those too close clutched their throats, gasping for air as the magic coiled around them like a tightening noose.

"Death to the prince! Death to the prince!" someone shrieked.

"Teyocel! Hurry!"

Mateo spun to the shouts, lifting his sword barely in time to deflect a downward strike. Another rebel lunged from the side. He met both, weapons flashing, the clang and grind of blades shivering through his arms. The fighters were skilled, not peasants with pitchforks. They were trained assassins, perhaps, or rogue soldiers. Sand Bluff loyalists.

"Teyocel!"

"Almost there!"

Mateo pivoted, ducked, and slashed. He drove one rebel back with a well-aimed kick to the chest. Then swung his sword into the gut of another.

"Get him!" a high-pitched voice screamed. "The prince!"

A deep, guttural roar like thunder exploded through the sky, the dragon's cry so terrifying it shook the earth's core.

"Dragon!" Voices called out in all directions. "Retreat! Retreat!"

Too late. A streak of shadow swooped from above, wings wide as sails and claws like curved daggers. *Teyocel* roared again, then dove. His talons raked through the chaos, snatching a rebel clean off the ground. Another tried to flee, but *Teyocel's* tail whipped sideways and sent the black-clad attacker flying into the trees with a sickening crunch.

"Stop!" Raelor hollered. "Save one!"

Mateo halted mid-strike, his blade inches from a fallen attacker's chest. The masked rebel beneath him shielded their face, bracing for the blow. It never came. Raelor's order cut through the haze of bloodlust and steadied his hand. Raelor was right. They needed answers more than corpses.

He angled the sword's tip to the rebel's throat. The mask left only the eyes exposed, wide and terrified. "Move and my blade will slice you through," Mateo said quietly.

He studied the camp as the rest of the skirmish wound down. Those not already dead had fled into the shadows. Marina moved swiftly, calling for the wounded to be put in the nearest tent and ordering the remaining guards to secure the perimeter. Karl strode up to Mateo, chest heaving, axe still dripping.

Raelor approached. "Well, well. Look what we have." He eyed the captive rebel, snapped his fingers and pointed at the makeshift command tent. "Take the prisoner over there."

Karl and one of the guards half dragged, half pushed the captive toward the tent. The rebel thrashed and kicked. They tossed him to the ground.

Raelor motioned to Karl. "Remove the face covering."

"With pleasure," he said, ripping off the cloth.

A cascade of red hair spilled out, the pale skin stark against the black outfit. She was young, maybe fifteen or sixteen. Her green eyes burned with the same defiant fire Mateo had seen in Selene Baffin before she was dragged to the dungeons.

"It's her," Mateo hissed, moving in closer to study her face. "Selene Baffin's sister."

The girl sneered and spat in his face. "Do not speak her name. Scum!"

Mateo wiped the dribble with the back of his hand. "You will regret that."

Karl lunged forward, axe raised.

Raelor held out a hand. "We need her alive," the witch commanded.

The tent flaps opened, and Marina stomped in. She held an attacker by the throat and tossed the body onto the floor next to Selene's sister with a grunt. "One more," the troll said.

"Thank you, Marina," Raelor said to her as she left. He tipped his head at Karl, who pulled off the face covering and hood with a rough grab.

This time, long dark hair spilled out. Brown eyes met Mateo's, and his heart lurched. *Camilla.* Not her, but someone who looked a lot like her. It was like facing a mirror of his childhood, of the place he'd called home.

"Girls?!" Karl yelled. "We were attacked by a bunch of girls?!"

Mateo backed up and turned away, his vision tunneling. Memories clawed their way up from the depths of his mind, uninvited and aching. *Camilla.* He had called her sister. He had chased her through the craggy rocks of Spirit Butte, laughed with her, and cried with her. She made the best tea and bread. She taught him how to braid Floriana's hair. Sun, Moon, and Stars. He hadn't thought of Floriana in how long? A plug like a stone clogged his throat. She had the Dragon's Bellow. Had it taken her?

And then there was Manny... Manny, who had raised him. Manny, who had lied to him. He had concealed the truth about Mateo's blood, his birth, his entire life. He was robbed of his birthright by Manny, kept away from his greatness by Manny. And the human had somehow called it love. How could he have done that to him?

Mateo's stomach twisted. He shoved through the flaps of the tent and burst into the cold night air. The damp grass clung to his bare feet, and a shiver ran up his spine. He wrapped his arms around himself, suddenly feeling exposed and fractured. Like a lowborn nothing again. A lowborn struggling to survive.

"You are not nothing or lowborn. You are the future King," Teyocel pressed in his mind. *"Do not forget your greatness, my prince."*

Mateo swallowed. "Future. King. Not lowborn." The pendant at his chest pulsed softly, heat spreading like a steady flame through his ribs. Strength and clarity flooded him. He had a home at Stromm Palace. He had a family—the mighty Stromms, including a little sister, Lily. He inhaled through his nostrils, sharp and cold, the truth hardening inside him.

"My prince." He turned to find Marina with his cloak. She held it out with a bow. "It is cold."

The dark, dragon-scaled cloak glinted from the firelight, almost beckoning him. He took it with a tip of his head and slipped it on. "Thank you, Marina."

The rich fabric molded to his skin perfectly. Power hummed through the seams, coiling around his shoulders like armor. He knew who he was.

Head held high, he stepped back into the tent. The

attackers were huddled together on the floor. He met their pitiful gazes. "Who are you?" he asked, his voice like a blade unsheathed.

"We've been trying," Karl said. "But they're not talking."

"We are waiting for your orders, my prince," Raelor added. "Say the word, and I will make them speak."

The girls exchanged glances but managed to put on a brave face. Mateo admired that. He also wondered how long it would take for them to break. Knowing Raelor's abilities, not long.

He stepped back with a sweep of an arm. "They are all yours, Raelor."

CHAPTER EIGHT

Mateo clasped his hands behind his back and began circling the room. He'd been a victim of Raelor's magic once, during the presentation of the hunters before the Summit Range Hunt. His fingers brushed his throat. He could still feel the pressure against his windpipe where the witch had held him in an invisible chokehold and dragged him across the floor with a mere hand movement. Would he do the same to the girls? Something worse? They and their band of riders could have killed him.

"Don't say anything," the dark-haired girl warned her accomplice, her eyes narrowing defiantly in Mateo's direction.

So, she was the leader, not the Baffin girl. Interesting. Mateo raised a brow at Raelor. His sharp gaze told him the witch was thinking the same thing.

"Well, then," Raelor snapped at the dark-haired girl. "You do not have to worry about your friend saying anything because she won't be able to." He flung his fingers out, crooked and curled at the knuckles. The Baffin girl sputtered. She grabbed her throat and fell to her side.

"No!" the dark-haired girl yelled. She slid in front of her friend and held out her hands, as if she could stop the witch. Mateo knew there was no way.

"Now, tell me," Raelor hissed. "Who are you and your friend, and where are you from?"

She clamped her lips shut as her friend's choking grew more strained. Mateo didn't think she had much air left.

"Have it your way." Raelor lifted his arm. The Baffin girl's body rose from the ground, her legs flailing while her hands grasped at her throat. "Your names. The name of your group. Where you are from."

"No," the girl uttered, tears welling up in her eyes. She lunged for her friend, as if she could pull her from Raelor's magic, but she stayed thrashing in the air. "I can't..."

Raelor snarled. "Can't? Or won't?"

"I have felt that pain," Mateo said. He continued circling the room, the sounds of the sputtering reducing to the choked silence that preceded death. "Her windpipe will crush any second now. Without air, she will perish." He stopped and faced the girl whose legs now dangled loosely, her face turning a dark, bluish red. "Tell us what we want to know, and she will live."

Tears streamed down the dark-haired girl's face. "Okay!"

Raelor's hand relaxed, and the Baffin girl crumpled

to the ground like a puppet whose strings had been cut. She gasped once, then twice, her body seizing as air finally clawed its way back into her lungs. She lay there, heaving, as her friend reached and grabbed her hand.

"I will end you before this is over," the brown-haired girl spat. Her eyes moved from Raelor to Mateo. "Both of you."

Raelor smirked. "No, you will answer my questions." He raised his hand again. "Or would you like a taste of what will happen if you do not give us what we want?"

The Baffin girl sputtered. "Just ... tell ... them." She grimaced as she squeezed her friend's hand. "Let them know."

Mateo stopped in his tracks. This should be good. He faced the girls. Whatever explanation they had for attacking them would be their last words. He was the prince. A Stromm. They were as good as dead.

"I ask again," Raelor said. "What are your names, the name of your group, and where are you from?"

The brown-haired girl rose to her feet. She brushed her long hair out of her face and raised her chin. She gestured to her friend. "This is Nyra of House Baffin from Sand Bluff. I am Isabelle, a Soltec from the Soltierra South."

Mateo's brow rose. A Soltec from the Soltierra South? He had never met anyone from there. Tales of the region drifted through the realm like smoke in the wind. They spoke of a land untamed by crowns or courts, where sunlight kissed the earth year-round, and the trees grew thick and wild with golden fruit. Vast beaches shimmered under endless skies, and jade-colored rivers cut through dense forests.

They were a people of mixed blood, fae and human, who called themselves the Soltecs, or sun people. They were unruled, unyielding. Undeniably dangerous. Legends claimed they had their own dragons—smaller, swifter beasts who lived in volcanic groves and stayed on their land only. But Mateo doubted their existence. If they truly existed, they would be here with their riders.

"Are you part human?" Mateo asked.

She threaded her hair behind her ears, exposing their roundness. "I am." She nodded once. "A lowborn, as you once were. Remember that?"

A fire sparked in his veins. She shouldn't have said that. "Do I remember the lies?" He stepped forward. "The deceit and trickery?" He balled his hands into fists. "Oh, I remember."

Her eyes widened. Her throat bobbed from a hard gulp.

"You had best watch yourself, girl," Karl warned. "Or you'll end up dragon food."

Should Mateo summon *Teyocel*? End the pair right here and now? He could drag them from the tent and let *Teyocel* do the rest. It would serve them right.

"Tell us of your riders," Raelor said. "Why did you attack us?"

The Baffin girl, Nyra, clambered to her feet and joined her friend. She stood so close to her their shoulders touched. She narrowed her stare on Mateo. "We are Oathriders. We ride because you, the Stromms, are killing Faevenly," she said. "You killed my father and hold my sister. You betray the realm with the evil you commit. We are prepared to stop you."

"Oathriders?" Mateo asked, the word foreign and bitter on his tongue. His jaw clenched. Oaths were sacred. Oaths were binding. Still their oath was not to the crown; that much was evident. "To whom have you given your oaths?"

Isabelle's back straightened. "We stand with the Only One. Bringer of peace. Uniter of bloodlines who lives and breathes in the Wild North."

Mateo stiffened, the words striking him like a blade through the gut. *The Only One.* The title echoed through him, dragging ice across old wounds. The weight of the pendant burned against his chest as visions of Avalynn hurtling through the clouds played in his mind. Had she survived? If one could, it would be her, and her only.

He searched Nyra's and Isabelle's young defiant faces, and for a fragile moment, he saw not rebels, but believers—ones willing to die for something or someone. Avalynn. *Alive.* The thought gripped him like a vice, tightening until rage surged to the surface. He wouldn't—*couldn't*—let her threaten everything he'd built.

His voice came out low and taut, his tone coiled like a whip, his face a mask of thunder. "End them," Mateo commanded Raelor.

The girls moved even closer together, as if one could protect the other from his death verdict. Foolish girls. They did not deserve life.

"No," Raelor said.

Mateo halted. *No?* Had he heard that right? He

turned to face the witch, heat crackling through him like a brushfire. "You defy me? Your prince and future king?"

"No, my prince. Not at all." He bowed low, holding the position for a few long seconds before he righted himself. "What these girls claim is nothing more than whisperings. I offer an alternative plan." He flicked his hands at the girls. "Bind them. Gag them. Get them out of here."

When they were gone, Mateo eyed the witch. "You'd better suggest something that will please me, and quickly." Teeth gritted, he pointed his finger. "If you do not, you will see your end in a blaze of flames." His mother might value Raelor's gifts, but he didn't need him, not with a dragon at his command.

"My prince," Raelor cleared his throat. "If Avalynn is truly alive in the North, we could use the prisoner rebels to draw her out."

"Bait the Only One, if she exists," Karl said with a grunt. "Makes sense. But what about the other Oathriders? Who knows how many more there are?"

"As long as we have these two, the others will attempt a rescue," Raelor said. "I am sure of it. When they do, we will be ready."

"Ahh. A sound strategy," Karl said, his bushy brow raised high. "What say you, my prince?"

For once, he agreed with Raelor. The girls had faced death. They still did, but not before they were used to capture the other Oathriders, and perhaps Avalynn too.

"Very well," Mateo said, voice smooth and sharp. "Let them be our lure." He turned to Raelor. "But if this fails, you will answer for it, witch."

Karl cut in. "What of Sand Bluff? We are nearly there."

"A wise observation," Raelor said, stroking his chin. "It would be a mistake to leave it unfinished. I suggest we complete the task as per the order of the king and queen. We must put in place a steward loyal to House Stromm before we move on. Only then do we head north." Then, as if remembering his place, he tipped his head in Mateo's direction. "If that is what you wish, my prince."

That witch was begging for a shortened life, but he saw the wisdom in the suggestion. Lucky for him. "Yes, I wish it." Mateo flapped his cloak behind him as he made his way to the tent opening. "We will complete our mission in Sand Bluff." He paused, the implications of their next stop halting him in place. "Then we head north."

CHAPTER NINE

North. The word rang like a distant bell in Mateo's mind, sending a chill down his spine. North meant the Vale. North meant confronting his choices. North meant her. *Avalynn.*

Could she truly be alive? The thought slid through him like a cold blade. After all this time. After what had happened. After what he had done. He let the memory surface cautiously, like touching a wound he had never allowed to heal.

She leaped from her dragon to his. He remembered the wild act—the flash of her body cutting through the wind, the shock of her hand slamming into his. She dangled beneath him, boots swinging through empty air as *Teyocel* beat his wings above.

"Pull me up!" she had shouted, her fingers digging into his wrist.

For a heartbeat, a small part of him had wanted to. The part that remembered who she had once been to him and what they had shared. Then the darker truth invaded, sharp and insistent. She had betrayed him. She had chosen herself. She didn't deserve to be saved.

He closed his eyes, tightening his grip around the wrist she'd clung to, her final, desperate words still echoing in his skull. *"Don't do it."*

But he *had* done it. His fingers had loosened. Her hand had slipped from his. She fell, hair whipping wildly, body swallowed by the clouds, her voice lost to the wind as the sky closed around her.

Mateo blinked now, throat tight, the memory leaving a dull ache behind his ribs. He exhaled slowly, trying to steady the tremor in his hands. He told himself it was the cold night air, the long ride, the skirmish with the Oathriders—not the memory, not her. It couldn't be her.

He dragged a hand down his face and walked into the darkness, away from the camp, as a thousand thoughts warred. Doubt and desire. Rage and ruin. The pendant around his neck pulsed, like a bolt from the blue, grounding him, reminding him of who he was. Whatever waited in the Wild North, whoever she had become, it would not matter.

He would face her. She would kneel or die. If she had her sword, he'd take that and claim the power that was rightfully his.

"My prince is wise."

Mateo glanced up, catching *Teyocel's* wings soaring through the night sky. Seeing his dragon brought a sense of calm, a deep inner peace he craved. He didn't need anyone or anything, only *Teyocel. "Thank you, my friend."*

The dragon touched down, quietly this time. He took soft, gentle steps closer to Mateo, sending out a tuft of satisfied smoke from his nostrils. "Ahh, friend," *Teyocel* said out loud. "That title has not been bestowed upon me in far too long." The dragon smiled, the faintest curl of his mouth softening the lines of his usually sinister face. "Thank you for that, my prince."

Power stirred between them, steady and sure, wrapping around the bond that bound their souls. Companionship, understanding, and trust flickered inside Mateo. Could their connection be something more than a bargain? Oh, how he wished it were so. He was tired of feeling alone.

He stepped closer, the link between them thrumming like a living thread. Heat shimmered off *Teyocel's* dark scales, the air still thick with smoke and ash. He lifted a hand and laid it between the dragon's dark eyes, fingers tracing the smooth ridges where power breathed beneath his skin.

Teyocel lowered his head and leaned into the touch. The warmth between them bloomed, the kind Mateo hadn't felt since Stormshroud. The memory of the wolf-beast flashed sharp and painful, his heart aching something fierce. The creature had chosen *her* in the end, had turned away when Mateo called her to him. How could Stormy have done that to him? When he had saved her as a pup and loved her for so long?

The dragon's pulse hammered under his palm, steady and sure. *Teyocel* would never leave him. At least, that's what Mateo let himself believe.

"Never fear, my prince. You are mine. I am yours," he

rumbled, his voice curling through the air and circling Mateo like a hug. "I do not abandon what is mine."

The words sank deep, settling somewhere between comfort and claim. Mateo's hand lingered against the warm scales, his chest loosening with something that felt dangerously like affection. Should he keep up his guard or settle into his chosen path? He desperately didn't want to be alone anymore. With *Teyocel*, he wasn't.

He closed his eyes and leaned his head against the dragon's cheek. "I will not abandon you, either."

They stayed that way as the winds of the night gently swirled around them. Mateo's breathing steadied, his shoulders easing for the first time in days. "*Teyocel*, where were you when I called for you earlier? You did not answer me, and I needed you."

"Ahh, yes. I hunt at night to keep my strength. It caused my delay, and for that, I offer you my most sincere apology."

"I see." Mateo let the quiet return, finding comfort in the stillness, tranquility, and companionship. Forget the betraying wolf. He didn't need Stormshroud after all.

His breathing fell into the same slow rhythm as *Teyocel's*. The steady rise and fall lulled him, a rare moment of peace, when a sharp pain pulsed between his eyes. He drew back, wincing. A dull ache spread behind his temples, deep and strange, like something pressing from within. He touched his forehead, then felt warmth trickle down his upper lip.

"My prince," *Teyocel* rumbled, pulling his head back with narrowed eyes. "You are bleeding."

"What?" Mateo swiped beneath his nose and stared

at the crimson smear glinting on his fingertips. "Why am I bleeding?" His voice came out thin, unmoored. He wasn't injured. At least, he didn't think so.

Teyocel stepped back, wings shifting. "The skirmish. The late hour. Even the strongest warriors feel their strain. Rest now. I will see you at dawn."

Before Mateo could ask the dragon to stay, he launched into the dark. A rush of air and a shimmer of heat swept across his face as the echo of departing wings trailed behind.

Mateo stood there swaying, the night spinning softly around him. *Exhaustion. That's all it is.* He forced his legs to move, each step heavier than the last, until he reached his tent. Inside, he tore off his coat, rubbing at his nose. The blood was gone, yet the dull pain remained.

He exhaled, ragged and unsteady, and lowered himself onto his pallet. *Teyocel* was right; he needed sleep. Tomorrow, they would secure Sand Bluff. The Oathriders would serve as bait for the others. And after that, he'd find Avalynn and finish what she started.

The tent walls shuddered, then went still, leaving only the faint pulse of the pendant and the quiet weight of the dark.

CHAPTER TEN

S onia walked for miles, creating distance between herself and the Sublands. With each step, her mind swirled with the different scenarios she might encounter in the Wild North—Avalynn held against her will, Avalynn wanting to stay, Avalynn no longer alive. She had given Manny hope that Avalynn still lived, but it was only a guess. She had no real information but chose to believe in the best-case scenario. It was the only thing that kept her going.

With the sky darkening and her thoughts spent, she found a clearing obscured by wild brush, the perfect place to vanish. After a quick scan of her surroundings, she slipped her hand beneath the collar of her dress and pulled out her necklace. She rubbed the opalescent stone's smooth surface, then pinched her thumb and forefinger together and tugged. The small, round, shimmery portal she'd hidden within slid out, weightless and warm.

She placed her hands on the edges and stretched. When it was big enough, she stepped through.

Her coven's hidden land unfolded like a beautiful tapestry. Thatched cottages where she and her sisters lived sat nestled beneath a towering mountain range. Purple leaves clung to thick trees, violets and elderflowers drifting in the crisp breeze. Time moved differently here. Days in paradise passed like mere minutes in Faevenly—plenty of time to plan her next move.

Drawing in a deep breath, she let her shoulders drop and her muscles relax. This was the only place where she was truly safe, a place where secrets lived and truth was shaped.

This was home.

She made her way toward the cottage tucked deep in the back, offering quiet greetings to the coven sisters she passed along the way. There, sitting on a log, was the one she needed to see, a trusted friend and confidant.

Rook Cailean, former steward of the Sublands, sat on a log in front of a small fire, its flickering glow catching the edges of his broad, muscular shoulders. The hulking human's thick hands moved slowly as he stoked the flames with a long branch. With each step she took closer, his features came more into view. Scars lined his face, across his cheeks and brow. His ears were cut into sharp points that poked through his thick, dark hair. The shape disguised his humanness when he lived in Faevenly, a life he was able to sustain by steady sips of Green Falls water and other potions Sonia had given him. But the water could do nothing to heal his mortal wounds, which he suffered at the hands of Kane assassins. And so, Sonia had brought him here to heal.

Now, he lived tethered to Sonia's homeland, the magical properties of the soil, air, and water the only things keeping him alive. She slowed her steps and stopped at the edge of the fire's glow. "Hello, Rook."

He glanced up, his deep brown eyes looking tired and even a bit bored. Life here was peaceful, so different from the chaos he had known in Faevenly. Sometimes she wondered if he wished he hadn't been saved.

"Sonia." His voice rolled out low and rough, like stones tumbling into a riverbed. "You're back."

She eased onto the log across from him. Seeing her friend brought a flicker of comfort, but it didn't last. The gravity of her mission settled back in. "I am," she said quietly. "But I cannot stay long."

"I see." He kept poking the flames. "Did you see my nephew?" Gareth was the only surviving member of the Cailean family, adopted into a loving family after Rook's injuries.

"I did not, my friend," she said.

The flames popped with a sizzle. "And what of Manny? How did he take the news about Mateo and Avalynn?"

"Like we thought he would." She sighed. "You know Manny. He's an emotional being."

"Yes, he is." Rook shook his head and smiled. "Still hard to believe that after all this time, he is still alive. Does he fare well?"

"He does, for now. Though I sense his time will end

soon. His humanity is catching up to him, especially since he's stopped taking the potion I gave him."

Rook offered a nod. "And he still refuses to come here?"

"He does." She wished she could change Manny's mind, but she knew it was impossible. He'd never leave his family and loved ones. "Maybe, when this is all over, he will come back with me."

Rook grunted. "It would be nice to see that little man again." He tossed the stick in the fire and picked up another one. "Any word on Verona?"

When Rook served as steward of the Sublands, Verona, her brother Adrius, and Leaf, Avalynn's father, were but young fae under his care. They had been close, and Rook would have done anything to protect them.

"No word. She is out there somewhere," Sonia said, rubbing her forehead. "Doing whatever she must." Her voice thinned with worry. "Between the Dragon's Bellow, the Mother of Rivers failing, Mateo becoming a Stromm, and Avalynn lost in the Wild North... She's holding the Sublands together with a threadbare grip."

"She will figure things out," Rook said. "She always does. At least the Sublands were spared banishment."

"At least." Sonia murmured.

Silence stretched between them, long and heavy, strangely comforting. They had weathered much together. Sitting there in the quiet with her old friend, it almost felt like time had paused, like the weight of the world had lifted, if only for a little while.

At last, Rook shifted. "So," he rumbled, eyes fixed on the flames. "What is your plan?"

Sonia's gaze roamed to the emerging stars beyond the trees, then back to her friend. "I need to retrieve Avalynn and her sword. Bring her back to Faevenly before it's too late."

Rook's head snapped up. "How? The Valians won't let her go. They'll see it as a threat."

"I know." She nodded with a sigh.

He narrowed his eyes at her and tilted his head. "Do you really?"

"Yes, I do. With the help of my home, I will be ready for their opposition." She moved closer to Rook. "This place is filled with magic." She inhaled deeply. "I need the glimmer in the air, the healing waters, the memory threads that run through the trees. I need the blessing of the land itself if I'm going to reach Avalynn." She rested her hand on his shoulder. "My friend, once I leave here, I may never come back."

Rook's jaw tightened, and he chucked his stick into the flames. "If this is your goodbye, I do not accept it." He rose to his feet, his nostrils flaring. "Do you understand me?"

Sonia held his gaze, her heart aching at the pain etched across his face. "I do," she said softly. "More than you know."

For a long moment, neither spoke. The fire lowered, and the forest sounds around them seemed to pause, honoring their parting. Rook sat back down, and Sonia leaned her head against his shoulder.

"You were the one who brought me back," Rook murmured. "Do not make me lose you again."

"You won't lose me," she said. "Even if I do not

return, I'll always be part of this place." She pulled back, and a smile touched her lips. "And you'll still be here, grumbling into your fire, pretending not to care."

Rook huffed, a sound between laugh and protest. "It's what I do. Grumble and pretend."

Sonia's gaze drifted to the flames. Shoulder to shoulder, their silence weaved together like an unspoken promise. With the flames dancing in her vision, Sonia let down her guard and revealed her fears. "I do not know how I will get into the Wild North without compromising my mind and my magic. As much as I hate to admit it, I am out of answers." She drew out the word *answers* as her mind spun and her back stiffened. "Answers," she repeated, her mind catching an echo from long ago.

"Answers?" Rook repeated. He turned to face her. "What do you mean?"

"Sun, Moon, and Stars." Her mind stretched, the words falling from her lips, the spell remembered. "When the way is lost, and your heart is heavy with doubt, remember this moment. Remember the fire we shared. The scale will answer when it's time."

Rook frowned. "What is that?" He searched her eyes. "Whose words are those?"

"*Izel's*!" She grabbed his hand, jumped to her feet, and took off toward her cottage. Her legs moved before her thoughts could catch up, the memory flooding in fully now—her flight with *Izel*, her magic and the dragon's fire intertwined as they crafted the magical boundary, her fingers prying off the dragon scale *Izel* had offered, then placing it in her pocket. "The dragon gave me the answer to this very moment, so very long ago when she and I created the boundary between Faevenly and the Wild North," she explained over her shoulder, dragging Rook behind her.

Sonia's boots struck the packed earth, scattering fallen leaves as she walked with haste, her cloak snapping at her heels. Rook kept pace, his footsteps heavy. The cottage came into view, a thatched and cozy refuge tucked between amber trees. Its windows glowed faintly in the twilight.

They burst inside, the door swinging wide before closing with a thud. The hearth's logs sparked with fire in her presence, sending warm light into the room. Herbs hung in bunches from the rafters, sage and lavender mingling in the air. Rook kept close while Sonia strode to the carved mahogany chest beside the fireplace.

"I put it here," she explained.

She knelt and opened the lid, her hands steady despite the tremor of anticipation in her veins. From within, she took out a small wooden box, its lid etched with leaves and flowers. With a glance at Rook, she opened it. Inside, resting on a square of white silk, lay the scale. It gleamed with *Izel's* iridescent hues of blue, purple, and pink.

"Incredible," Rook uttered.

"It's just as I remember," she murmured.

She reached for the scale. The moment her fingertips brushed its smooth curve, warmth bloomed against her skin, soft at first, then thrumming with a steady pulse. It felt alive, like a heartbeat answering her own.

Rook's eyes widened. "Is it..." He peered closer. "Moving?"

Sonia nodded ever so slowly. "It still carries *Izel's* magic. Her memory, breath, and life."

They stood together, haloed by the soft firelight, the air in the cottage teeming with possibilities. "See," he said with a rare smile. "You do have answers."

Sonia's heart swelled, hope sparking within her for the first time in a long while. "*Izel's* magic lives within this scale. She gave it to me for this moment. For Avalynn, the Only One. For all of us."

The words settled between them, fragile and bright. For so long, she'd felt adrift, praying for signs that never came. But now, holding the scale, the flame within her, long dimmed by grief and doubt, flickered anew.

Rook stepped closer, his presence steady and grounding. She let herself lean into him, the warmth of his arm a quiet promise in the cool evening light. Outside, the wind rustled the leaves like soft applause.

For the first time in a long while, Sonia dared to believe the path ahead wasn't lost.

CHAPTER ELEVEN

Ava pulled and stretched her fingers, pacing the perimeter of her hut. Where were Rien and Axe? She approached the window and peeked out. Her gut clenched. The village had gone dark. The fires had long been snuffed, and the glowing orbs dimmed. It would be just like Zalarae to figure out that they were up to something. For all she knew, Rien and Axe could have been caught by now, shackled and put away like that stranger.

Tap, tap. She rushed to the door. She held her breath. She inched her hand around the doorknob and pulled. Axe's blond bushy beard popped into view. Rien loomed nearby, his lavender eyes tight and narrow. *Finally.* Ava stepped out and closed the door softly behind her.

Rien placed a finger over his lips, then pointed to the forest. With a nod, they tiptoed around her hut, eased their way to the brush, and slipped between the trees. The bright moonlight trickled through the branches, illuminating enough of the path ahead as they took quick and soft strides. They found a shadowy spot and huddled together, their breath vapors drifting between them.

"Now what?" Axe whispered in his husky voice. They hadn't thought that far ahead.

"We locate that stranger," Rien said. "Find out who he is and what he knows."

"Where do we look?" Ava asked. As far as she knew, the village had no holding areas. The only place where he could be was the healing lodge.

"You thinking what I'm thinking?" Rien asked.

She nodded. "The healing lodge."

"Me too," Axe said. "It's the only place."

Ava eyed the path. The healing lodge sat at the far edge of the village. It stood apart from the cluster of Valian dwellings, isolated and silent, rarely used. She'd never been there and never needed to. The thought of creeping over there made her chest tighten. If the stranger was being kept there, that meant guards were present, especially after the way he had been dragged out of the training circle.

"We have no weapons." The words felt heavier than they should, like the start of something she couldn't take back. Was she prepared for all that?

With a grunt, Axe raised his hands and curled them into fists. "These are all we need."

Really? She rolled her eyes. "We need more than that."

Rien pulled a stone-carved dagger from his trouser pocket, then another. "I have these."

Ava stared at the makeshift weapons. "Well, well, someone's been busy."

So that's what Rien had been doing all those hours alone. She'd seen him whittle wood before, smoothing branches to pass the time. But this was different. Weapons, other than the wooden ones provided by the Valians, were forbidden.

He eyed his handiwork with a shrug. "I wanted to be ready for anything."

She took a closer look. The blades were rough, carved from river stone and crudely sharpened along the edges. The handles were wrapped in cloth strips and stained, perhaps from Rien's blood. They weren't perfect or balanced, but they'd do damage. He kept one and handed the other to her.

"There's no going back now," she muttered, taking the weapon. "Too bad we don't have swords." She hadn't told them about the empty scabbard tucked under her palette. Now was not the time.

Rien met her gaze, something fierce glinting behind his eyes. "Fists and daggers. That's all we need."

A smile crept across Axe's face. "Let's go, then."

They moved in silence, their footsteps muffled by the thick forest ground. As they drew closer to the healing lodge the rush of each heartbeat amplified. When the thatched structure came into view, her heart hammered with a crazed beat.

They slowed and crouched low. Ava eyed the door. "No guards," she whispered.

Axe shrugged. "Maybe they're inside?"

She gulped. Were they walking into an ambush? She pictured Dorn waiting inside, sword held high. Fists and daggers wouldn't touch him. Were they foolish to attempt this? Undoubtedly. Should they turn back? No way. That stranger knew something, and she wanted answers. They all did.

"Let's find out," she said.

Rien crept forward; Ava and Axe followed close behind. They stopped in front of the door. Rien pressed his ear against the wood and held it there for a few seconds. Satisfied, he eased the door open. The hinges creaked as they stepped in. They found the room partly illuminated by a single oil lamp on a nearby mounted wood shelf. Dried herbs and something acrid like blood and metal hung in the air. And there in the dim room lay the stranger strapped to a wooden table, motionless.

Oh no. Ava sucked in a sharp breath. Were they too late?

Rien rushed in, the floorboards groaning beneath his boots. The stranger's red, matted hair streaked against his cheeks, a thick gag shoved in his mouth. The top of his tunic was torn and crusted with dried blood. Bruises and cuts darkened his jawline, cheekbones, and neck. Rien reached out a shaky hand and touched his shoulder. The stranger's eyes flew open, wild and alarmed. When he recognized Rien, his expression softened. He mumbled against the cloth in his mouth.

"Shhh." Rien stopped him, pressing a finger against his lips. "Quiet."

The stranger nodded, his gaze roaming to Ava's. Her chest lurched as it had in the training circle, but this time with force and clarity. She saw an image of the stranger bleeding on the frosty ground and Rien holding him. They were friends. They all were. They had to be.

"Hurry," Axe urged, untying the stranger's ankles and pulling Ava into action. She started working on the wrist closest to her while Rien freed the one nearest him.

The stranger yanked out the wad, sat up, and hugged Rien. "Um, yeah." Rien patted his back. "I'd say we know each other."

"Let's go," Axe grunted, ending the moment. "You can hug later."

They started for the door when the stranger pulled them to a halt. He pointed at the back of the room. Ava, Rien, and Axe peered at the darkness, then at each other. Now what? They followed the stranger, finding a stack of weapons piled high in the corner. Swords. Daggers. Axes. Fighting sticks. Bows and arrows.

"Stars above," Ava muttered. "So many." She faced the others. "Why would they have these?"

The stranger rifled through the choices. He grabbed an axe and handed it to Axe, took an axe for himself, then grabbed a dagger for Rien.

"What about me?" she asked.

The stranger moved his hands, trying to tell her something. He flicked his thumb out from under his chin and then held his palms up and moved them in a small circular motion.

"I think he's saying you don't have one," Rien said.

That was dumb. Even though she had one of Rien's daggers, she wanted a real weapon. She reached and grabbed a sword. "I have one now."

With their new weapons in hand, they rushed out the door and burst straight into Zalarae, Dorn, and two armed Valians.

"Thunderation." Ava stumbled back. Getting caught had always been a risk. Still, she hadn't expected it to happen so close to their getaway. The Valians must have been watching and waiting.

"Now what?" Axe muttered.

The stranger's eyes went wide. He shook his head frantically and darted behind Rien, clutching his sleeve like a lifeline.

Instinct took over. Ava and Axe moved without a word, flanking Rien and blocking the Valians' advance. No way were they going to let the stranger be taken. Not again.

"My friends," Zalarae said, opening her palms. Her face stayed calm, but her eyes narrowed into sharpened points. "What are you doing?"

The cold air moved around them, the faint trails of moonlight trickling down. Ava's palms grew slick as her body tensed. She started to answer, when Rien beat her to it.

"Who is this stranger?" he demanded. "Why is he being held?"

Zalarae stepped forward. "He is an invader who means us ill."

Dorn moved next. "We had no other choice but to hold him."

The stranger mumbled a grunt that sounded like a no, and Ava believed him. The Valians weren't telling them the actual story. She flashed a look at the others, confirming they felt the same.

"We don't believe you," Ava challenged. No way was the stranger a threat.

Dorn lifted his hand, and the Valians raised their fighting sticks. Ava raised her weapon, as did the others. Was this happening? All she wanted was to be a Valian, but now she was going to fight them?

"Life in the Frost Vale works because we keep to ourselves and protect our own." Dorn's words came out hard and deadly. "You all know the ways."

"The ways?" Axe jerked his weapon at them. "What of the weapons in the healing hut, huh? What of them?"

The Valians stepped closer. "Those are there to protect us. All of us," Zalarae answered.

"How did you get them?" Rien demanded, his voice laced with suspicion.

The Valians tightened their grips on their weapons and stepped closer. Ava's pulse kicked hard as Dorn's eyes fixed on her.

"Give us the stranger and the weapons you found," he said, voice flat and steady. "And we won't hurt you."

"We can forget this happened," Zalarae added.

"Or what?" Ava asked.

Dorn advanced another step. "Or, we will make you."

Silence pressed around them, heavy and hot, making every exhale feel too loud. Ava's throat went dry despite the sweat trailing down her neck. They were outnumbered and standing on Valian soil, but something inside her refused to back down.

With their backs nearly up against the lodge wall, and the Valians closing in, a sudden chuckle broke the tension. *Axe?* Ava and Rien snapped their gazes toward the dwarf, then toward each other. Even the Valians hesitated. What in the stars was he doing?

Axe's laughter echoed through the trees, rolling through the forest like thunder. He jabbed Rien in the ribs. "They will make us!"

Um. Okay. Axe had lost it.

Ava shifted her weight, muscles coiling tight, sword raised and ready. There was only one way out of this.

"Charge!" Axe shouted, and then he was gone, racing forward like a wild boar.

A glance at Rien, and they rushed after him. Steel met wood, the clash sharp and echoing through the night. Dorn barreled toward her, swinging his stick in a blur. She caught the strike on her blade, then twisted and slashed, missing his shoulder by inches. He pivoted fast and brought the stick down again. The blow rammed her back, knocking the breath from her lungs and sending her sprawling. Her face hit the cold earth. She rolled, dirt scraping her cheek as the next swing cut the air beside her. Twisting more, she thrust upward, her sword meeting Dorn's weapon with a jarring crack that shook her to the bone.

"You cannot win," Dorn seethed, bearing down on her.

Thunderation, was he right? Her arms trembled, her muscles screaming beneath his weight as she struggled to hold the sword. "You. Are. Hiding. Something," she seethed.

The words came out between ragged breaths as she bucked her hips, trying to throw him off. He pressed harder, the ground biting into her back. Spots flashed at the edges of her vision as her head swam. The clang of battle dulled, fading beneath the thump of her pulse. She couldn't lose here, not like this, not so fast.

Her lungs burned as she dragged in another breath, willing her body to move, when sudden warmth flooded her insides. This time, it wasn't a flicker. Blue light ignited around her hands. It shone brightly, spilling from her skin in a flare that lit the night. The shockwave blasted into Dorn, ripping him off her. He was launched backward several feet before crashing hard into the ground.

The pressure vanished as quickly as it came, leaving Ava gasping, the blue light collapsing back into her skin as if it had never existed. Her chest heaved. Her hands shook.

"What in the—" she whispered, staring at Dorn.

He stared back, eyes wide. He scrambled to his feet, weapon already rising. "You *are* real." He charged.

A growling howl tore through the night. A blur of black-and-white fur vaulted over Ava, plowing into Dorn with bone-jarring force. She blinked. *A wolf?* She staggered to her feet and backed away fast. The massive beast snarled, circling Dorn, teeth bared and fur bristling.

With a sharp twist, Dorn swung his staff in a brutal arc, the strike cracking against the wolf's flank. The beast yelped and skidded through the dirt. Ava's breath hitched. The wolf shook itself and turned its blazing eyes on her.

Visions filled her mind in quick, disjointed flashes— the wolf bounding toward her and licking her face, the two of them surrounded by attacking foxes, then lying side by side in a cave. And always, the dark prince was with them.

"I know you," she stammered.

A hand clamped around her wrist and yanked. "Run!" Rien shouted.

He took off toward the trees, dragging her with him. Ava glanced back. Axe and the stranger stood with the wolf, the scene a blur of black-and-white fur and flashing weapons.

"Axe!" she cried.

"Go!" he shouted.

With her heart in her throat, Ava turned and sprinted. She jumped over rocks and dodged trees, the cold air slicing through her lungs. When the sounds of battle finally fell away, she slowed. Her chest burned. Her legs shook. And suddenly, Rien wasn't beside her. Panic flared.

"Rien?" she hissed, spinning in a tight circle. The forest stretched empty in every direction, trees packed close, shadows thick between their trunks. Had she lost him?

A soft crunch caught her attention. *The Valians.* She pressed her back against a wide trunk and held her breath when a twinkle of silver filled the space. Ahead, between two snow-dusted pines, stood a horse. White as frost light, bright against the darkened woods. Taller than any horse she'd ever seen. Its coat gleamed, catching a glow that didn't exist anywhere else. Its mane fell in a pale, silvery cascade. Its dark eyes watched her—steady, calm, knowing.

Ava's breath caught. It was the same horse. The one

from the brook. Her fear eased without reason. The horse shifted its weight and turned its head slightly, as if beckoning. Ava stepped forward, following as it moved deeper into the trees, always ahead of her, never rushing.

"Wait," she gasped. "Are you," she swallowed, "helping me?"

The horse slowed, glancing back. Then a shout rang out. "Ava!"

She spun toward the sound. "Rien!"

When she turned back, the forest stood empty. Her guide had vanished, leaving nothing but frost-laced earth and shadow.

"Over here," Rien called, waving her toward a cluster of thick brush.

Heart still pounding, Ava ran to him. Relief flooded her chest. She grabbed his arm. "Did you see it? The silver horse?"

"A horse?" He glanced around. "No, but I saw your blue light." His brows lifted. "What was that?"

She shook her head, her breath still uneven. "I wish I knew." Her fingers curled over her heart as she studied the trees. "Rien, are we safe here?"

He lunged for the brush, tearing at the thick greenery until it gave way with a snap, revealing a tight, shadowed opening. "We are," he said firmly. "In here."

Ava shot him a sharp look. "First daggers. Now secret hideaways?"

He lifted a shoulder. "You have your light. I have my preparations."

Fair enough. Except she'd only seen that light once before and had no idea what it was or what it meant. She peered into the near-total darkness, searching for the others. "Where are they?"

"If they follow where we went, they'll show," he said.

She craned her neck. Come on, come on. The moonlight barely pierced the canopy, silvering the branches and rock. Her pulse drummed in her ears. Her eyes scanned the trees.

Finally, she detected movement. Axe burst through the shadows, the stranger close behind. Where was the wolf?

"This way!" Rien hissed, motioning toward the cave mouth.

"Hurry!" she urged, beckoning with frantic sweeps of her hand as she stepped into the cave.

The stranger slowed. Even in the dim light, she could see the dark stains spreading across his clothes. *No, no, no.*

Axe darted through the opening, rolling in with a tumble. The stranger followed. And just as he made it into the cave, he went down hard.

Ava gasped. Arrows jutted from his back, their shafts glinting in the faint light. The Valians shot him.

She dropped to her knees. "Stay with us." Her hands hovered uselessly over the blood-soaked shirt. "You're going to be all right."

His lips parted, but no sound came, just quick exhales.

Axe crouched beside her, ripping a strip from his tunic. "We have to stop the bleeding."

"Help him. Hurry!" Rien pleaded, yanking the branches across the cave's opening and shutting out the moonlight. A sharp strike like flint on rock echoed, and a small flame flared to life, casting amber light across the walls.

The stranger's breath came in short, shallow gasps. With a grunt, he angled himself and pulled his hands out from under him. He trembled as he lifted his arms toward Rien, moving his fingers.

"I don't know what you're saying," Rien said gently, kneeling at the stranger's side now.

The stranger touched his chest, pointed at Rien, then locked his forefingers together. The gesture lingered, desperate and heartfelt, before his hands fell limp and his eyes closed.

Ava froze. Tears blurred her vision. Something in that final gesture tugged at her chest, an ache cutting deep inside her. Her gaze drifted to Rien. He stared down at the stranger, a hollow look breaking across his face.

"Is he—" Rien gulped, his eyes watering over. "Dead?"

Reaching in, Axe placed two fingers on the stranger's neck. The silence stretched, pressing in from the thick, cold walls. Ava watched in horror, counting the seconds.

Axe drew back his hand. His voice came out low. "He's gone."

Rien bowed his head, shoulders shaking. He pulled in a breath that sounded like a sob, turning away from them as he wiped his face.

Ava did not understand why tears packed her eyes. She didn't even know his name. None of their reactions made sense. Still, she felt his loss deep within her, as if something steady and familiar had been torn away. She sank to the ground, her mind in a whirl. They had set out to save the stranger and get answers. Now he was dead.

The Valians weren't at all who they thought they were. "What do we do now?" she mumbled.

A scratching noise sounded against the branches across the cave opening, followed by whimpering. Axe rushed to the spot. "The wolf," he said. "She fought with us."

He started pulling away the branches, and Ava joined him. A snout pushed through the opening, followed by a paw as the wolf eased inside. She padded forward, circling Ava's legs with a soft huff, tail swishing. Then she stopped. Those wise, golden eyes drifted to the stranger, then back to Ava. Her ears folded back as a low, mournful whimper slipped from her throat.

Tears slid down Ava's cheek.

The wolf stepped closer to the body, slow and deliberate, and lay down beside the stranger. Resting her chin on his chest, she released a sound that was almost human in its sorrow.

"How?" Ava mumbled, swallowing the lump in her throat and wiping her eyes. She stared at Axe and Rien, who stood beside her as the wolf paid homage to the stranger. "The stranger knew us, and now this wolf." She clutched her chest. "I feel the loss."

Rien shook his head. "I feel it too."

No one spoke after that. Everyone was shocked, mourning the stranger they couldn't save. "What do we do now?" she asked.

"With his body?" Axe asked.

She replied with a slow nod. She had never experienced death and had no idea what to do. Still, something in her demanded they honor the stranger, some act to prepare him for his journey.

Rien scanned the cave. "We can't go outside with the Valians out there, but we can pull him farther in. Give him some sort of sending."

They worked in silence, carefully moving the body deeper inside where the faint light flickered against the walls. Rien and Axe knelt, pulling the arrows from his back, then carefully rolled him over. Ava swallowed hard as she threaded her fingers through his red hair, brushing the strands from his still face. His expression was calm now, as if in death he had found peace. At least, she hoped he had.

When they were done, they smoothed out his tunic and trousers with care, then stepped back in quiet reverence. The wolf circled the stranger, then took her place beside Ava, the heat of its body steady against her trembling knees. She rested a hand on her head, grateful for the solid, living warmth beneath her palm, a reminder that not all was lost.

Axe broke the silence. "Should we say something?"

"Yes." Ava looked to Rien. "You should start."

Rien hesitated for a moment. "I didn't know his name," he said softly. "But he fought for us when he didn't have to." He paused, eyes flicking toward the body. "Wherever you're going, may you find peace there."

Ava bowed her head. "May your next life be kinder."

"You'll be remembered," Axe said. "Even if we don't know who you were."

They stayed that way for a long moment, the cave quiet. Then, slowly, they walked back toward the mouth of the cave.

Ava stopped near the covered entrance, listening to the hush beyond. Somewhere out there, the Valians were searching for them—former friends turned enemies. Her stomach twisted. They'd gotten the stranger killed. For what? A cause they didn't understand? A truth they couldn't remember?

Rien crouched near the entrance, peering through the cracks in the branches. "We can't go back to the Frost Vale," he said quietly. "Not after this."

"True," Axe said with a grunt. "So where do we go? We don't even know who we are."

Ava thought of the scabbard back at her hut, the one with no sword. In the healing hut, there was no sword for her there either, not a single blade meant for her. The realization pricked at her, sharp and unwelcome. She should tell Rien and Axe, but needed some sort of explanation first.

Then there were the dreams. The dark prince calling to her from the shadows, his voice threaded with longing and danger. Half-remembered words. Half-formed warnings. It all felt tangled together—the missing sword, the memories they didn't have, the stranger who'd known them, the wolf and the horse. None of it made sense. But somehow, the pieces were part of the same truth. They had to be.

"We need answers." She looked at Rien, then Axe, then down at the wolf pressed against her legs. "About this place, about who we are."

"You're right," Rien said.

"So, what do we do?" Axe asked.

Ava drew a breath, the moment settling deep. "Forget the trials. Forget all of it." Her voice steadied, the spark inside her catching flame. "I say we search for the dragons. They'll tell us who we are. They'll tell us what's going on."

For the first time since the night began, something shifted inside her. Not hope. Not yet. Direction. Somewhere beyond the frost and fog, the dragons waited and with them, the truth Ava feared as much as she needed.

CHAPTER TWELVE

M ateo awoke to the muted rustle of his tent and the faint scent of lemon oil. Pale morning light filtered through the canvas walls, glinting off his freshly polished boots that gleamed in the half-light. Marina's work, no doubt. The troll had taken it upon herself to tend to his needs, not that he minded. She was useful, and her strength was an asset.

He sat up, and the world swayed for a blink before righting itself again. *Not again.* He drew a steadying breath, waiting a few seconds, then wiped below his nose. He studied his fingers. No sign of blood. He wiped again to make sure, still confused as to why he'd had a nosebleed. As *Teyocel* had said, the fatigue and the skirmish were surely to blame. But after a solid night's sleep, why did he still feel off?

"My prince, may I enter?" Marina called from outside.

"Come in," Mateo replied.

The tent flap lifted, and Marina ducked in. Tall and broad-shouldered, her gray-green skin caught the light. Her face was rough, the texture uneven like weathered stone, but her movements were careful and deliberate. Balanced on one hand was a small wooden tray with bread, dried fruit, and a glass of golden juice.

"You slept late," she said, her voice deep and steady.

"Did I?" His tone came out flat. He didn't think he'd had enough sleep at all.

"You did." She set the tray on the ground beside his pallet. "It is near time to break camp."

Mateo reached for the glass. "Anything to report?"

The troll paused at the flap. "The prisoners are awake." She hesitated, then pointed to the table at the far end of the tent. "Your water basin is low. The creek nearby is drying."

He raised a brow. "Drying?" The Mother of Rivers never dried. "Does Raelor know?"

"He does."

"Very well. Thank you, Marina."

He took a sip of the juice, finding it sweet with honey. Let Raelor deal with the rivers. He had more important matters to worry about. He stretched his neck with a pop, gulped the rest of the juice, then eased himself to his feet.

Stripping off his tunic, he dipped his hands into the cool water—what little there was—and splashed his face. The liquid soothed him, clearing some of the heaviness behind his eyes. He cupped his hands again, rinsing his face once more before running the water along his neck, shoulders, and chest. Snatching the nearby towel, he dried off. If all went as planned, they would reach Sand

Bluff before nightfall. That's when the real work would begin. He had to be ready. The sooner Sand Bluff was dealt with, the sooner he could set his sights on the North.

Dressed for the day and with his sword at his side, Mateo stepped out from his tent and into the bright morning sun. Smoke from last night's fires still clung to the air, threading through the damp scent of trampled earth. Stromm warriors moved about the camp with low murmurs, tightening saddle straps and packing their weapons. Every motion was purposeful, but their eyes flicked away the moment they landed on them, the way he liked.

With his boots crunching over the dead grass, he made his way toward the carriages. He hadn't gone but a few paces when the pulse throbbed behind his eyes again, sharp enough to make him wince. He paused for a moment and steadied himself. This wasn't going to work. He needed to rid himself of this nagging pain. But how?

"*Teyocel*," he called in his mind, sure the dragon could help. "*Are you near?*"

Silence answered him. Again. Like when they were attacked. He formed a fist at his side. He needed the dragon, needed the reassurance and clarity *Teyocel* always brought him. This vanishing, this ignoring him, it would have to stop. A bond like theirs demanded obedience, not absence. He would speak to *Teyocel* about it. Dragons were mighty, but so was he.

Karl approached with a measured pace. His jaw was set, his expression unreadable. Every line of his posture radiated rigid duty and obligated respect.

"My prince," he said with a quick bow. "Cleanup is complete. Tents repaired, dead cleared, wounded tended. We lost two. They lost six."

Too bad the attackers hadn't lost more. "And the prisoners?" Mateo asked.

Karl's nostrils flared. "The zealots are bound and ready for departure. I hear they've refused food."

Something tightened in Mateo's chest, his thoughts on the so-called Only One they worshipped, but he didn't let it show. "They are fools." The words came out as sharp as intended. "Fools with delusions. They can starve for all I care."

"On that, we can agree," Karl huffed.

Mateo kept his eye on the camp. "Have you seen Raelor?"

"Last I saw he was at his tent, gathering his things."

Mateo lifted his chin. His voice dropped in volume. "And *Teyocel*?" He felt weak asking for his own dragon. He should know where he was at all times.

The slight tilt of Karl's head suggested he thought it a strange question as well. "I have not seen the dragon."

"Very well. Continue preparing the caravan," he ordered.

Another quick bow, and Karl jogged off to issue commands. Mateo watched him go, then turned away from the camp. He narrowed his eyes and scanned the tree line beyond the last row of tents. There he spotted his scaled companion. The familiar dark shape rested on the ridge above the camp, wings folded tight, watching everything with predatory stillness, and ignoring Mateo.

Heat crept up his neck. How dare the dragon sit on

his perch, paying no regard to his calls. He headed toward the beast, boots striking the ground in a determined rhythm. If *Teyocel* wouldn't answer him in his mind, then he would answer him face-to-face. He'd make sure of it. With each step, his heart sped up while emotions swirled within him. Anger and frustration, but also something like hurt and abandonment. How dare *Teyocel* make him feel less than.

The dragon launched into the air, spread his dark wings, and glided toward Mateo. His massive form cut across the early morning light like a storm shadow. He circled twice, then landed several paces away.

Mateo stopped, feeling every inch of distance between them. They may have been standing on either side of the Majestic Chasm. "Why did you leave me so abruptly last night?" he asked. "I was injured."

Teyocel's molten-lava eyes blinked. "I sensed you needed rest." His tone was smooth and calm. "I am here now."

"What about moments ago?" Mateo snapped. "I called to you, and again you did not answer."

Teyocel's head extended, a faint ripple passing along his neck. His next words came with a bite. "You expect me to answer every thought the instant it crosses your mind, little prince?"

Mateo stiffened. He took a step back. The dragon hadn't called him that in a long while. How dare he do it now. "I expect loyalty," he shot back. "Especially after what I have done for you."

Thick silence stretched between them. Had Mateo said too much? He'd given *Teyocel* half his soul in exchange for his power. When Mateo was done and his enemies were slain, *Teyocel* said he'd return his soul and go back to the mountain. But Mateo was not done, not by a long shot. The provinces planned to rise against House Stromm. There was also Avalynn and the Oathriders. If she lived and possessed her sword, he'd need *Teyocel* more than ever. Should he take back his words?

The dragon lowered his head slightly, his voice smoothing to velvet. "I meant no disrespect. You are my anchor beyond the Vale, my prince. My strength outside its borders. You are also, like you said, a friend. I would never abandon you."

Mateo's anger faltered, dulling beneath the warmth of those words. *Teyocel* spoke like he *chose* him. Like he *believed* in him. Like he was more than the Stromm prince destined to rule. He was simply Mateo. The thought sank deep, soothing his insecurities.

"I would never abandon you, either," he admitted.

The dragon moved forward. "I felt your pain last night. Your fatigue. Even now, it clings to you." A slow exhale of warm air washed over him. "You push yourself harder than any in your camp. Harder than any prince before you. They do not see it, but I do."

Mateo pressed his hand against the pendant under his tunic. His rigid stance eased. "I try my best, but I'll admit that I do not feel like myself," he uttered, the words coming from a place he did not know.

Teyocel dipped his head, voice softer still. "Trust me, my prince. As long as I fly beside you, you will not fall."

The twinge behind Mateo's eyes eased, and the morning steadied around him. The sound of *Teyocel's* voice had a way of settling the noise inside him, quieting everything until only purpose remained. For the first time since waking, he felt clear. Certain.

He swallowed, holding on to that feeling. "Thank you, *Teyocel*," he murmured. "We head for Sand Bluff soon. We should return to the others."

Wings rustling, *Teyocel* shifted his weight. "Then I will take to the sky. From above, I can watch the path from all angles. If the Oathriders strike again, I will see them first."

I will take to the sky? He wanted to fly without Mateo? He paused. Although he recognized the strategic positioning, a part of him wanted the dragon to lower himself, to offer his back the way he had before. The height, the speed, the command of it. He almost craved it.

But *Teyocel* didn't offer. And Mateo refused to ask. "If that is what you think is best."

"It is." *Teyocel* inclined his head, a slow, measured gesture. "It will keep you safest."

Reluctance tugged at Mateo's chest, but he forced it down. "Very well," he said again, quieter this time.

The dragon's dark wings spread wide, catching the morning light. "I will fly above you," he promised, voice low. "Always."

Mateo returned to camp as the last of the preparations snapped into place. Soldiers rushed into formation as horses stamped restlessly. The carriages creaked with each movement as the maidservants climbed into their designated spots, followed by the supply boxes.

Overhead, a rush of wind rippled the Stromm banners. *Teyocel* circled the caravan before settling into a steady watch overhead. Mateo felt the shift inside him—quiet, settling, aligning. The dragon overhead was a sound move. He should trust him more.

At the front of the line, Karl barked orders, every word sharp and efficient. Behind him, two soldiers led the Oathrider girls forward. The prisoners sat double on a single horse, tied at the waist, wrists bound before them, ankles secured beneath the horse's belly. Their long hair hung tangled with dirt, their faces smeared, yet their eyes blazed like flames—defiant, unbroken.

Mateo returned their glares. "Keep them moving," he ordered the warrior, tugging them along.

Pressing on, he strode to the middle spot where the core warriors rode. A sleek black horse awaited him, and he mounted with ease. Guards fell in around him, forming a protective ring that made the space feel tight.

A few horses back and to the left, Raelor sat atop his horse, posture straight as a blade. Mateo glanced over his shoulder as the witch's diamond eyes slid his way—measuring, prying, hungry for something Mateo couldn't name but didn't like.

He looked away first. Did the witch know about his nosebleed? Or his conversation with *Teyocel?* The thought clawed at him. Raelor had a way of *seeing* things, of digging into thoughts not meant for him. Mateo's fingers twitched against the reins. He would not be read like an open book. Not now. Not ever. Least of all by the likes of Raelor.

He nudged his horse forward, then called out to Karl in front. "Signal when ready!"

Karl raised his fist to the sky. "Move out!"

The front line surged into motion with Karl in the lead, hooves drumming against the packed earth. The prisoners' horse was pulled along with them, flanked by four guards and one in front leading the rope.

When enough distance had been made, Mateo called out. "Core column, forward!"

His guards echoed the command, and the line behind him lurched into movement. Wagon wheels creaked to life. Horses huffed. A shadow passed overhead as *Teyocel* glided from above, wings outstretched, lowering into a watchful orbit. Every beat of those vast wings pressed something steady into Mateo's mind, quieting the dull ache that pulsed behind his eyes. Nothing could touch him while his dragon soared. *Nothing.*

Ahead, the road cut a clean path toward Sand Bluff. Mateo set his shoulders, letting the rhythm of the march settle into his bones. Sand Bluff by nightfall, he reminded himself. He would install a Stromm loyalist as steward. And after that, the Wild North.

"Do you think she's alive?" he asked *Teyocel*. He didn't even have to say her name.

"The Only One?" Teyocel's voice rumbled in his mind, low and silken. *"If she breathes still, we will find her. And when we do, we will end what was begun. Together."*

Mateo believed in himself, his family name, his power, and especially his dragon. Those were the only truths that mattered now. The only ones he could trust.

They rode in silence as the land unfurled before them. Fields of green turned golden, the air growing warmer with every mile. The low hills rippled along the horizon like sleeping beasts, dotted with twisted oaks and the occasional burst of lavender and indigo wildflowers. Above him, *Teyocel's* shadow glided across the changing terrain, a dark shape moving against the daylight.

The closer they drew to Sand Bluff, the more Mateo's thoughts cluttered with scenarios of what they'd find when they arrived. With a Baffin in custody, would others be there, armed with swords and daggers? Or maybe she was the last one, and there was no one to fight for the name. None of it mattered. If anyone opposed him, he'd burn the whole place down. His hands tightened around the reins. He wouldn't mind that.

CHAPTER THIRTEEN

After a long day of travel, the sun began to set. The road narrowed. A bit farther, and a small cottage came into view, shutters drawn tight. Another stood nearby with its door hanging open, creaking faintly in the wind. Then another. Mateo's instincts flared. He straightened in the saddle, scanning each silent home. Where was everyone? Had they fled when they lost their steward?

Then he saw it—the signs he'd missed at first glance. The ground was cracked and pale like broken pottery. The usually grand oaks drooped, their leaves curled brown at the edges. This wasn't right.

Up ahead, Karl lifted a fist and signaled the column to halt. He rode back toward Mateo. "This is not natural." His voice came out low and uneasy. "Sand Bluff should not look like this."

Raelor's horse moved close, the witch's gaze flicking over the thirsty earth and the dying trees. "The Mother of

Rivers fails," he said. He brought his attention back to Mateo. "But nothing can be done about this now. She is not our mission. Our course is set."

The sight unsettled Mateo, a crawling wrongness beneath the soil. Raelor was right. It wasn't his problem, not today. The rivers had nothing to do with him or the Stromm goals.

He eyed the group. "We continue on."

"Very well, my prince," Karl said. "With night falling, I propose the caravan stay here while a smaller detail proceeds to the manor house."

Mateo nodded. "Agreed."

Karl turned to the caravan and began barking orders. "The carriages and prisoners will stay here." He motioned his arms, directing the carriage drivers. "A small detail will ride forward with the prince, Raelor, and myself."

"And me, my prince!" Marina called, hopping from her carriage with a lumbering thud.

Mateo raised an eyebrow. She had handled those Oathriders with ease, swinging her thick arms like clubs. Having her and Raelor close, and *Teyocel* overhead, would make him nearly impossible to reach. And with the outskirts of Sand Bluff appearing abandoned, who knew what lay ahead?

"Yes, Marina is with me," Mateo said.

The troll grunted her approval, then took the largest available horse and mounted with ease despite her size. She spurred the steed up close to Mateo.

"Alright then," Karl said. "Let's see what awaits."

Karl, the prince, Raelor, Marina, and a handful of

guards moved forward toward the manor house, the horses shifting into a choppy trot, snorting and huffing.

"*Stay sharp,*" Mateo said to *Teyocel.*

"*I will,*" *Teyocel* said, circling above in a slow, deliberate sweep, wings cutting wide shadows across the caravan.

The road bent toward the first cluster of homes, more shuttered cottages. Somewhere deeper in the village, a plume of dark smoke drifted skyward, burnt grass and herbs in the air. The place felt like an injured warrior waiting to be sent to the Passing Place.

When the road curved, the manor rose from the ridge. It loomed tall, turreted, and unmistakably proud, even with neglect clinging to its edges. Ivy had clawed too far up the walls. The pale stone appeared weathered, scuffed by wind and sand. But the structure itself stood firm, resolute against the darkening sky. Mateo's grip tightened on the reins. It wasn't as bad as he'd expected, but the too-quiet air troubled him all the same.

As the group emerged into the courtyard, movement stirred at the manor's entrance. A small group stepped out, led by a young fae with silver hair and a sword too long for his slim build at his waist. Behind him were two older fae with short-cropped dark hair dressed in hunting clothes of brown and green. In the back, a small maidservant in a brown dress hovered.

The young fae held his arm up in an uncertain and timid-looking wave. "Welcome, Prince Mateo." He bowed low. "Welcome to you all."

Mateo raised his brow at Karl. No ambush. An empty village. A rundown manor. Now a young fae seemingly in charge. He hopped off his horse, as did the others, and strode forward. When Mateo neared, something about the fae's features tugged at his memory.

"Thank you for your welcome," he said. "Who are you?"

The fae's throat bobbed with a hard swallow. "There are no Baffins here," he said carefully, almost rehearsed. "I was sent to receive you in their stead. I am Heiric Lind of House Lind, betrothed to Selene Baffin, who remains in your custody." He bowed again, voice thin. "I present this province to you, my prince, and ask only that you accept its loyalty."

Mateo narrowed his gaze. "You are brother to Eiric Lind," he said, the name curling his lips, "and future mate to Selene Baffin?"

Heiric flinched. "Y-yes, my prince."

Mateo scoffed. Images flashed in his mind of Eiric and Selene at the Summit Range Hunt, all smirks and deceit, the two of them working together until Eiric was impaled and Selene abandoned the competition. His blood boiled. He despised them both. Now this trembling sibling dared present himself as if he deserved recognition, deserved mercy. Pathetic.

His hand slid toward the hilt at his side. He should run the boy through and call it justice. Clean. Simple. Final. But a hand closed around his shoulder.

"Patience, my prince," Raelor whispered low enough for his ears only. "Let us hear what he knows, what he wants."

Mateo held still, though the urge to end the exchange with his weapon pulsed in his veins.

"Please," Heiric pleaded, bending low with his arms out. "Come in and let us offer you what we can. Evening approaches. We have food, drink, and beds prepared for weary travelers." His gaze darted between Karl, Raelor, and Marina before snapping back to Mateo, wide and desperate. "All we ask is a chance to serve you and your House. Please, Prince Mateo. I beg you."

Mateo lifted his chin. Perched atop the manor's highest turret, *Teyocel* watched, wings tucked tight. *"He begs, Teyocel."*

"He does indeed. And is doing a fine job. It will not hurt to hear his words, my prince." The dragon's voice coiled through Mateo's mind. *"Information can be as sharp as any blade."*

With a slow exhale, Mateo brought his gaze to Heiric's trembling form. "Very well," he said at last. "Lead the way."

Mateo followed Heiric when a jolt zapped behind his eyes. *Not again.* He couldn't afford any weakness, least of all now. Pushing through, his boots echoed against weathered stone as he scanned his surroundings. The entrance hall was dim, lit only by a few guttering lamps. Cobwebs veiled the corners. A tapestry of the Sand Bluff banner hung crooked and limp.

The young Heiric led them through the echoing corridor toward the great hall. "Forgive the state of things," he said, wringing his hands. "There are not that many hands to maintain the manor."

"Why is that?" Raelor asked.

"When word spread of the elder Baffin and his..." He gulped. "Untimely demise, along with the demise of the other stewards, the manor was abandoned. I only came to help and offer my services for the good of the crown. The Stromms."

"And to get your betrothed back?" Raelor asked.

Heiric stopped and bowed. "Only if it pleases the prince."

Mateo's nostrils flared. It would not please him, not in the least. Still, let the young fool think otherwise. "We will have to see," he said.

They entered the dining chamber. The long table that had once held feasts now bore only a modest spread: one loaf of bread, a small plate of dried fish, and a lone pitcher.

Karl scanned the offering with a huff. "Is this all?"

"Supplies run low," Heiric explained. "The Mother of Rivers is fading. I am certain you witnessed it on your journey here. The streams and basins dry faster each day, and there is no water to spare. Without water, everything suffers."

"What of Cuesta?" Raelor asked. "Does House Lind suffer there too?"

Heiric nodded. "It does, my lord."

"We will take what you have," Mateo said, settling into his place at the head of the table where Heiric led him.

They ate in a silence sharpened by growing unease. The bread was stale, the fish tough, the wine barely enough for one glass each. Heiric's gaze kept flicking about, as if searching for something or someone. Karl remained stiff, taking his bites with one hand while his other stayed on the axe he'd set near his plate. Marina ate as quietly as possible, her chewing slow and measured. Raelor declined the meal but remained standing in the shadows of the room.

With each swallow, the dull pressure behind Mateo's eyes increased. At first, he ignored it, but the throb deepened slowly, like something tightening inside his skull. His vision blurred at the edges. The room swayed with every movement. He steadied himself with a hand on the table, jaw locking as he forced his breathing to even. He needed this meal to end. He needed to lie down. And he needed no one to notice.

When the plates were cleared, Heiric cleared his throat. "May I make a formal petition to the prince now?"

"No," Mateo said quickly. "We require rest first. You may petition in the morning."

"Of course, my prince." He motioned to the young maidservant. "Ellira will show you to your rooms for the night," he said. "We hope to make your stay comfortable, though we can only offer what remains."

After a quick bow, Ellira led them out of the hall and down a dark corridor where the sconces burned low. Mateo followed last, his eyes drifting to the windows where night settled thick and heavy across the village. He flexed his fingers. Something was wrong here. Something unspoken. But for tonight, he would rest.

Tomorrow, he would pry Sand Bluff open until its secrets spilled like blood.

CHAPTER FOURTEEN

A va stayed close to the cave opening, realizing they couldn't stay there. Not with the stranger's body cooling behind them or the memory of Dorn's fury still echoing in her bones. And the air. It had turned thick, hard to breathe, and every noise outside their hideout sounded like Valians moving in. For all she knew, Dorn and Zalarae were getting closer and closer.

"We have to move," she whispered. "Before they find our tracks."

"You're right," Rien said. "We shouldn't stay here."

"I agree." Axe moved for the branches. "Let's go."

They quickly parted the branches, just enough for them to slip through, then moved them back into place. With silence all around, and the wolf at her side, they eased into the trees, every breath held tight. They scanned their surroundings, catching their bearings.

The Vale stretched out around them, dark and unfamiliar. Ava had never been this far from the village before. Mist threaded through the trunks, low and drifting like pale fingers. Far above, the jagged peaks of Skywatcher Mountain loomed against the brilliant stars.

"That's where they are," Ava said in a low voice.

"Assuming the Valians have told us the truth," Rien said.

Axe pointed skyward. "If the dragons live anywhere, it's up there." He huffed. "I'd bet my beard on it."

The mountain looked impossibly far, its slopes steep and rimmed with snow and mist. The trek might be the most dangerous thing she'd done so far. And yet something inside her tugged toward it—an instinct, a pull, the same one that had throbbed in her dreams.

"Then we go," she said, tightening her grip on Rien's borrowed dagger, the sword she had used against Dorn had fallen near the healing lodge, though luckily Axe and Rien still had their weapons. She hoped they wouldn't need them again.

Rien nodded, his eyes flicking back toward the village, toward the false life they were leaving behind. "We keep to the trees. Travel by night and rest during the day."

They moved—without memories and now joined by a wolf who seemed to know them better than they knew themselves. A wolf she instinctively thought was a girl, though she had no proof. They maneuvered their way around evergreens and brambles and picked their way across roots slick with ice and dew. Now and then, Ava looked back, half expecting to see Dorn's silhouette crashing through the trees. But the night stayed still. No footsteps. No shouts. No Valians. Just the mountain rising higher and higher with each step.

As the dark sky softened to gray, a cold awareness threaded through her. They weren't Valian trainees anymore, preparing for the Frost-Forged Trials. They were seekers of a truth that had been stolen from them. She had wanted nothing more than to prove herself in the trials, to earn her place as a Valian and stand beside a dragon. And yet, as she scanned the looming mountain-top, something else stirred within her—something truer. Something better. Meeting the great dragons like this, stripped of deceit and false histories, felt right. They would face the dragons as themselves.

"I wonder who we are," she uttered quietly. Her boots crunched against the frosty land.

"I wonder who *you* are," Rien said.

"The blue light," Axe said in an almost reverent tone. "You don't see that every day."

Ava kept her focus on the mountain. "I hope they can tell me."

They moved forward quietly. "Well, I know who I am," Axe said. "A warrior." He lifted his weapon, the metal catching the glint of moonlight. "Maybe my name's the only thing that remembers that."

She raised a brow at him. He was right. He had all the makings of a warrior. "Fine, you're easy." She laughed.

"And you, if you are not some sort of witch, I'd say you are a spoiled princess." Axe's teeth flashed with a grin. "I'd bet my beard ... again."

"Spoiled to the core," Rien chimed in. Then he

stopped, his eyes narrowing. "And maybe even the reason why we are here."

"Hey, now." She pushed his shoulder. "I am not the reason, you are. You, with all your secrets, like making forbidden weapons and finding hideouts. You are nothing but trouble." They walked a few more paces while her mind churned. How dare he accuse her of getting them into this mess? She stopped and jabbed her finger at him. "And while we are at it, I think *you* are the one who's spoiled royalty, Rien. I am just a noble lady."

Axe covered his mouth, muffling a laugh. He nudged Rien. "You gonna let her get away with that?"

Rien shook his head. "It doesn't matter." He kept walking. "Nothing matters but finding those dragons and figuring out the truth."

"And getting out of here," Ava finished. "Don't forget that part."

They pressed forward—toward the dragons, toward answers, toward whatever truth waited at the top of the mountain. But when the first threads of sunlight began weaving through the branches, they slowed their pace.

"We need cover," Rien murmured. "Someplace hidden from view where we can catch our breath before the ascent."

Ava scanned the area—and froze. Between the trees on a gentle ridge stood the horse. White. Luminous. As if carved from frost and moonlight both. Its mane fell in a pale cascade, silver catching the early light. Those calm, knowing eyes met hers across the distance, steady as the mountain itself. There was no fear, only a profound, grounding certainty, as if something ancient had found her and wanted to help.

The horse lowered its head once, slow and deliberate. Then it stepped aside. Only then did Ava see what lay beyond it. A cluster of jagged stones jutted from the mountain's base, half hidden by frost-kissed brush. A narrow gap between them led into a shallow alcove where the trees leaned close, their branches a draped curtain of needles and shadow. It wasn't a cave, but a pocket of the world overlooked by everything else.

She turned to the others. "There." She raised her arm and pointed. "Between those boulders." Another glance at the spot and the horse had vanished.

"Good eye," Axe said with a stiff nod.

Ava swallowed and nodded, her heart thudding. Where had the horse gone this time? And why didn't it want the others to see it?

They quickly closed the distance and slipped inside the natural shelter. Ava sank against the stone, exhaustion pulling at every part of her. The wolf circled once before settling at her side, warm and solid.

"I have to close my eyes," she mumbled. "For a little while."

"Go ahead," Axe said. "We'll keep watch."

Ava let her eyes fall shut, leaning her head against the wolf's soft fur as darkness folded around her. She snuggled into her companion, the warmth soothing her. The beast's heartbeat thrummed against her cheek like a comforting lullaby. With her body relaxing, she floated, unsure if she was awake or asleep, and not even caring, until she felt the ground beneath her boots.

Shadows gathered and parted, revealing hints of carved stone walls, tapestries she couldn't quite see, a window of black glass. What kind of dream was this?

The air shifted. The skin at the back of her neck tingled. She wasn't alone. A figure in the corner came into view, shrouded in shadow. She couldn't see his face, only the outline: tall, strong, familiar in a way that tightened her chest for reasons she couldn't name.

"Come to me," a voice crooned—low, velvety, dangerous.

Ava stepped closer, and the shadows peeled back, revealing the interior of a bedchamber—grand, but dimly lit. Thick fabric hung from the ceiling beams, draping the room in shifting shadows.

She inched forward. The darkness thinned even more, and a shape took form on the bed. She gasped. The dark prince. He lay on his back, the covers pooled low around his bare hips. Moonlight spilled through a high window, washing over the sharp lines of his body, the rise of his collarbone, the powerful sweep of his shoulders, the perfectly carved planes of his chest.

Beautiful. Terrible. Mesmerizing.

At the base of his throat hung a gold pendant. She leaned forward. It was etched with an S, and it pulsed faintly. She swallowed. Was that thing alive?

Her pulse stuttered. She didn't know why she was there or how she had crossed into this place—if it was even real—but terror wasn't the only thing stirring in her. Something deep and unbidden tugged her toward him, impossible to ignore. She wanted to know him. To understand the tingle in her body when she thought of him. To see the expression on his face when he opened his eyes and saw her standing there. What would he say? What would he do?

Her fingers curled at her sides. Should she wake him? Should she speak? She took one silent step closer to the bed, drawn by a force she didn't understand, a force that frightened her, and thrilled her, when something cold slid through her. Terror. Not of him, not entirely. But of the gold pendant lying against his skin. It glowed faintly in the moonlight, shifting and completely dangerous.

An overwhelming urge shot through her to rip it off. But would touching it hurt her? Would it hurt him? And could she even touch it in this state whatever it was?

Before she could decide, his breathing changed. Slow, then sharp, then rapid and panicked, like someone drowning in a dream they couldn't wake from. He twitched, muscles tightening. A low sound escaped his throat. Ava flinched as his back arched slightly, the pendant's light flaring. She reached for him on instinct when his body jerked. He shot upright with a gasp.

Their eyes collided—surprise slamming into shock, shock into recognition, and recognition into something deeper, older, aching. Hope. Longing. Loss.

"Avalynn," he breathed.

The name struck her like a blade. *Who?*

He reached out, his hand sweeping through her, like she wasn't there at all. But she was. She knew she was. Not her body, but her spirit, somehow pulled across the Wild North by a force she didn't understand.

His chest rose and fell in sharp, quickened breathing, like he was stunned by the sight of her. His long dark hair spilled around his shoulders in wild, storm-tossed waves. "Are you alive?" he asked, voice cracking. "Are you dead?"

"I'm alive," she said, the words trembling from her lips. "I don't know how, but I'm here."

His shoulders slackened, only for something to shift in his eyes. That soft, aching recognition drained out, replaced by a cold calculation that whispered against her like a warning. A shadow crossed his expression, dark and hungry.

"Where are you?" he asked.

Her mind quickly processed. He didn't know. He didn't know where she was. Every instinct screamed at her to stay silent, to tell him nothing, to protect whatever thin thread tethered her to her real body. She met his gaze with a forced steadiness. She couldn't let him feel her fear.

"Who are you," she demanded, her voice sharp, "and how do you know me?"

He tilted his head slowly, almost curiously. Whatever warmth had been there a heartbeat before was long gone, smothered under something vicious and sinister. His fingers grazed the gold pendant at his chest, its surface glowing faintly, pulsing like evil incarnate.

"Ah," he murmured, voice lower. "You don't remember me. You don't even remember yourself." He pushed the covers aside and rose, completely bare, every inch of him carved in the kind of perfection that looked designed to tempt and ruin.

Ava's breath hitched, her eyes roaming over every flawless inch before she could stop herself. She had no idea how, but heat washed over her spirit form. Something buried deep inside her reacted first, a pulled string vibrating with recognition her mind couldn't name. Her stomach flipped, her pulse skittering wildly. She took a step back. Then another.

Whatever that pull was—whatever her body insisted it remembered—her mind recoiled from him, from the shadows in his steely eyes, from the way the gold pendant at his chest pulsed like a second heartbeat. Fear curled through her. He was beautiful in a way meant to devour and destroy. Yet something in her wanted... *No. No. No.* She couldn't.

She swallowed hard, her shimmery form moving back toward the wall as she held out her hand. "Stay back."

He advanced anyway—slow, unhurried, predatory. He licked his perfect lips, his gaze so intense she thought she would melt. He braced his hands against the wall on either side of her, caging her in. Spirit or not, she felt trapped. Heat coiled low inside her—unwanted, confusing—born of a pull she didn't fully understand.

"That's all right," he murmured, lowering his face to hers until they shared the same breathless space. "I already know where you are."

Her pulse thundered in her ears. He knew? But how? *He can't. He can't.* But the certainty in his voice chilled her.

"And I'm coming for you."

Their gazes locked—his dark and devouring, hers as fierce as she could muster despite the fear. She forced herself to look away, dropping her gaze to the gold pendant glowing faintly against his chest. A vision slammed into her — Wind screaming against her face. A dragon beneath her, surging through the clouds. The dark prince riding beside her. A leap into open air. His hand clamping around her wrist. Her free hand reaching for the pendant at his throat, desperate to rip it away. Her voice breaking as she begged, *Don't do it*. His grip loosening. Her fingers slipping. The world falling as he released her into the sky.

Ava's breath tore free as the vision shattered. She lifted her gaze to his. "You let me go," she whispered.

He recoiled a fraction, as if the words struck something buried deep within him.

Fear knotted inside her, twisting into something sharper. He was darkness given form. So was the necklace. He needed to be stopped, like the Valians had said.

She raised her chin. "Then come, dark prince," she said, her voice trembling. "Find me so I can tear that cursed thing off you."

For a single heartbeat, they stared at one another—charged, dangerous, inevitable—and then the room blew apart.

CHAPTER FIFTEEN

A crack like the world splitting open ripped through the chamber. Stone buckled. The far wall burst inward with a thunderous roar, chunks of rock hurtling through the space like a storm of jagged daggers. The dark prince's eyes flared with anger, fear, and something monstrous colliding in their depths. He whipped his head toward the destruction.

Ava twisted away and jolted awake with a gasp, someone shaking her hard. Axe's voice cut through the haze, raw and urgent. "Ava! Get up!"

Her vision snapped into focus. Trees blazed with crimson fire, smoke coiled like serpents into the sky, and the forest howled with heat. Everything was burning! "What is happening?" she hollered.

Rien skidded into view, eyes wide. "The dragons!" he shouted over the roar.

Axe dragged her upright as a streak of flame tore across their hideaway, setting the branches above them ablaze. "They attacked. Out of nowhere," he said, eyes darting wildly. "Two silver dragons."

What? The dragons were attacking? She had wanted to stand by them, craved the honor of passing the Frost-Forged Trials and being a Valian, but now the beasts wanted them dead?

The wolf responded before Ava could, ears flattened, fur bristling, a deep, trembling growl rolling through her chest. She dashed around Ava's ankles, then lunged toward her and clamped down, not hard but firm, on the sleeve of her tunic.

"Hey—" Ava staggered, then froze as the wolf tugged, her golden eyes burning with purpose. "Sun, Moon, and Stars. I think she wants us to follow her."

"The wolf? Follow her?" Axe shot Rien a wide-eyed look, the smoke around them thickening.

Rien crouched low as the flames above him roared. "We've got nothing better." He studied the wolf with a raised brow. "She better know what she's doing."

"She does." Ava patted the wolf's head. She hoped.

Terror clung to her, the leftover shards of the dark prince's presence swirling inside her, but the world around her was burning. She had no time to worry about him. Her instinct screamed that nothing made sense except following the wolf.

The wolf dropped her hold on Ava's sleeve and paced in a tight circle, nails scraping stone. Then she stopped abruptly. Her ears pricked. Her whole body went rigid as she faced the exit with the thickest smoke.

Rien cursed under his breath. "That's the way *toward* the fire."

Axe swallowed hard. "She wants us to run *at* the dragons?"

The wolf huffed, sharp and impatient. She stepped in the same direction, glancing back at them with a piercing, urgent look.

Certainty rose in Ava's chest. "She wants us to face them," she said softly. "Not run."

Axe's mouth fell open. "Are you both mad?"

Another spray of fire blasted overhead. Maybe the wolf *was* mad. Perhaps she was too, but right now, they really had no other choice. They were boxed in between the boulders.

She looked at the wolf, giving the animal her complete trust. "Let's go, then."

"Fine," Rien blew out.

"I hope we don't regret this," Axe grumbled.

The wolf bounded ahead. Ava followed, squeezing between the jagged boulders until the sky burst open above them. Heat slammed into her face as another spray of fire cut across the cliffside, flames licking the stone feet away.

"Stop blasting!" she shouted, voice cracking into the open air. "We're coming out!"

Rien and Axe flanked her, weapons unsheathed. She didn't bother with her own; she knew it couldn't touch those beasts. The wolf stood a few steps ahead, growling. They moved fully into the clearing.

Two silver dragons circled above them, their scales catching the pale dawn light like shards of crystal. Their wings cut the air, sweeping currents of wind that sent Ava's hair whipping across her face.

Without warning, they dove. Ava braced herself, her legs itching to run, but the dragons pulled up at the last instant, landing before them with earth-shaking force. Dust spiraled. Heat rippled. The ground trembled beneath her boots.

The dragons stared at them, their silver eyes blinking. And then, they glowed. Silver light rippled across their bodies, scales liquefying into streams of shimmering magic. Their forms twisted, folded inward, reshaped—until where two dragons had once stood now stood Dorn and Zalarae, dressed in silver dragon-scaled tatters.

"No," Ava whispered.

Axe shook his head slowly. "Absolutely not. No way."

Rien stumbled back a step. "The Valians are dragons?" He gripped Ava's arm. "Dragon shifters?"

She couldn't move, could barely think. All she managed was a single shaking whisper. "Yes."

Axe jabbed his weapon at them. "You tried to kill us!"

"And you killed that stranger!" Rien hollered.

A thunderous roar cracked through the air as a third dragon swept over the treetops—massive, breathtaking, radiant, and much larger than the others. The beast soared with an effortless grace that left Ava frozen in place, her thoughts scattering beneath the sheer magnitude of it. Light danced along the scales, each one catching and splitting the morning sun into ribbons of lavender, gold, and soft rose pink. As the dragon descended, the air itself hushed.

"Look at that," Ava said, unable to tear her eyes away.

The dragon touched down with a sound like rolling thunder. Its wings folded with slow majesty. Up close, it was even more magnificent—sleek and ancient, with a ridged head crowned with jagged horns like sculpted starlight. And the eyes were striking molten gold, burning not with fury, but with depth like wisdom, power, and even sorrow.

The dragon studied Ava, Rien, Axe, and the wolf at Ava's side before resting her gaze on Dorn and Zalarae. "My children." Her voice flowed into the clearing, soft as a lullaby, and powerful enough to silence the mountains themselves. "What is happening here?"

The words vibrated through Ava's bones—ancient, commanding, impossibly gentle. Her knees almost buckled. Had she called Dorn and Zalarae children? Had she heard that right? She exchanged glances with Axe and Rien.

Dorn and Zalarae fell to their knees. "Mother," Zalarae said, voice trembling. "We were trying to bring them back to the village. To finish the Frost-Forged Trials."

Dorn held out his hands, his palms up. "We did not mean to end the stranger's life. We meant only to protect the Frost Vale." His hands shook. "To protect you and the entire Wild North."

Zalarae kept her gaze down. "Please, forgive us."

Protect. Ava's heart thudded. She knew precisely what Dorn was referring to. The dark prince. But seeing the magnificent dragon before her, why would such a creature fear any prince?

The great dragon lowered her head, her gaze ancient and wise. "You are forgiven. You acted out of fear," she said. "Fear clouds judgment. Even the judgment of a guardian."

Zalarae flinched but nodded. "Yes, Mother."

"But, Mother, the dark prince is coming," Dorn urged. "He will not come alone. The signs are clear. The omens. The sickness in the South. The Mother of Rivers failing." His jaw clenched. "We know *Teyocel's* strength. We *must* prepare."

Ava stiffened. The name hit her like a slap of cold water. "*Teyocel?* Who is that?"

Zalarae whipped her head toward Ava. "Tread carefully when you speak that name. He is the Bringer of Darkness. He is the dragon who will bring the prince."

A chill rolled through her. *Dark prince. Dark dragon. Teyocel.* Her dreams. Seeing the dark prince in the crumbling bedchamber. And the pendant. Nothing made sense, yet all of it felt connected.

The mother dragon sent a tuft of heat from her nostrils. She kept her attention on the Valians. "Fate has already decided our future. But I assure you, we will be prepared."

Dorn and Zalarae pressed their palms together in thanks, slowly rising.

The dragon shifted her vast form toward Ava, Rien, and Axe. "I am *Izel*, Mother of the Vale." She stepped closer, her gaze settling on Axe. "You are Keeth Graddor of High Meadow, Master of the Blade for House Stromm."

Her gaze settled on Rien. "You are Lirien of the Sublands."

Her gaze fixed on Avalynn as she tipped her head in

a slight, reverent gesture. "You are Princess Avalynn Strong of Strong Haven. Last of your name. Human blooded and fae blooded. You are the Only One."

Axe whipped his stare on her. "I knew it," he whispered.

Ava's breath caught, her pulse stuttering painfully against her ribs. "What?" The word rasped out, thin and shaking.

Only One. Strong Haven. Fae blooded. Human blooded. None of it should have meant anything. But the moment *Izel* spoke her name—her true name—something inside her cracked like ice under a blade.

Images flickered. The same ones she had seen when her spirit had found its way to the dark prince. Snow. A blue-etched sword in her hand. Tumbling through the clouds. The face of the dark prince. Then her body free-falling.

"I don't understand." Ava swallowed hard. Who was the prince to her? How had she and the others ended up in the Vale? Without their memories?

Izel kept her eyes on Ava. "There is much more to learn." She shifted forward. "Come with me, and I will tell you all."

"Absolutely not." Axe stepped forward.

Rien joined the dwarf. "She's with us."

"Fear not," *Izel* assured, unfurling her wings. "I will do her no harm. There is truth she must hear alone, and only I can speak it."

Ava's stomach flipped. Questions cluttered in her mind, swirling like a tempest. The dark prince's threat. The scabbard with no sword. The wolf who knew her.

The stranger who died for her. She needed answers to that, and so much more. If the dragon could tell her what she wanted to know, then she needed to go.

She sheathed the dagger Rien had given her and wiped her palms on her trousers. "Okay, I'll go." She faced her friends. "I'll be back."

They moved to block her, trying to convince her to stay.

"I'll be all right," she reassured.

Izel lowered herself, offering her a wing like a bridge. "Climb," the dragon said.

Axe looked terrified—eyes wide, knuckles white around the handle of his axe. Rien stood rigid and wary, shoulders lifted in a guarded line. His gaze narrowed in sharp distrust as it flicked between the dragons-turned-Valians and the shimmering creature before them.

But the wolf pressed her muzzle firmly into the back of Ava's leg, nudging her forward with a deliberate, insistent push.

Ava stepped toward the ancient dragon. She rested a hand on the warm, glowing scales and climbed. With careful steps, she maneuvered to the base of *Izel's* neck and found a perfect spot to sit.

She wrapped her hands around the ridge, then said in her mind, "*Is this good?*"

"*Ah, you remember the mindspeak,*" the dragon said, soothingly.

"*Yes. I guess I do.*"

"*Now, hold on.*"

The dragon launched skyward. Wind ripped past them, cold and sharp, as the ground fell away in a blur of snowy rock and pines. They climbed higher, past jagged peaks that glinted like shattered glass, until a wide rock ledge appeared near the mountain's misty crown.

Izel circled, then descended in a smooth, spiraling glide. She landed with a grace impossible for her size. Nearby, a wide cavern mouth glowed. Three smaller dragons emerged from its depths, their scales shimmering like *Izel*'s. Their eyes fixed on Ava as they stepped forward. They were smaller than *Izel*. A closer look revealed slightly different shading—one was more purple, another more white, and yet another more gray.

"*These are my brood,*" Izel said. "*Zahni, Mixi, and Coyotl.*"

Ava lifted herself from her perch and took careful steps down the wing. Unsure how to greet the three dragons, she offered them a nod.

"These are your brood," she echoed out loud in a questioning voice. She looked from the three young dragons back to *Izel*, confusion knitting her brows. "And so are Dorn and Zalarae?"

Izel's golden eyes softened with something like pride and something like sorrow. "These before you now were made from my body." Her wings curved inward elegantly. "The Valians? They were made from my flame."

A chill swept through her despite the dragon mist warming the mountain. "What do you mean?"

Izel lowered her head closer to Ava's. "Zalarae was the first. She lay dying on the slopes of this mountain, her spirit crying out for life. I could not leave her in agony. And so, I breathed dragon fire onto her, the flame designed to mark, not destroy, and she rose anew—the first dragon shifter and guardian of the Vale." The dragon's gaze drifted toward the distant village. "Then came others, all of them near death and asking for life. Dorn came later. He entered the Wild North with grave wounds. Another flame gifted."

"Dragon shifters." Ava swallowed. "But you and your brood are—"

"Full-blooded dragons. We belong to the Wild North. This is our home."

Ava tried to make sense of these impossible truths. "All Valians are dragon shifters?"

"Yes. Zalarae and Dorn created the ritual. Those who wished to shed their old lives and become a protector of the Frost Vale and its dragons would climb the mountain after completing the Frost-Forged Trials. I offered them my fire. They accepted it eagerly. Every one of them."

Ava's throat tightened. The training. The secrecy. It had all been leading trainees to the moment she had so desperately wanted. But to become a dragon shifter. Did she want *that*?

Izel stepped closer, so close Ava could see her reflection in those golden eyes. "Dorn and Zalarae and the other Valians guard the Wild North because they are bound to me and were created by me." She paused with a low rumble. "You, child of storm and sword, are bound to something far older."

A shiver raced down Ava's spine. "Something like what?"

"Come," *Izel* said, turning toward the shadows deep

in the cavern. "There is much you do not know, and much you must learn before he comes."

"Before who comes?" Ava asked.

A cold certainty coiled low in her stomach, tightening with every breath. She already knew. She felt his pull in her dreams and even in her waking bones. She had seen him in his bedchamber, almost feeling his touch and tasting his breath. She knew him, and somewhere in her past, she had been with him completely and intimately. She had loved him.

"You know of whom I speak." *Izel's* gaze held a gravity older than the mountain itself, a knowing that transcended time and space.

"I do," Ava whispered. "The dark prince."

"Yes," *Izel* confirmed. "His name is Mateo Stromm."

The name struck like a bell tolling in Ava's chest—final, inescapable. Somewhere, far beyond the Wild North, something ancient and terrible stirred in answer.

CHAPTER SIXTEEN

Stone screamed. Air ripped. Mateo jerked around as the far wall of his bedchamber burst inward, shards of stone and marble spraying like arrows launched sideways. Heat rolled through the room as a shockwave nearly knocked him off his feet.

"Avalynn!" he shouted before the thought even formed, her name a raw cry dragged from some part of him he thought he'd buried and hardly recognized.

She was gone.

Another blast hit, harder, and the ceiling cracked in a jagged line above his bed. Mateo stumbled, grabbing for the trousers at the foot of his bed, yanking them on in a hop. His boots and tunic next. Dust choked the air. The floor buckled.

"*Teyocel!*" he shouted in his mind.

"*I am here,*" the dragon answered at once, the steadiness in his voice only sharpening Mateo's fear.

"*What is happening?*" Another shudder tore through the manor.

A pause. "*I circle above,*" he finally said. "*No threat stalks the land. Whatever strikes you comes from within.*"

The words punched through Mateo's ribs. Rage flared hot at whoever was tearing down the manor house to get to him. But beneath it, something colder lurked. *Avalynn.* She was the reason for all of this. He could feel it in his bones. He needed to end her.

The door flew open. "Prince!" Marina barreled inside, her hulking form looming over him. "We need to move!" Her thick arm looped around his waist before he could protest.

"What is happening?" he demanded. She didn't answer, already dragging him with her as another quake shook the manor.

They dashed into the corridor as the ceiling crashed down behind them. Flames licked through the cracks in the walls. Smoke curled through the air. Screams rose somewhere deeper in the manor. Soldiers? Villagers? Heiric Lind, who was their host? He couldn't tell.

"Karl!" Mateo shouted as they ran. "Raelor!"

He could hear only the thunder of collapsing stone and the troll's labored breathing as they hauled down the buckling hallway. Another explosion rocked the manor, the floor pitching under their feet.

"Go. Go!" Karl hollered.

Mateo glanced over his shoulder, spotting Karl darting through waves of dust. He swung his axe wildly from side to side, as if it could deflect the debris. "Keep go

—" A chunk of wall slammed into him, wiping him away and leaving only a solitary boot.

Stars be damned. The dwarf was gone in a swoop.

Mateo met Marina's terrified eyes, then pushed her forward. "Don't stop!"

She growled, pumping her arms, picking up speed, and pulling him with her.

He turned his thoughts inward. *"Teyocel! We need a way out!"*

"Hurry to the closest exit. The structure bends from all sides. It will not stand much longer."

The entire structure? He pulled Marina to a stop, gasping for air. If *Teyocel* was right, they didn't have time to snake through the corridors. He pointed at the exterior wall. "Knock it down!"

Marina shoved Mateo behind her, planted her feet, and rammed her shoulder into the stone. The wall shuddered with a moan. She staggered back with a snarl and hit it again harder. Cracks spider-webbed outward as not just the wall but the entire manor groaned, beams snapping like brittle bones.

"Hurry!" Mateo barked.

"One more!" she bellowed. With a final, brutal slam, the wall gave way, bursting outward. Marina grabbed Mateo and launched him through, both of them tumbling into the dirt as the manor behind them folded and crumpled like a dying beast. A choking cloud of dust ballooned, swallowing the early morning sky, the ground, everything in its wake.

Mateo stayed down, covering his head, his ears ringing and his head pounding. Warm blood dribbled over his lips. From the crash or his constant headaches, he wasn't sure. But at least he was alive.

Marina's thick hands grabbed his shoulders, helping him to his feet. "My prince." She eyed his face. "You are hurt."

Before he could answer, a figure tore through the plumes, cloak whipping, boots skidding. "Prince Mateo!" Raelor emerged, face smeared with dirt, eyes blazing with frantic relief. "You're alive!"

Mateo spit, then stared at him, chest still heaving. "Thanks to Marina."

Raelor looked around at the destruction. "And Karl?'

"Gone," Mateo said. What was it with him and dwarves? Seemed they never lasted around him.

Raelor swallowed and gave a solemn nod. "Sad news."

The world throbbed, the ache behind Mateo's eyes pulsed like it wanted to split him open. Above him, *Teyocel* roared, the sound trembling through the scorched air. Mateo lifted his gaze to the devastation— the shattered manor, the fallen stone, the cratered earth.

Something inside him snapped.

He clenched his jaw. His fingers curled into fists. "Who did this?" he whispered. Fire lit behind his eyes. "Who," he growled, louder this time, "did this?"

"*I am searching and see no one,*" *Teyocel* responded.

Mateo's gaze snapped to Raelor. The witch was covered in dust, his breath ragged, his eyes glinting like fractured glass. He lived, and *Teyocel* had said the source was from within.

Mateo wiped the blood from his mouth with the back of his hand and stepped toward him. "Was it you?"

Raelor blinked, not once, but twice. "My prince?"

"Was it you?!" Mateo shouted.

"Destroy my life and yours?" Raelor stepped back. "The one whom I serve and whose family I am bound to? No!"

Mateo kept his hands curled at his sides. The desire to throttle someone with his bare hands burned inside him. If it wasn't the witch, then how did something so heinous happen under his nose?

"Then what is your worth," he hissed.

Raelor's brows drew together. "What are you saying?"

"You know what I am saying!" Mateo's voice cracked like a whip. "You should have sensed the danger. You failed to do so!"

Raelor flinched as Mateo advanced, his explanation spilling out of him. "My prince, whatever happened was not magical. I could not have—"

"Excuses!" Mateo spat. "The so-called most powerful witch in the realm could not sense an ordinary threat." Mateo barked out a bitter laugh. "Whoever brought this place down wanted us dead. All of us. You did nothing. You did not shield the manor. You did not warn us. You did not even help."

Raelor lifted his chin. "I was asleep. It all happened so fast. My prince, please."

"Please what?" He raised a fist. "Please don't execute you for incompetence?"

Raelor opened his mouth, then clamped it shut.

"Hear this, Raelor," Mateo added, his voice dropping to a low, venomous growl. "The moment I find a better witch—or the moment my mother stops protecting you—I will tear that crystal stare right out of your skull."

A gust of wind rippled overhead as *Teyocel's* shadow swept across them like a punctuation mark.

"If you will allow my counsel," Raelor said, clearing his voice, "I suggest we leave here at once and rendezvous with the rest of the caravan. There may be other dangers lurking here."

It was the wisest thing he'd said yet.

"*Shall I transport you?*" *Teyocel* asked.

"*No. Keep scanning the skies. If you find anyone suspicious, bring them to me.*"

"*I will.*"

Mateo dusted off his trousers and the sleeves of his open tunic, realizing his chest and stomach were scraped and bleeding. He touched the pendant resting against his bare skin, feeling the steady warmth pulsing there. At least that wasn't harmed.

"Let's go," he said, turning toward the outskirts of the village. "Before anything else happens."

Marina stayed close to Mateo's side. Raelor followed several paces back, silent, but Mateo could feel his eyes crawling all over him as they should. The witch was one order away from being burned to a crisp. His magic be damned. *Teyocel* could take him.

They hadn't gone far when the rest of the Stromm guard came into view, rushing toward the manor with blades drawn, shouting orders, scanning the skies for threats. They spotted Mateo and hurried to meet him, relief flooding their faces.

Mateo didn't return the sentiment. Their new Master of the Blade was gone. His life could have ended, too. Raelor had failed him. There was nothing to be relieved about.

He left the witch to explain what had happened and strode into the heart of the caravan, making his way to his tent. The horses stamped nervously. The maidservants bustled about. The prisoners sat bound beneath a canopy. And something about their posture stopped him.

They were whispering, heads together. They knew something. Mateo redirected his path and headed straight for them, his rage flaring. "What do you know?"

The Oathriders separated, and the dark-haired Soltec, Isabelle, spoke first. "I know that your Sand Bluff welcome did not go the way you expected."

Raelor was beside him now and stepped forward, palm glowing faintly as threads of magic spiraled around his fingers. "Do you want me to make them talk?"

"We'll talk," the Baffin girl, Nyra, said defiantly. "No magic needed."

Mateo swept his hand back, motioning for Raelor to halt. "Talk," he said.

Nyra narrowed her stare on Mateo. "The Oathriders stand with House Baffin," she said. "And House Lind stands with the Baffins. And *all* of us stand with the Only One who will restore peace to Faevenly and forever unite the bloodlines. Her name is Avalynn Strong of Strong Haven."

Mateo's pulse slammed against his skull. His insides

ignited, leaving him to see only red. *Avalynn.* Again, with Avalynn. "You all formed an alliance against me for the daughter of Strong Haven?"

"That's right," the Soltec rebel said with a smirk. "Long before you arrived, we emptied the village, emptied the manor, and filled it with enough powder to bury you and your witch."

Mateo's blood boiled. Beside him, he felt Marina stiffen.

The Baffin girl continued, her voice rising. "We knew you were coming. Everyone knew. The whole province prepared for the prince who burns his enemies alive." Then she yelled, "Burned my father alive!"

He'd heard enough. He snapped his fingers at the closest guard. "Untie her. Now."

"Teyocel, you are needed."

"Coming, my prince."

"Stop!" the Soltec girl hollered as the guard untied her Oathrider companion's wrists. "Haven't you done enough?!"

Mateo smiled with a wicked grin. "Not nearly enough."

"What do you want me to do with her?" the guard asked.

"Let me go, you evil filth!" she hollered, trying to wrench away from the guard's hold.

"Stop!" Isabelle screamed again.

Mateo scanned the caravan, set up not far from a deserted cottage. "Tie her to that fence post."

The Baffin girl's voice rose higher as she was dragged away. Her yelling mixed with her friend's cries. "You are on the wrong side of history! All of you! Following a mad prince and a mad crown!"

Mateo wrapped his fingers around his pendant, feeling its strength coursing through him. The only ones on the wrong side of history were those who opposed him. They would understand that in time.

"You are right, my prince. They will come to learn the truth when all is said and done." Teyocel glided in, circling the camp. *"Now, what will you have me do?"*

Out loud, so all could hear, Mateo said, "She says I am the prince who burns my enemies alive. And she is my enemy." His gaze scanned the guards before landing on the Baffin girl, her red hair matted against her tear-filled face. "Burn her."

Screams pierced the sky, followed by a torrent of flames. Mateo didn't watch. He turned, striding away from the camp, his glare facing the North. *Avalynn.* She had tricked him, knocked him down inches before crossing the hunt's finish line. The ultimate betrayal. Now, she still plotted against him, gathering so-called believers and turning the realm against him and his name.

He marched into his tent and strode to the basin. He washed himself off quickly with a rag, his blood filling the cotton threads. He needed to end her and find that sword. Clenching his jaw, he pulled on a fresh tunic. With the sword in his grasp, the Oathriders and all of Faevenly would see him as the Only One. He would be the realm's savior, not her. Never her.

He tore open the tent flaps, his breath coming out in bursts as he searched the skies for *Teyocel.*

"*The prince recognizes his true destiny,*" *Teyocel* said. The dragon soared above, landing a few feet away. "*Now it is time to claim it.*"

"It ends today," Mateo hissed.

Teyocel stretched out his wing, and Mateo climbed on. His anger and rage erased the pain and filled him with renewed energy. "I want her burned," he said out loud, needing to feel the words on his tongue. "And all those standing with her."

"*It shall be done, my prince.*"

THE
FRACTURE

CHAPTER SEVENTEEN

Sonia trekked through the snow-draped trees. They grew taller here, their branches arching overhead like silent sentinels. Frost glittered along the trunks in delicate spirals, catching the dimming light. Finally, the trees thinned until the forest opened into a frost-lit clearing, her breath misting in the cold air. Every step hummed with old magic. She was close now. Close enough she could sense the vibration nearing. But where was it?

She stopped, her gaze sweeping the landscape, when a spark twinkled. She moved closer, angling her head just so, and there it was. The thinnest curtain of pale blue radiance rippled ahead, a veil of living, shifting light. The boundary between Faevenly and the Wild North. She'd made it. Though the last time she had been here, so long ago, she didn't recall blue hues in the magic.

Sonia drew her cloak tighter and slipped her hand in her pocket, feeling the warm, thrumming pulse of *Izel's* scale against her fingertips. Her heart steadied. She approached the boundary, the magic stirring like a cool breeze, brushing across her face. Then it pushed at her, hard enough to stop her in her tracks.

Huh, that was strange. Why was it resisting her? She had come too far to falter now.

She stepped forward again. Tendrils of air brushed across her face again, moving into her long dark hair, whispering through her thoughts. Her breath hitched—not from pain, but from the sudden sense of being seen. The magic did not strike, or tear, or claw. It simply reached out, brushing all around her, as if getting to know her.

"Do you not remember me?" she asked.

Shh, it whispered back as if telling her to let it finish. She stood still and opened her mind. The ancient magic glided across her thoughts, echoing her name, her memories, her lineage. Recognition shivered through the boundary, like a lock clicking open.

"You are back. You are here... We have been waiting." The magical veil parted.

She smiled. "Yes, I am here." She exhaled slowly, trusting the scale in her pocket to protect her memories, her magic, her purpose. She stepped forward.

"Well," a musical voice piped from beside her. "That's a first."

She turned sharply. A faun perched atop a snow-slicked boulder, cloven hooves dangling, tawny fur shimmering in the light. His almond-green eyes were wide, curious, and a bit unnerved. A grin tugged at his dimpled cheeks.

"What's a first?" she asked.

"That grand entrance of yours. So very dramatic. But first, allow me to introduce myself." He stood atop the rock and pressed a hand to his chest and swept into a bow. "I am Bramble. Keeper of the Boundary, and, apparently, witness to miracles."

"I am pleased to meet you, Bramble." She offered him her own bow. "I am Lady Sonia."

His tail flicked. "A fae witch crossing without losing her memories? No need for my magic seeds? The boundary hasn't greeted someone like that in ... well, ever." He hopped off the boulder in a graceful swirl of hooves and theatrics, circling her with a flourish of his arms, studying her as if she were an experiment gone awry. "No seeds. No bargains. No screaming." He sniffed lightly. "And no unraveling." He leaned closer, squinting. "How are you still ... you?"

Sonia's hand brushed the shape of the scale in her pocket. "I have help."

"Help?" Bramble echoed, skeptical.

She withdrew the scale and showed it to him. "Yes, help."

"Sun, Moon, and Stars." He staggered back, one hoof slipping in the snow. "You carry *her* mark—dragon-blessed magic. You should have opened with that. I was about to drag you out myself."

"It is a good thing it did not come to that," she said.

He paced in a tight circle, muttering, "No seeds, no crying, no screaming—yes, yes, the boundary will be talking about this for weeks." His hooves slipped in the snow, but he hopped back into place and straightened his simple green tunic. "The boundary tested you, of course. It tests all who approach. But once it felt the scale..." He tapped his temple with two fingers. "Memory recognizes memory. Guardians walk freely."

Sonia stilled. "Guardians?"

"You heard me," Bramble said, wagging a finger at her. "Do not pretend to be surprised. The North remembers what the South has forgotten."

She did her best to unravel his message, but she was having trouble understanding its meaning. "I am not sure I am following you, Bramble."

He rolled his eyes. "You Faevenly fae are all alike. Thick as brick." He hopped once. "Let us start over with the basics." He slowed his words, stretching them out as if she were a young child. "Why," he drawled, shrugging, "are you here?" He flicked a hand at the ground.

She swallowed, both amused and annoyed. "I am here for Avalynn Strong, the Only One."

Bramble blinked. "Of course you are. Avalynn, Avalynn. Everyone wants Avalynn. Sheesh."

That did not sound good. "What do you mean, everyone?"

"Everyone means everyone!" His ears twitched sharply. He turned toward the southern trees, a shadow crossing his expression. "But I say this, there are whisperings in the wind of those seeking the girl."

Icy dread threaded Sonia's veins. She knew the answer but asked anyway. "Who else searches for her?"

Bramble's nose wrinkled. "A dragon and a rider will come, or so I have been told." His tail puffed. "The veil will push back. It wants no part of either one."

"Can he get in?" Sonia asked.

"Unknown." Bramble's gaze turned grave. "But the veil is tired. Strained. Too many forces stirring at once. If he presses hard enough..." He jumped and pounded his hooves against the ground. "Something may break."

Sonia's pulse quickened. She needed to hurry. "Do you know where the girl is?"

Bramble pointed toward the towering peak in the distance. "Up there with *Izel*. Learning truths that should have reached her sooner."

"I see." The news that she was with *Izel* was a spark of light in her darkening thoughts.

"And, lady..." He moved in closer, his mischievous eyes softening. "The North always remembers its guardians."

A prickle danced at the base of her spine. *The North always remembers its guardians.* The words rang like a forgotten truth resurfacing. The Valians still had a significant role to play in all things. But what role? And what of her role? She had always known her path would eventually lead here. But not like this, not with the veil straining, not with Mateo twisted by shadow, not with Avalynn teetering on the edge of awakening. She had little time to reach her.

She tipped her head at the faun. "Thank you, Bramble."

"My pleasure." He bowed low. "Now, I take my leave. Until we meet again." He flicked his tail and wiggled his ears. "*If* we meet again," he added with a snip, then slipped backward into the boundary's shimmer, dissolving into ribbons of light.

"Wait!" she called out. She had wanted to ask about the sword, but the faun was gone. No matter. She would find out soon enough.

Sonia squared her shoulders and drew in a deep breath. Avalynn and *Izel* needed her. All of Faevenly needed her. If she didn't act quickly, the entire realm would not survive what was coming.

CHAPTER EIGHTEEN

Ava followed *Izel* into the cave. The temperature shifted at once, the crisp bite of the mountain air replaced by a breath-warm heat that wrapped around her like a cozy blanket. A few steps deeper and the narrow entryway opened into a broad chamber, its ceiling arching so high she couldn't see where the stone ended and the shadows began.

"Incredible," Ava said, tilting her head back.

Her gaze swept from the cavern's towering roof to the thick walls, where the stone wasn't smooth so much as scored with claw marks, some old and faint while others were sharp enough to look freshly carved. Threads of luminescent blue-green veined the rock, glowing softly like frozen rivers of light. Ava stepped closer, mesmerized, the glow catching along *Izel's* scales as the dragon moved deeper into the chamber, each clawed step clicking against the stone.

When they reached the back of the cavern, *Izel*

stopped. She circled once, her massive body moving with grace. She lowered herself, curling her tail neatly around her body, and folding her wings.

"Come closer," *Izel* rumbled, her voice echoing through the cavern. "There is much you must understand."

Ava stepped forward, each footfall light and hesitant. The cavern felt ancient and alive in a way that made her skin prickle. This place held secrets. Old ones. Heavy ones. Was she ready for that? She stopped at an arm's length from the dragon, suddenly aware of just how small she was. How fragile.

"Is this good?" she asked.

"It is." *Izel's* luminous eyes studied her, calm yet piercing, as though looking not at her but *through* her. "What you have learned so far is only the surface of who you are," she said.

Ava's pulse quickened. She hadn't realized how tightly she was gripping her own hands until her knuckles ached. "I want to know," she said, voice barely above a whisper. "Everything."

"Then sit," *Izel* instructed gently. "Your legs may tremble before we are finished."

Ava lowered herself onto a rise of stone opposite the dragon. Warmth seeped through her clothes, anchoring her, steadying her breath even as her heart hammered.

Izel watched her for a long moment, as if measuring her readiness, weighing her strength. "Ask, Avalynn Strong," she said at last. "Ask what you fear most. I will not lie."

Ava didn't have to think twice. She knew exactly

what her fear was. The dark prince. Her throat tightened as her hands wrapped around her knees. "Why do I feel drawn to the dark prince?"

The question hung in the air, fragile and precious, like something she had never meant to speak aloud. *Izel* stilled. The air in the chamber paused. "Avalynn," she said, her voice softening in a way that made Ava's stomach flip. "The pull you feel is no accident. No illusion. No trick of memory."

Ava's pulse throbbed painfully at her neck. "He calls to me in my dreams," she admitted. "Once, his call was so loud it pulled me to him. To a place where he slept. Not my body, but my spirit. I don't even know how I did that. And when I saw his face, it felt like I knew him."

"You drifted to him using your innate human magic, which you inherited from your mother, Gabriela, and Gabriela's father, your grandsire, Julio. Your human magic is strong." *Izel* paused, as if waiting for Ava to say something, but she was speechless. "As for the knowing feeling, that is because you *do* know him."

She knew it. Deep down inside, she had always known. "But how?"

Izel lowered her head until her luminous eyes were level with Ava's. "You and Mateo were bound before you crossed the veil. Before your memories were whisked away by the Wild North's protective magic."

Her stomach twisted. "Bound how?"

Izel exhaled a plume of warm air that brushed Ava's skin like a mother's caress. "By fate," she said. "By bloodlines entwined since birth. Strong and Stromm. By a

172

prophecy whispered. And by something far more dangerous."

Ava's fingers trembled. "What's more dangerous than that?"

Izel's gaze softened. "Love."

Ava's breath collapsed out of her in a broken gasp. A flood of tears surged in her throat. *Love.* She couldn't remember him. Couldn't recall a single shared moment. Yet the word struck something buried so deep inside her it hurt to breathe.

"But if we..." She shook her head. "Then why would he want to kill me?"

Izel's nostrils flared. "Darkness has wound itself around his heart like a noose," she growled. "The queen poisoned his path long before you were old enough to choose yours. He believes ending you will end the pain inside him."

Ava's vision blurred. A shattering ache bloomed in her chest, not from memory but from grief for something she didn't fully know she had lost.

Izel's voice dropped to a whisper. "He does not remember the truth of you. The truth of both of you. The truth of what you shared. He does not even remember himself."

Ava pressed a hand over her heart, as if trying to keep it from breaking open. "Then what am I supposed to do when he gets here?"

"Face him," she said. "Face the one you loved, now twisted into a dark prince who believes he must destroy you." She let her words settle like falling embers before adding, "You will not be alone. I will be with you."

"And so will I!"

Ava spun around. A woman strode through the cave mouth, her long dark hair whipping around her shoulders, a dark cloak billowing behind her like a shadow tugged by the wind. Ava shot to her feet, glancing from the stranger to *Izel*. The dragon was steady and calm. If *Izel* was not alarmed, then this lady was no enemy. Still Ava's mind offered nothing, no sign of memory or recognition.

"Who are you?" Ava asked.

The woman stopped before her, bent slightly with breathless effort from the climb. "I am Lady Sonia," she said with an exhausted smile. "A friend."

"The lady arrives when she is needed," *Izel* said, dipping her head with a rare note of fondness. "As she always has."

Sonia reached into her cloak and withdrew a shimmering, pearlized scale. "I had a little help getting in," she said, holding it up.

Izel's eyes warmed. "A piece of my heart fire," the dragon rumbled. "Given to you long ago. No magic forged by dragon flame would deny you while you carry it."

So, they did know each other. If *Izel* trusted her, then she would too.

Sonia's expression shifted, urgency tightening the edges of her mouth. "There is one more thing we need, though," she said. "The sword."

A shiver raced down Ava's spine. The sword. Flashes burst behind her eyelids of the empty scabbard tucked beneath her bed. Then the blade spinning end over end as she plummeted through the clouds.

She pressed her fingers against her temple. "I had it when I fell. I remember watching it drop faster than I did. I have no idea where it landed."

"Never fear," *Izel* said. "I know exactly where your sword lies."

"You do?" Ava blinked.

Wisps of smoke curled from *Izel's* nostrils. She rose from her resting place, her wings unfurling in a slow, controlled sweep. Ava shuffled back, watching as the dragon lifted herself to her full height. "I am the Mother of the Vale," she said, her voice low and resonant. "Every shift of frost, every heartbeat under this mountain, every breath of wind through the boundary—I feel them." She tilted her head. "Do you think a sword of power could fall into my domain without my notice?"

Ava lowered her head, feeling smaller. She hadn't meant to question *Izel*. Not at all. "Of course, you would know." This was a dragon who had lived long before Ava was born, long before the kings and queens of Faevenly rose and fell. "I did not mean to offend you."

Lady Sonia spoke, her voice steady but urgent. "Then we must go for the sword. The hour is late. Mateo is coming. Now."

Fresh fear prickled across Ava's skin, sharp as frostbite. Bond or no bond, past or no past, he was the dark prince now. He wanted her dead. They needed to be ready.

Izel turned her head toward them. "Both of you," she said, extending a wing, "climb on."

Ava didn't hesitate. She climbed the scales, gripping a ridge at *Izel's* neck as she lowered herself. Sonia followed, settling in behind her with steady, practiced ease.

"Hold fast," *Izel* warned. Her body shifted beneath them, then she launched herself.

The cavern vanished behind them as they burst into open air, *Izel's* brood following as the mountain fell away in a blur of silver rock and frost-blue shadows. Below them sprawled the icy Wild North. Endless forests dusted with frost. Rivers gleamed like steel. Streaks of blue light threaded through the land like veins. Far ahead, a shimmering wall of silver-blue light stretched across the horizon. The veil. The boundary between the North and the rest of Faevenly.

"What is happening to the veil?" Lady Sonia asked *Izel*, their minds somehow linked together so Ava could hear.

Ava's heart slammed against her ribs. *"What do you mean?"*

"The blue streaks," Izel answered. *"They are wrong. The magic should be unseen. You will see why when we land."*

Izel angled her wings, descending in a long, controlled glide until her talons struck the ground with a jolt. Snow erupted around them. When the flakes settled, Sonia slid off, and then Ava. They stood side by side, staring.

The sword had not simply fallen at the boundary. It had dropped *within* the boundary, the blade embedded halfway inside the shimmering magic. Blue cracks trickled outward from the embedded onyx—thin at first, then widening, pulsing with a dangerous rhythm. It was as if the magic was trying to contain the weapon, and the weapon was attempting to break free.

Sonia stepped closer, her face pale. "By the Stars."

Izel's wings folded close, her brood landing behind her. "The boundary stretches from the sky to the deepest roots beneath the ground," she said. "It is not a curtain, but a wall that touches the core of the land." Another crack widened, pulsing brighter. "If it breaks," she added, "the boundary will collapse."

Lady Sonia whispered, "And the Wild North with it."

The sword hummed, a deep vibration Ava felt in her bones. "The sword. I hear it," Ava said, voice tight. "I feel it."

Izel nodded. "Your blade calls for you. But touch it now, and you end everything we stand on."

Before Ava could respond, something tumbled out of the magic in a burst of shimmering light. A faun. He landed in a heap of limbs, fur, and indignation, skidding across the frost and falling face-first.

"Ow! By the ancient roots of the First Tree, why is it always the face?" he groaned, rubbing his nose. He staggered upright, eyes wild, tunic askew, one hoof missing its ankle wrap. "You fools are finally here. And not a moment too soon!" He paced in a flurry. "The boundary is breaking. The Mother of Rivers is drying. And the dark prince comes."

Ava pulled her chin in. "Bramble?"

"Yes, it's me! Are your eyes not working?" His ears twitched violently. "Before you start asking questions—

no, I am not drunk. Yes, the boundary is unstable. YES, the North's guardians are the only ones who can stop it from collapsing!"

Behind them, a rush of wind announced new arrivals. Dorn, Zalarae, and the other Valians, dressed in pure silver. All armed with ice-colored spears. Even Axe and Rien were with them, wearing their training clothes.

"We're ready to fight," Axe said, wielding his axe.

"That's right," Rien added, a dagger in each hand.

They formed a semicircle around Ava, Sonia, and *Izel*, weapons raised toward the fissured veil.

Reinforcements. Avalynn let out a sigh of relief. "The North's guardians. The Valians," she uttered. "Of course."

"Them?" Bramble's eyes widened. "Are you daft?" he sputtered. "Why in all the frozen hells would I mean them?"

Dorn bristled. "Watch your tongue, faun!"

"I mean, look at you!" Bramble snapped. "You all are competent. Fierce. Muscular and all that. But magical guardians?" He barked a laugh. "Not even close."

"Bramble, please," Lady Sonia said.

The faun clamped his mouth in dramatic fashion, rolling his eyes and stepping aside.

"The faun means *Izel* and me." Sonia lifted *Izel's* scale in her palm, its light pulsing in rhythm with the boundary. "The boundary was fashioned by dragon fire and a witch's spell. It breathes because we breathe. It stands because we stand." She turned to face *Izel*. "I know that now."

Izel's great head lowered, her voice a low, reverberating thunder. "Lady Sonia speaks the truth. She and I are the guardians." Behind her, the sword pulsed, the mountain groaned, and somewhere in the distance, a dragon's roar carried on the wind.

"Now that we have established that, it is time for the guardians to activate." Bramble clapped his hands. "Quick, quick. Before *Izel's* mate returns with that villainous prince. I hear him even now!"

Ava's head spun. *Teyocel* was *Izel's* mate? What else did she not know? Other than, basically, everything.

Sonia stepped forward, the scale gleaming in her palm. Her voice steadied, firm and resolute. "I am ready."

"Proceed, lady," *Izel* said with a reverent nod.

Sonia approached the boundary. She extended her hand into the shimmering wall of magic. Her arm disappeared up to the elbow, then the shoulder, until only half her body remained visible. She grasped the sword's hilt. The blade shrieked, a high, ringing tone vibrating deep in Ava's bones. Or was it the boundary that shrieked?

Slowly, Sonia pulled the blade free, the blue cracks pulsing brighter, faster, like a dying heartbeat. The sword slid loose, and Sonia extended it toward Ava, arm shaking from the magic engulfing through her.

"Take it," she gasped. "Hurry."

Ava dashed forward. She wrapped her fingers around the hilt. A surge of power poured through her, fierce and warm, and familiar. She stumbled back, clutching the sword to her chest.

"Thank you, Lady Sonia," Ava said, her voice shaking. The sword's warmth pulsed through her fingers. But it did nothing to ease the cold knot forming in her gut. Her throat tightened. "What about you?"

Sonia met her eyes with a soft, steady resolve. "I will endure. The magic knows me. It will not unmake me. When this is all over, you will come back for me."

Ava reached a hand out but let it fall before touching her. "I will." *If I can...*

With a nod, Sonia stepped fully into the veil. Her silhouette blurred into the shimmering blue, swallowed by the flickering light. The cracks along the boundary stopped spreading, their angry glow dimming to faint scars.

Bramble let out an explosive breath. "Finally! I have been holding that in for a full minute. Do you know how undignified that is?" He waved dramatically. "Anyway. Good luck facing *Teyocel* and the dark prince, you brave fools! Bye-bye now!"

With a flick of his tail, he vanished back into the magic. Sonia's voice echoed faintly from within the shimmering barrier. "I will hold them back for as long as I can. But if they breach the boundary, you must be ready to fight."

Ava tightened her grip on the sword. She lifted her eyes toward the distant roar breaking across the sky, one she knew in her bones.

Mateo was almost there.

The clearing shifted into motion at once.

"My brood and I will take to the skies," *Izel* said. She turned to the Valians. "Valians stay on land." Her wings snapped wide. With a guttural roar, she launched herself skyward, the others rising with her.

Dorn and Zalarae stepped forward, Dorn barking sharp commands. "Form the line!" Spears dropped in perfect unison, tips aimed at the boundary. "Axe, Rien, Ava." Dorn jerked his chin. "Behind us. Now." He tossed Ava's scabbard at her. "This is yours."

She hadn't noticed it strapped to his back. "Thank you," she said, slinging it in place.

Falling into trainee mode, they moved into position. Axe and Rien flanked Ava. A low growl rumbled beside her as the wolf bounded up, massive and shadow-sleek, fur bristling as she took her place at Ava's heels—no hesitation, no fear, as if this was exactly where she belonged.

"I was wondering where you were," she said to the beast. Her mind took her to another beast, the silver horse. Where was she?

Teyocel's roar split the air again—closer now, powerful enough to vibrate through Ava's ribs. This was it. Standing with all her courage, and even her fear, a whisper brushed along the edges of her mind. A saying. A promise. A truth.

Ava tightened her grip on her sword, the blue light within the blade and within her skin pulsing to life between her fingers. "Faith is a warrior." She lifted her chin as the sky cracked open with a roar. "And so are we."

CHAPTER NINETEEN

Mateo crouched low atop *Teyocel's* back, hands gripping the ridge at the dragon's neck as the wind whipped across his face. Each beat of *Teyocel's* wings hurled them forward, the landscape beneath blurring from the grass and brush of Sand Bluff to the rolling meadows of High Meadow, and finally, to the frostbitten pines of the North.

"We near the boundary," Teyocel said.

"Good," Mateo said, when another thought crossed his mind. *"Will I lose my memories when we cross?"*

"Not while you are with me, and not if the boundary fails. But something is amiss."

Mateo peered forward, unable to see anything but open skies. *"What is it?"*

"The veil. It is clouded and streaked."

"Clouded and streaked?" Mateo craned his neck. *"How?"*

"A witch's hand," Teyocel hissed.

Mateo's mind spun. *Avalynn.* She had witch abilities from her human bloodline. He had seen her blue light. "*Avalynn's?*"

Teyocel drew in a sharp inhale. "*Not of her, but from her. And another.*"

Mateo's grip tightened. "*It doesn't matter who.*" He braced his legs tight around the dragon. "*Just get through.*"

A roar blasted from *Teyocel.* Then another. A few more beats and Mateo spotted the shimmery boundary. Blue and silver streaks lined the mist, like thin spider webbing. This was what *Teyocel* meant. He crouched low, ready for *Teyocel* to bust through, when a surge of energy slammed against them like an invisible tidal wave.

"*Teyocel!*" Mateo hollered.

The dragon screeched, his wings faltering. Mateo tensed, gripping and clinging to the mighty beast as they soared downward in a spinning freefall before *Teyocel* righted himself with a growl and glided upward in a wide arc.

"*She will not bar my entry!*" *Teyocel* bellowed.

The dragon flew around until he hovered midair before the boundary. His chest rumbled like a mighty storm, building until a torrent of red and orange flames erupted. The fire slammed against the magic, enveloping Mateo in heat waves mightier than the sun. Eyes slammed shut and head down, Mateo stayed low. When the flames thinned, he opened his eyes. Holes riddled the veil—some as small as fists, others wide enough for dragons. Through them, he saw the frozen Wild North. Waiting for them, the Valians in glimmering silver battle leathers, spears glinting like icicles. Above them hovered *Izel* and her three offspring, wings taut, ready to strike. Mateo barely registered them. Standing behind the Valians, he spotted *her*.

She stood with blade in hand. Jaw set. Eyes fierce as winter stormlight. Her brown, white-streaked hair almost stirred with power. Seeing her ripped the air from his lungs. Then he saw another face and froze. *Lirien*. Childhood memories screamed through him—hunting, laughing, bleeding together, sleeping under the same stars. His wolf at his side, his friends always with him. He spotted the traitorous beast beside Avalynn. But where was Gareth?

"Prince! They mean to deny us glory!" Teyocel roared.

Mateo shook his head, his hand resting over his pendant. *Teyocel* was right. They had betrayed him. They were his enemies. They would take his crown, his legacy, his destiny—unless he destroyed them first.

"Go," Mateo snarled. *"Burn them to ash."*

Teyocel tucked in his wings, hurtling through the largest tear like a bolt thrown from the skies. Shouts from the Valians filled the air as they blurred into movement, their spears zipping through the sky as *Teyocel* unleashed his fire. In a flash, the spears collided with a ringing crack as the poles linked, locking into a lattice that curved like a shield of woven ice and silver. *Teyocel's* fire struck a heartbeat later. The flames crashed against the shield with a deafening roar, but the blaze did not break through. It sputtered, then died, a ring of steam hissing outward as the flames dissolved.

Teyocel snarled in outrage as Mateo's heart thundered. They had blocked dragon fire. "Go again!" Mateo hollered.

"You will not," a voice said in Mateo's mind.

It was not *Teyocel*, but someone more ancient. It rang low and resonant, threaded with warmth and wrath and a power that carried the weight of centuries. *Izel.* Mateo's breath caught as if the air around him had thickened. He had not invited her into his mind. Yet *Izel* was there. And she was furious.

"Out of him!" Teyocel bellowed.

"Out of the Vale, Destroyer!" Izel roared.

Izel and her brood advanced. They sliced through the air from all sides, swooping and circling *Teyocel* in a frenzied rush. The movements jerked Mateo from all sides. His legs lost their hold, his hands their grip, and he tumbled. He crashed to the ground, smashing face-first into a pile of snow.

Clambering to his feet, he saw *Izel* and her brood chasing *Teyocel,* blurring together in flashes of scales and fires as they soared out of sight.

"Well, well. The dark prince is without his dragon."

The voice halted him in place before he turned and faced Avalynn, the Only One, his once loyal wolfbeast at her side. He dusted himself off. "*Prince* Mateo Stromm," he corrected.

Lirien and Keeth stayed close to her. The Valians held their ground just beyond, their silver spears somehow back in their hands and raised at him. He didn't care about any of them. He wanted Avalynn dead and that sword in his possession.

She moved forward. "Do you remember me?" Her

gaze narrowed on him. "Remember who you were before that pendant around your neck corrupted you?"

A low hiss drifted upward from his chest where the chain hung, its warmth pulsing softly against his skin. "I know who I am." He drew the sword from his scabbard. "And I remember you. Your trickery. Your deceit. How you thought me a fool and betrayed me."

She stepped forward. "I don't know any of that. But I do know that I don't want to harm you." She edged closer, Stormshroud mirroring her every move. "I don't want to fight you. But I will if I must. Only me." She glanced over her shoulder. "Everyone, stay back."

Mateo barked a humorless laugh, slicing his blade back and forth. "You have no idea what you are doing."

"You may be right. But I still have to stop you."

She struck first in a blur of blue and motion. Mateo parried with a quick sidestep. She pressed again, throwing an angled cut aimed for his shoulder. He blocked, then twisted out of reach. His pendant thrummed, cold power curling around his ribs. He drove her backward with a brutal kick to the gut. Stormshroud snarled but stayed at her flank, waiting for her order.

"You don't stand a chance against me, Avalynn," he said with a wicked smile.

"Oh yeah?" She regained her footing but stayed slightly bent over, her breath labored, sending puffs of vapor into the cold air. "We'll see about that."

Then she was on him again. Their blades collided, ringing like clashing bells echoing off the treetops. Valians shouted behind her. Lirien surged forward a step.

Keeth lifted his axe. Yet they stayed back. Stormshroud paced, ears pinned, muscles tense but restrained.

Mateo lunged, blade sweeping in a deadly arc. Avalynn ducked, rolled, and came up swinging. Her strike grazed his ribs, enough to draw blood, and he groaned. She had learned a thing or two from the Valians. Her moves were unpredictable and wild. She'd gotten stronger, too. But she still wasn't enough.

He tightened his grip and hammered his sword at her. His return blow sent her sprawling, her sword skidding several feet away. Stormshroud leapt in front of her, hackles raised. Lirien and Keeth charged forward, but Avalynn forced air into her lungs and slammed her palm against the ground. "No!"

The wolf froze. So did Lirien and Keeth. "Ava, come on," Lirien hissed.

Mateo raised his brow. "Ava? Is that what you are called here?"

"Yes," she answered. She stood again, unsteady but resolute, gulping in air as she caught her breath. "What are you called?" She retrieved her sword. "Dark One? Evil One?"

"Dark Prince." Mateo lifted his weapon in a ready stance. "You should've stayed down," he growled.

"You should've taken that necklace off," she countered.

He approached, fury bubbling within him, when *Izel* and *Teyocel* screamed overhead. Their roars shook the frost from the pines as they barreled over the mountains. They collided, jaws snapping and claws shredding scale. They tumbled, locked in a whirl of rage, force, and power, spinning in a blur of white, purple, and black until they crashed. They hit the ground like fallen gods, the ground cracking beneath them. Ice shattered, snow and dirt exploded upward. Mateo staggered as the great dragons lay motionless in the crater they'd carved.

"Sun, Moon, and Stars," Avalynn whispered.

Another roar ripped through the air. *Izel* spread her wings and launched from the spot, spiraling up and away. *Teyocel* stayed down.

"*Teyocel!*" Mateo sprinted across the uneven ground. He dropped to his knees, hands hovering over the dragon's head, unsure if he should touch him. "*Teyocel, I'm here.*" The dragon's chest heaved, smoke trailing from wounds that pulsed deep, ugly, and dark across his side. "*Talk to me.*"

The dragon's head lifted only an inch, but he stayed silent. *Teyocel* was never weak, never vulnerable.

"*How do I help?*" Mateo's hands shook as he stroked *Teyocel's* cheek. "*What do you need?*"

Teyocel's wings shuddered, folding tight against his body. "*There is a place called the Green Falls.*" His voice barely touched Mateo's mind, the weakness audible. "*The waters... They will mend me.*"

"*I know it.*" Mateo remembered the place the Enbarr had taken him and Avalynn during the hunt. His thoughts landed for only a second on what they had shared there before he pushed it all away. "*Do you know how to get there?*"

"*I do, though I am weak,*" *Teyocel* whispered. "*There is power in your pendant. It might help. Climb on.*"

Mateo didn't hesitate. Sheathing his weapon, he

scrambled up *Teyocel's* wing, carefully gripping the ridges along his neck. "*Let's go.*"

The dragon inhaled sharply as if drawing strength from the cold air itself. With a grunt that was more pain than fury, *Teyocel* forced his wings outward and launched. The earth dropped away beneath them. Wind slammed against Mateo's face as they climbed, banking hard into a rising current. His heart hammered with fear, not of falling, but of losing *Teyocel,* the one creature who had stayed by his side when everyone else had turned against him.

"*Please, Teyocel. Please be okay. I need you.*" He pressed his cheek against the dragon's scales, as if he could will *Teyocel* to fly faster, but the dragon only slowed. "*Hold on,*" Mateo muttered, not sure whether he meant it for the dragon or himself.

Teyocel teetered, then descended in a staggering swoop. He nearly brushed the very ground, his wings dragging against the air as though they weighed mountains. Mateo held on, hands digging in, legs clamped tight. They needed to make it. They had to. *Come on. Come on.* He glanced down, watching the cold landscape give way to meadows and grasslands.

"*I think we're getting close,*" he said.

"*We... are,*" *Teyocel* said between ragged breaths.

Finally, they reached the familiar hills. A minute later, they crashed into the dirt. Mateo jumped, his boots striking the ground. He nearly lost his balance before spinning toward *Teyocel.*

The dragon collapsed halfway on his side, chest heaving. "*My strength wanes.*" Smoke wheezed from his nostrils.

"No, no, no," Mateo said out loud, dropping beside him, pressing a hand to *Teyocel's* head. "You'll be all right. You just need water from—"

The words cut off as he turned toward the falls. The once gushing cascade was now a barren cliff, streaked with dried mineral lines and brittle moss. Not a single drop flowed. The ground beneath their feet, which should have been a rippling pond, was evaporated and empty.

"The Green Falls is no more," Mateo uttered. "The Mother of Rivers is dying. Faevenly is...."

"Dying, like me," *Teyocel* snarled, pain in his voice.

The air shuddered with beating wings. Mateo whirled as *Izel* descended, Avalynn on her back, sword in her grip. They landed a short distance away. Avalynn slid off the dragon, eyes filled with surprise as she scanned the dry dirt.

Mateo stiffened. Rage surged hot and seething through his chest. "You did this," he spat. His hands curled into fists. "Somehow it was you. I know it!"

Avalynn took a single step forward and shook her head. "No," she said quietly, desperation tangled in her throat. "I did not do this. I swear it."

Mateo's vision wavered, anger blurring the edges of everything. "You would take my dragon. You would take my throne. You would take my destiny!"

She took another step. "I don't care about thrones or destiny," she pleaded. "But I know in my heart that I care about you. That we shared something." She gulped. "I don't want to fight you, Mateo."

"Stop talking," he snarled, "and defend yourself."

He drew his sword and charged. Their blades clashed as he drove forward with brutal strength. He pounded and sliced. She parried, barely deflecting the impact. He swung again. She dodged, his blade scoring through the ends of her flowing hair. With a growl, he pushed forward. She ducked, rolled, and came up with a strike that split the air with a whoosh. But he was stronger, faster. He was darkness made flesh. He whipped his arms back, then struck with relentless speed, her arms shaking under the weight of his fury.

"Don't do this," she gritted out.

He pulled back, then slammed his blade so hard she staggered. Another hit, unrelenting, and she broke, dropping to one knee, gasping.

"Mateo, please," she sputtered out. "Stop."

He had her. Then something changed. Not in her stance. Not in her eyes. In the air itself. Heat curled against his skin, subtle at first, like the kiss before a blaze. His grip tightened as his gaze snapped to her hands. A faint blue shimmer traced her fingers, then deepened, light bleeding outward in slow, deliberate threads. It crept along her skin, spiraling up her arm, brightening with every heartbeat.

Her light. He had seen it before, during the hunt. And by the look on her face, she had no idea what it was.

She stared at her hand as if it didn't belong to her, then lifted her gaze to him. "You know what this is," she said quietly. "This light."

A smile touched his lips. "Oh, I know." He stepped closer. "Allow me to extinguish it for you."

He towered over her, his body shuddered, his breath heaved, his muscles shook. He had loomed over her like this once before, choosing whether she lived or died. Back then, flying through the skies, his mind had been in chaos. Now it was cold and clear. She deserved this. He raised his sword, but something in her shifted.

She blinked, her head shaking as she sucked in a breath so sharp it sounded like something tearing inside her. "Sun, Moon, and Stars," she whispered. "I remember." Her eyes widened, not with fear but with awareness. Her gaze found him—raw, broken, impossibly vulnerable. "I betrayed you," she choked out, tears welling in her eyes. "I did it to save you. What I didn't tell you was that I was also saving myself, and Lily." She swallowed. "My fath—I mean, the king—he threatened me. Hurt me. It was his marks you saw on my arms." A tear rolled down her cheek. "I should have told you about him, but I didn't think I could. My duty had me in shackles I didn't even know I was wearing."

"Stop," his voice shattered out of him. His mind rattled. His stomach wound so tight he thought he might collapse. He reached for his pendant, pulling it out from under his tunic, and clutched it like a life source.

She rose to her feet. "Mateo, please." Her voice trembled. "Listen to me. That pendant is poisoning you. It's twisting your thoughts. It made you drop me. I know it."

He staggered back. The pain of what she'd done to him—what he'd done to her—flooded his mind so viciously he almost blacked out. Yet the truth remained. She had ruined him. There was no going back.

Her gaze lifted, but not at him. Through him. As if she saw something beyond the world itself. Then, softly, with a steadiness that froze his blood, she uttered, "Some prophecies are meant to be broken."

"What?" he whispered.

She lowered her sword. "In the twilight of transformation, there will arise like a mighty storm, one born of the union between realms. With a sword of blue in hand and the heart of a champion, this Only One will restore peace to Faevenly and forever unite the bloodlines."

The words slapped him. Burned him. Killed him. The Only One prophecy. It should have been his, not hers. She had stolen it from him.

She raised her free hand—open, gentle, as if in offering. "You want the blade?" she asked. "I give it to you. Willingly." She stepped toward him. Slow. Careful. She placed the sword's hilt into his palm.

He stared at her, stunned and helpless, horrified by how her touch felt like a memory he both longed for and hated.

Teyocel's voice curled through his mind. "*Run. Her. Through.*"

Mateo's grip tightened around the hilt. His hand shook from the thrumming power within the sword. Finally, it was his. The power. The glory. The destiny. In the same instant, her hand snapped upward. Faster than lightning. Faster than thought. Her fingers closed around the pendant. She ripped it from his neck. And the blade slid through her stomach.

CHAPTER TWENTY

Mateo broke.

  He collapsed as though someone had ripped every bone from his body. His knees hit the ground. Pain detonated behind his eyes. His vision blackened at the edges, pulsing in and out like a dying heartbeat. The roar screamed in his ears before he knew it was coming from his mouth. It tore out of him like something feral, something unmade, something dragged from the depths of his soul.

Every nerve in him burned. Then froze. Then burned again. He fought to breathe but sucked in nothing but knives. The ground swayed beneath him. The sky spun. Faces flashed before his eyes—Manny, his sisters Camila and Floriana, Lirien, Gareth, Keeth, and Avalynn. Everywhere Avalynn. A voice screamed his name, urgent and unrecognizable, but it dissolved into ringing. Then another roar, a deeper one, *Teyocel's* agony, or fury, or both. It echoed somewhere close, but Mateo couldn't see him, couldn't process him.

Just kill me.

That thought sliced through him, wild and raw. Anything to stop the pain. *Anything.* Tears stung his eyes, but he couldn't wipe them away because he didn't know where his hands were. Did he still have hands? Did he still have a body?

Red light pulsed before his eyes. Then blue. Then white. Then silence. The pain snapped and vanished, leaving him trembling and face down in the dirt, panting like someone dragged him from drowning. And in that abrupt stillness, clarity slammed into him with merciless force.

He blinked. The ringing died. The haze cleared. He lifted his head, his gaze falling on Avalynn. She lay on the ground, the blue-etched blade piercing through her, her hair fanned out, her eyes half-lidded, glassy, and empty.

Everything inside him collapsed, imploding into a howling void where his heart had been. A sound tore out of his throat, broken and raw. "No..." His voice shook, barely more than a whisper. "No, no, no!"

He crawled toward her, hands shaking, a hollow scream stuck inside his throat. He couldn't feel the pendant anymore, couldn't feel the darkness. He could only feel the devastating, unbearable truth that she wasn't moving. And it was his hand that had done it.

"Avalynn," he choked. He placed one hand on her shoulder, the other on her cheek. "What have I done?"

"You rid yourself of your torment, my prince," Teyocel said coldly.

Mateo stilled. Every muscle locked tight. A slow, searing realization cracked inside him. It hadn't been Avalynn twisting him. It hadn't been fate damning him. It had been the pendant, and *Teyocel.* The pendant's influence swirled in his mind while the dragon's whisperings magnified and stoked. They steered him, pushed him, goaded him to destroy everything he loved.

A wildfire ripped through him. "You," he rasped. "You made me do this."

The dragon stirred weakly. "*I only touched what was already there.*"

Mateo shook his head, the agony in his chest flaring into a blazing inferno. "No!" he shouted. "You hollowed me out! You took everything good left in me! You made me—" His voice cracked as he glanced at Avalynn's motionless form. "You made me kill her." He added softly, "And so many others."

A sinister laugh slipped from *Teyocel's* mouth. "The little prince awakens."

Little prince? His anger flared. He didn't think so. He staggered to his feet, vision swimming, heart split wide open and bleeding. He wrapped his hand around the sword's hilt, the metal burning in his palm like molten guilt. With a shaky breath, he eased it from Avalynn's body, the blade sliding free and slick with devastation.

He stumbled toward *Teyocel,* each step fueled by grief, hatred, and the agonizing truth that he had loved Avalynn and had let darkness use him to destroy her. He reached the dragon's side. He raised the sword over *Teyocel's* heart, hands quaking, shoulders trembling, breath ragged.

"You don't get to twist me anymore," he said, raw as an open wound. "You don't get to own me."

"But I do own you." *Teyocel's* evil glare glued to Mateo. "Remember? I have half of your soul. These last few days, I have been siphoning more. If I die, you die."

A momentary hesitation stalled him, but he pushed it away. After what he'd done, his life wasn't worth living. "Then let's die. Together."

His grip tightened. He was ready to end this. Ready to kill the monster who had helped make him one. But something clicked. His mother, father, and his sisters came to mind. The lessons of faith and love he had been taught bubbled to the surface. He could almost hear his father saying, *"This isn't you, Mijo."* And he knew his father was right. He could not become the very nightmare that had ruined his life.

A sound escaped his lips, not a sob, not a roar, but something inhuman and shattered. He refused to be like *Teyocel* or the Stromms. He was a Vela. A lowborn from the Sublands. With his whole body convulsing, he drove the sword downward into the earth. The blade slammed deep into the ground beside *Teyocel*. Mateo collapsed beside it. He sobbed into the dirt, every muscle shaking, every memory cutting into him like sharp glass.

He was not a monster. Not anymore.

"You have done well, Mateo," Izel said softly in his mind, her words like a gentle breeze. *"Now, look..."*

He lifted his head. A blue sheen was coming from the sword. It pulsed once. Then again and again, easing into a slow, steady heartbeat of blue. Threads of light spilled from the hilt, curling like wisps of smoke, not drifting upward, but spreading outward across the barren grass and dirt. The mist swirled over Avalynn's body, winding around her like ethereal ribbons, painting her body in shimmering cerulean.

Mateo rose to his feet, watching the magic expand. It unfurled across the ground where the waterfall had long since dried, tracing every crevice, every jagged fracture. The color brightened, swirling faster, gathering, building like a storm coiling across the earth. The air hummed. The ground vibrated. A jagged fissure snapped open in the ground with a CRACK. Another followed. Then another. A tremor rolled through the land, low and rumbling, as though Faevenly itself was awakening, remembering something it had forgotten.

What was happening? He stumbled back, chest heaving, eyes wide. The cracks kept appearing when a gurgling sound beneath the surface met his ears. A thin trickle burst from the crack. Then another. Then a rushing surge.

He darted to Avalynn's side, scooping her up in his arms as a geyser of water exploded upward, spraying the air and cascading over broken rock. The fissures widened, and water poured forth, gathering, sweeping, racing and desperate to reclaim what had been lost. The dry basin at his feet filled in mere seconds.

"Sun, Moon, and Stars," he whispered. The lost waterfall roared to life like a forgotten god waking from centuries of sleep.

Izel soared above, swooping back and forth. *"The Mother of Rivers has healed. The Green Falls returns."* In the same breath, *Teyocel* screeched, launching up and away in a chaotic splash.

Healed. He looked down at Avalynn's pale face, then at the rising water all around them. The water could bring her back!

Pressing her body close to him, he began scooping handful after handful of the water, pouring it over her wound. The liquid shimmered as it touched her skin, swirling green and blue where it met blood.

"Stay with me, Avalynn," he urged, voice cracking under the weight of everything inside him. He cupped more water and let it spill across her chest, her neck, her face, willing it to seep life back into her veins. "Come on."

He scooped faster frantically, the water slipping between his shaking fingers.

"Sun, Moon, and Stars," he begged, his voice shaking. "Hear me. Don't take her. Please don't take her." The old prayers he had learned as a child tumbled out of him, broken and tangled. "Our Father, wherever thou art, in heaven, God of my father, of Manny's human faith... Anyone. Anyone listening... Bring her back to me."

He pressed his forehead to hers, the cool water dripping from his brow onto her skin. "I'll trade anything," he choked. "My life. My last breath. Just bring her back."

The water rose around them, swirling with blue-green light as his hands moved in desperate, shaking motions. He drenched her, pleading with the world to undo what he had done. He could barely breathe, barely see, barely think—only pray.

"Come back to me," he whispered, a gasp more than words. "Please, Avalynn. I'm so sorry."

His tears fell with the water, her body limp in his arms. She was gone. He brushed the hair from her eyes. It was over. He studied her face, wanting to remember every inch of her, when a glowing ripple swirled around her. It flickered, brighter this time, and began spreading all over her. It traced her cheek, her throat, down her chest until it gathered over her wound. It was as if the Green Falls itself was sketching her back into existence.

"Avalynn?"

Her lips parted with the slightest shift, as if the faintest breeze had brushed them. Her brows twitched; her eyes moved behind the lids. A sharp inhale tore through her chest, her body arching as air flooded into her lungs. She gulped, then gasped, coughing in ragged spurts until her breathing finally eased.

Mateo choked on a sob. "Avalynn. You're alive."

Her lashes fluttered, her blue eyes still unfocused as if lost between worlds before they finally landed on him. She shuddered, a broken whisper escaping her cracked lips. "Mateo?"

He folded around her, holding her as if he could keep death itself from ever reaching her again. "It's me." He squeezed. "The real me."

She moved her hands to his chest and pushed him back, staring into his eyes, as if to make sure it was really him. She placed her fingertips on his cheek, then pulled back and slapped him before burying her face into his neck.

"Don't ever do that again," she mumbled between sobs, her fingers knotting weakly in his tunic.

"I won't," he promised, his voice breaking on a half laugh, half sob. "I swear it."

They clung to each other, trying to make up for every lost moment and every wound carved into the space between them. For a few breaths, nothing else existed but them. Her heartbeat against his, his tears in her hair, and the water rising around them like a blessing.

The peace would not hold, not yet. Beyond the roar of the renewed falls, the realm still teemed with danger. *Teyocel* had fled, taking half of Mateo's soul with him. The queen and Raelor would not stop. The prophecy, broken or not, had been stirred.

Their fight was not yet finished.

CHAPTER TWENTY-ONE

Avalynn clung to Mateo for one breath longer before forcing herself to let go. She moved slowly, her heart quivering beneath the weight of emotions she didn't yet know how to name after everything that had happened.

"Mateo..." Her voice wavered. "What did we survive?"

He cast his eyes down, unable to answer. He set her down carefully, turned, and sloshed a short distance. He plunged his arm into the water. He reached down, then pulled out her blade. He carried it back to her and held it out with both hands.

"This is yours," he said quietly.

Avalynn stared at the sword, the memory of it piercing her stomach flooding her mind. Despite the trauma, she felt no pain. She curled her fingers around the dripping hilt, and the blade pulsed with soft blue light—alive, aware, answering her. Maybe even saying it was sorry. Yet, she had no idea what had happened after being wounded.

Her gaze slipped past Mateo to the mist curling off the Green Falls and toward a familiar shape in the distance, the weathered boulder. She and Mateo had once lain tangled together there beneath the sky. It wasn't that long ago, but it seemed like a lifetime.

"Our boulder," she said. "Let's go there."

Mateo followed her line of sight, his shoulders rising and falling in a shaky exhale. "All right."

She brushed the wet strands from her cheek. "There's a lot we need to talk about."

He offered her the slightest nod.

She tightened her grip on the sword, steadied herself, and met his wounded eyes. She took his hand and held it tight. "Come on."

Side by side, they walked toward the boulder, the roar of the reborn waterfall surging behind them like a promise and warning. They had much to discuss, much to figure out. Where would they go from here?

Mateo climbed up first, then reached for her hand and helped her onto the warm stone. In the sunlight, she stripped off her outer layers and laid them aside to dry. He took off his tunic. He lowered himself near the edge of the boulder, facing the glittering water below.

She joined him, and they sat together in a long, aching silence. Finally, she spoke. "I have so many questions."

He kept silent.

"I guess we should start with the—" Her breath

hitched, and she stood abruptly. "The necklace. I must have dropped it in the water."

Mateo flinched as though struck. "Let it stay there. No one should ever wear it."

She eased back down beside him, her chest tightening at the strain in his voice. "Will you tell me about it, Mateo? Tell me about the necklace?"

He picked up a thin stick and dragged it through the dirt. "It was a gift. From the queen. She gave it to me on my first day at the palace." He snapped the stick between his fingers. "I thought it meant I belonged. That I was being welcomed into my real family. But it was something far more sinister and I had no idea." He tossed the broken pieces. "It was her way of controlling me. Raelor's design, I'm sure of it."

His eyes drifted toward the water. "And when I met *Teyocel*, I thought he was a blessing that could help protect House Stromm. But he only magnified the pendant's hold on me." His voice thinned. "I gave him half my soul, Avalynn."

She gasped, covering her mouth. "Oh, Mateo..."

He shook his head. "The pendant blinded me," he said, voice cracking. "Made me crave power." His fists slammed into the dirt. "I hurt people." He struck again, harder. "Ordered their deaths. And you—" His voice broke. Tears gathered at the corners of his eyes. "I drove that sword into you," he choked out. "I didn't even hesitate."

Avalynn slid in front of him and cupped his face in her hands, tears pricking her eyes. "It wasn't you." He tried to turn away, but she held him still. "I know you," she whispered.

His tears spilled over. "You don't understand," he rasped. "I'm no good. The magic only amplified what was already inside me." He swallowed hard, looking away from her. "I will never forgive myself for what I have done."

She brushed away his tears with her thumbs. "Mateo," she said, "look at me."

He shook his head weakly. "Don't—"

"Look at me." Slowly, he lifted his gaze. The heartbreak in his eyes nearly undid her. "You are not the monster you think you are," she said, her voice soft but steady. "I know you. Really, truly know you. That darkness wasn't you. It was something that sank its claws into you and twisted until you weren't you anymore."

He closed his eyes, chest shuddering. "It used what was already inside me."

"That doesn't make you evil." She leaned closer, her forehead touching his. "It makes you someone who was hurting, manipulated, and used."

He drew in a rough, unsteady breath.

"I know your heart, Mateo," she said. "Even when I lost all my memories, I still felt you. Even now, sitting here." Her voice softened. "I feel you."

He let out a trembling exhale, leaning into her touch as though he feared the moment would dissolve if he breathed too hard. His fingers curled around hers, tentative at first, then desperate, gripping her like she was the only steady thing left in a world that had been ripped apart at the seams.

"I'm so sorry, Avalynn," he choked out, his voice raw enough to bleed. "Please forgive me."

She pressed a soft, lingering kiss to his forehead, letting it anchor him. "I forgive you. Now and always." She kissed him again. "And in case you didn't already know... I love you."

His breath fractured on a quiet, broken sob. She slid her arms around him, drawing him close. He clung to her, arms winding around her waist, face buried against her shoulder, as if bracing against a tide that had tried to drag him under for too long.

"I love you too," he whispered. "With everything I am and everything I will ever be."

For a long heartbeat, they clung to each other—two souls bruised and battered yet somehow still standing, still choosing each other despite everything.

She pulled back, taking him in, softly touching his face. His nearness and the desperate longing in his eyes sparked something deep inside her, a slow, undeniable pull—a wanting that rose from the devastation and threaded through the wounded edges of her heart. She closed the gap between them, their mouths meeting in a tender kiss, a collision of grief and longing and the fragile hope that maybe, despite everything, they would somehow come out of this together.

His hand cupped the back of her neck, holding her there, the one steady thing left in a world that kept breaking. The forest hushed. The roar of the falls ceased. All of it dimmed beneath their connection. She slipped off her top laces, then took his hands and pressed them to her bare skin.

"I want to feel you, Mateo. All of you," she breathed. "Everywhere."

He lowered her gently to the stone, removing the remainder of her clothing, then his own, every movement unhurried as though time itself had slowed to give them this moment. He braced himself above her, his hands trembling as they slid along her sides. The rock at her back faded beneath the warmth of him, beneath the way he fit perfectly against her.

She reached for him, her legs drawing him in, her hands finding his shoulders, his back, bringing him into the space where their bodies met. He kissed every inch he could find, slow and savoring, and when his mouth found hers again, it was softer, deeper. She answered him with a quiet moan, her fingers tightening in his hair, holding him to her. This closeness was the only thing that mattered.

They moved together slowly, guided by the ache they carried, every touch a reassurance: you are here, I am here. Grief lingered between them, woven into the moment, but it did not pull them apart. It made everything more precious. In the gentle joining of their bodies, comfort and longing tangled together, a silent promise neither dared to speak aloud. The quiet understanding that they had each other.

When they finally broke apart, they kept their foreheads pressed together, their breath mingling in shaky, uneven exhales. Their fingers remained threaded, their bodies still held close, neither wanting to be the first to let go.

"I could stay here forever," he said softly. "With you, hiding away from all I have done."

"We can always come back here," she said. "When this is over."

A ribbon of fear wound through her—Raelor's power, *Teyocel's* rage, the storm waiting for them in the North. She didn't know if they'd survive it, or if they'd ever really come back here, but she had to believe they would.

He sat back, as if sensing her shift, his gaze searching her face. "I guess we should figure out what to do next."

"We probably should." She reached for her discarded laces while Mateo pulled on his trousers.

They stayed close, his hand finding hers. "You said some prophecies were meant to be broken. What was that?"

"I learned when I was with Manny and Lady Sonia that I inherited gifts from my human bloodline," she explained. "An aura power—"

"The blue light," he finished.

She nodded. "Yes. I can see spirits, too. I met one on Spirit Butte, a girl named Abigail. She told me that some prophecies are meant to be broken." The girl's long white hair and big green eyes sprang to mind. "I didn't understand what she meant, not until she appeared again while you and I were fighting. That's why I handed you the sword."

"She somehow knew what would happen."

"She must have," Avalynn said. "The sword's power healed the realm because of you."

"The prophecy," he muttered. A heavy silence settled before he finally nodded. "We need to figure out the rest of what must be done, and quickly. Before *Teyocel* comes back for what is his."

"With help," she added. "We need Lady Sonia." She paused, everything that had happened in the Wild North coming into focus. "There's something I need to tell you." Her grip tightened. "Mateo, it's Gareth... He's dead."

Mateo's lips parted, but no sound came. He stared at her, grief sweeping over him in a slow, crushing wave. "Gareth." His voice sounded strangled. He swallowed hard, eyes glossing over. "I have to tell his family. And mine." He drew in a shuddering breath. "We need to go to the Sublands. I need to see them, especially my father. We can regroup there."

Avalynn clutched his hands and squeezed. "Then let's go."

He hesitated. His expression darkened, not with cold fury but with something far more deliberate. He slid his hands down her arms, holding her as carefully as if she were made of fine crystal.

She tilted her head. "What is it?"

"He will pay, Avalynn," he said. "He will pay for hurting you. For every bruise, every threat, every harm inflicted." His jaw worked, tight with barely contained emotion. "He will never touch you again."

She went rigid. The bruises her once-father marked her with had long since faded, but the memory of being his daughter for all those years still echoed deep in her bones. Tears stung her eyes, but she refused to let them fall. Not now. Instead, she pressed her hand over his heart, feeling it beat strongly beneath her palm. "We will face him together."

A single nod—a promise—and he rose, helping her to her feet. They finished dressing quickly. Avalynn slid the sword into its sheath, the weight of it grounding her.

She turned toward the roaring Green Falls, scanning the skies, hoping *Izel* had not left them. "*Izel*," she said in her mind. "*Are you here?*"

A few long seconds passed before a shadow swept across the sun. "*I am.*" With a thunderous beating of wings, she descended from the sky, her scales catching the sunlight, turning her into a brilliant, colorful prism. She lowered herself onto the boulder's surface. "Climb on, Avalynn Strong. Mateo Vela. It is time to finish what was started."

Together, they climbed onto *Izel's* back. As the dragon surged upward, the wind whipped through Avalynn's damp hair, the world tilting beneath them as the earth fell away. She pressed closer to Mateo, and his arms wrapped tighter around her waist. She felt the weight of the sword at her side, the weight of fate in her chest.

Whatever darkness awaited them, they were coming for it.

CHAPTER TWENTY-TWO

The wind cut across Mateo's face as *Izel* carried them toward the Sublands. Avalynn sat before him, her hair snapping in ribbons against the stark red horizon. Below, the wild terrain unfurled in scorched ridges and canyon-deep shadows. He should feel joy at returning home. Instead, every beat of *Izel's* wings pulled the knot inside his chest tighter.

He had left his home determined to prove himself. Now he returned as a son who had failed in every way that mattered. His pulse hammered against his throat. He had chosen the Stromms over the only family that had ever loved him, believing it was the only way to rise. Instead, he'd fallen farther than he'd ever imagined, losing himself piece by piece until he could no longer recognize who he'd become.

The shame and guilt strangled him like a tightening noose. Manny's parting words echoed in his skull, sharp enough to cut. *Always remember who you are.* If only he had listened. If only he had rejected the pendant when it was offered. If only he had returned home and told Manny everything instead of letting the palace swallow him whole. Gareth would still be alive. The others, too.

He dreaded telling them.

Avalynn shifted slightly, her shoulder brushing his chest. Somehow, he had fixed what was broken between them, miraculously, undeservingly. But family wounds ran deeper. He prayed his father would forgive him. He prayed he deserved it.

Izel dipped lower, the desert heat rising in shimmering waves that smelled of cracked earth and looming storms. Mateo tightened his grip around Avalynn's waist as they circled the village. Below, Sublanders poured from their homes, shielding their eyes as the dragon descended. Some looked awestruck, others terrified. Either way, they had seen him. There was no going back now.

Izel descended in a sweeping arc, stirring sand and grit into whirling spirals as her talons touched down at the edge of the village. Mateo slid off first, then turned to steady Avalynn as she dismounted. The moment their feet hit the earth, *Izel* lifted her massive head, eyes gleaming like twin suns.

"I am only a call away," she said out loud. With a single mighty leap, she vanished into the sky, a streak against the burning horizon.

Silence settled in her wake. Hand in hand, he and Avalynn began walking through the village. It felt like walking through memory—only the memories hurt. Faces appeared in doorways. Families lingered in shadows.

Whispers rustled like dry leaves, low and sharp and unhidden.

"He's back..."

"Is that Mateo Vela?"

"Is that a dragon they came on?"

"And the girl—"

No one stepped forward. No one greeted him. They parted for him all the same, moving aside in instinctive ripples, creating a narrow path through the dusty road.

Each footstep felt heavier than the last. Avalynn's fingers tightened around his, but it didn't stop the pressure building in his chest—the dread, the shame, the terror that his father would look at him and see only what he had become, not the son he used to be.

They reached the far edge of the village, where the Sublands opened into the jagged horizon. The Vela home stood alone beneath the towering rust-red cliffs. Mateo slowed. His palms grew damp. The knot in his throat tightened until swallowing hurt. And as they rounded the final corner, he stopped in his tracks.

Manny Vela stood in front of their home, shoulders hunched, face carved in stone. He looked older than Mateo remembered. Wearier. His eyes—dark, steady, unflinching—hit Mateo like a blow to the ribs. For a long, searing heartbeat, neither of them moved.

Then Manny spoke. "Mateo." His lip trembled, and tears flooded his eyes. "*Mijo.*"

The single word tore straight through him. Before he knew it, they were locked in an embrace. "Father," Mateo choked out. "Please forgive me."

His small-framed father held on tighter. Camilla and

Floriana joined in, squeezing him so fiercely they almost fell over.

"Of course we forgive you," little Floriana bawled, grasping his legs.

"We all do," Camilla answered, her voice shaking between sobs.

Manny pulled back and cupped Mateo's face, studying every inch. "Are you okay, *Mijo*?" He patted Mateo's arms and chest. "Are you hurt?" He reached for Avalynn and pulled her into his arms for a hug. "*Mija, are you okay?*"

"I'm okay. Thank you, Manny," Avalynn said.

"We're both fine, Father."

"*Gracias a Dios.*" Manny wiped his eyes, then made the sign of the cross. Mateo's hand instinctively went to his pocket, where the wooden cross his father had made used to be. He gulped as a surge of guilt flooded him because he had tossed it into the fire. He wanted it back more than anything.

"We prayed every day," Floriana said proudly.

"Oh, we certainly did. Lit candles too," Manny added.

"We almost burned the house down with all the candles," Camilla smiled as she wiped her face.

"Come, come in." Manny opened the door wide. "Tell me everything."

Inside, the warmth of home wrapped around Mateo like a long-lost memory. A small fire crackled in the hearth, throwing soft gold across the stone walls. The room smelled of fresh bread and spices—cinnamon, cumin, something sweet his father and Camilla must have baked that morning. They were always cooking together.

Layered rugs softened the floor, worn in places, patched in others. Manny settled into his favorite chair, its cushions flattened from years of use. Mateo could still picture Manny falling asleep there, mid-prayer with his rosary from the human realm tangled in his fingers.

"Sit, *Mijo*," Manny said. He gestured toward Avalynn. "Please, sit."

Mateo guided Avalynn to the sofa across from his father. She perched beside him, close enough that their legs touched. Camilla leaned against the wall, fidgeting with her hands. Floriana dropped to the floor at Mateo's feet, folding her legs beneath her as if this were any ordinary evening and not the moment Mateo had feared since being stripped of the dark magic.

Manny leaned forward, elbows on his knees. "Now," he said quietly. "Start wherever you need to."

Mateo drew a breath, steadying himself. "When I left for the hunt," he began, "I meant everything I told you. That I would make something of myself. That I'd help the Sublands."

Manny nodded, eyes fierce with love and worry.

"But then," Mateo continued, "I found out the truth that I was born a Stromm, and I didn't know what to think. I didn't know who I was anymore." Mateo took a second to steady himself. "Then I remembered, and I decided to stay there for a while, to use my position to help everyone here. To be someone who could change things for the better." His jaw tightened. "But the queen gave me a pendant. A curse, meant to control me. Its magic worked so slowly I didn't know what was happening. And I ... I lost myself."

Camilla's breath hitched while Floriana got up and moved closer to Manny.

"Then I bonded with a dragon, *Teyocel*," Mateo said. "I thought he was a blessing. But he only magnified the pendant's influence."

Manny's lips parted, disbelief and horror warring across his face. "*Mijo*."

"I know." Mateo looked down at his shaking hands. "Avalynn got the necklace off me. She saved me. And her sword was used to heal the Mother of Rivers." He glossed over the lives he had taken, including Avalynn's. Perhaps one day he'd tell his father.

"Then it is over?" Manny asked. "You are free of the curse?"

"I'm free of the pendant, yes." Mateo's breath faltered. "But things are not over."

With a blink, Manny straightened, dread sharpening his features. "What do you mean?"

Mateo swallowed hard. "Half my soul belongs to *Teyocel*."

Floriana stifled a cry while Manny leaned back as if struck. "My son," he whispered. "My boy."

Mateo couldn't look at him. He couldn't speak another word. The shame burned too hot.

"There's more," Avalynn said softly, taking over. "When we crossed into the Wild North, Lirien and Gareth were with us. And a dwarf named Keeth."

Camilla's face snapped toward her. "Lirien and Gareth? They found you?"

"Are they okay?" Manny asked.

"Well..." Avalynn's voice wavered, but she pushed through. "Lirien and Keeth are fine. But Gareth... I'm so sorry to say, he lost his life protecting us."

Manny bolted upright. "Gareth is—no. No, no, no." His hand pressed hard to his chest as his face crumpled. "Where? How?"

In an instant, Mateo was at his father's side, steadying him before he collapsed.

"He met his end bravely in the Wild North," Avalynn explained. "Lirien, Keeth, and I prepared him for the Passing Place. I am sure he's there now."

Manny made the sign of the cross again, whispering a prayer.

"You should also know that Lady Sonia is in the Wild North," Avalynn said softly. "She's in the magical boundary, guarding it until we return."

Manny blinked rapidly, absorbing far too much too fast. "Sonia? Inside the boundary?" He shook his head violently. "I must go to her. Now. I must—"

"We know, and we will," Mateo said, easing his father back into his chair. "We need her wisdom and counsel." His voice cracked beneath the weight of everything. "We need to figure out what to do about *Teyocel*."

Manny sagged into the cushions, staring up at Mateo. After a long moment, he rasped, "We will go to the Caileans, tell them about Gareth. Then head north."

Mateo nodded and, only then, noticed something strange. His father hadn't coughed once. "Father, your cough. Is it gone? Did everyone get the healing seeds I sent?"

"Seeds?" Manny blinked. "Sonia brought a few, but we received no seeds. But yes, the Dragon's Bellow has left the Sublands. The cough simply went away on its own."

On its own? So, the seeds he'd fought to have delivered never arrived. And he knew why. The king and queen must have intercepted the shipment or never sent them in the first place. But how did the cough disappear? Mateo forced the question aside. Right now, it didn't matter. Only Gareth and his family mattered.

Manny exhaled shakily, wringing his hands on his lap. "Let's go to the Caileans now," he said at last, rising to his feet, his voice thin but steady. "We will tell them what happened together."

They gathered in the center of the room—Mateo, his father, his sisters—and they wrapped their arms around each other. Mateo reached for Avalynn, pulling her in. She belonged in their circle now, drawn together by the same aching truth, hugging each other as if the embrace would be their last. Shoulders shook. Soft sobs escaped. The grief moved through all of them, weaving them closer in their sorrow. When they finally stepped apart, it was only to walk together into what came next.

They left the house quietly, the door closing behind them like the soft fall of a curtain. The path around the corner felt impossibly short. Mateo wished it were miles, wished grief could be delayed by distance. But the Cailean home appeared before them too soon, warm light glowing through the windows, the scent of hearth fire drifting into the dusk.

Manny knocked. The door opened. Gareth's mother

stood framed in the light, her eyes brightening with hope as she searched the faces gathered outside. Behind her, little Poppy peered out, her small hand clutching the edge of her mother's skirt. The moment Poppy saw Mateo, she broke into a run, wrapping her arms around his legs with a relieved little sigh, as if she believed Gareth must be right behind him. But Gareth wasn't.

His mother's gaze moved over each of them again, slower this time. When she didn't find her son, something in her expression flickered, hope dimming like a candle losing its flame. She let them inside. Manny took her hands, voice low, carrying the weight no parent should ever have to hear. Mateo couldn't listen to the words; he only watched the moment they landed. The moment Gareth's mother understood. The moment her knees buckled.

Mateo caught her as she collapsed, and the room folded into grief. Poppy dropped beside her mother, wailing. Manny, Camilla and Floriana knelt with them. Avalynn wrapped her arms around Poppy, whispering something softly. And Mateo sank to the floor, his vision blurring with tears he couldn't hold back.

The family he had grown up with—his second home —shattered in front of him. He bowed his head. Someone would answer for this. The king. The queen. Raelor. *Teyocel*. Every hand that had shaped Gareth's fate, every force that had turned Mateo into the blade that severed so many lives. They would pay.

By the time they returned to Manny's home, the moon hung low over the Sublands, casting long shadows across the quiet village. Floriana had fallen asleep in

Mateo's arms, her small body quivering in rest. He carried her into the house and tucked her gently beneath her blankets, brushing a strand of hair from her face.

In the dim glow of the hearth, the rest of them silently agreed on what had to happen next. At first light, Manny, Avalynn, and Mateo would ride north. There was no time to waste. They needed answers and a plan. *Teyocel* would have healed by now. Mateo was sure he'd be coming for him.

They drifted to their rooms without another word. With Avalynn taking his bed, Mateo stretched out on the narrow couch. The cushions were familiar, worn by years of evenings spent laughing with Gareth and Lirien and cuddling with Stormshroud. But tonight, they felt wrong, unable to hold him steady. Sleep refused to come. His mind kept spinning. His chest ached with a sharp, restless hurt, the kind that made it hard to breathe.

What kind of son was he now? What kind of brother and friend? The questions burrowed into him like thorns. He stared at the ceiling until the edges of dawn smudged the darkness into gray. His body felt carved hollow, scraped clean, yet somehow still unbearably heavy. And somewhere between anguish and exhaustion, he finally slipped into slumber.

"*Mateo.*" The voice curled into his mind—soft, low, like a secret whispered against his ear. "*Mateo.*" Louder this time. Sharper. Then a roar tore through his skull. "*PRINCE!*"

Mateo jolted awake with a strangled gasp. His body lurched upright, heart hammering, air tearing from his lungs. *Teyocel.* He whipped his head around the dim room, chest heaving. For a terrifying heartbeat, he expected to see wings, fire, teeth. He only saw darkness. The dragon's voice had been inside him.

His pulse spiked. "What do you want?" he spat into the dark.

A low, velvety hum whisked through his mind, the way smoke slipped through cracks. "*I want what is mine.*"

Mateo's hands clawed at the blanket, his fear giving way to anger. "I owe you nothing."

A soft, amused rumble followed. "*Oh, little prince. You owe me everything.*" The words slithered through Mateo, intimate and violating. "*Half your soul still burns in my chest. When I want the rest, all I need to do is pull.*"

Mateo's stomach twisted. "*What do you mean, pull?*"

"*The headaches, the nosebleeds. That was me. Pulling.*"

Realization slammed into him. That explained what he had been feeling. He should have known.

"*You were magnificent, by the way,*" Teyocel purred. "*To run her through, to claim your rightful destiny. I have never been more proud.*"

Mateo's vision blurred red. "*Shut up.*"

"*But then you faltered.*" A hiss, like talons scraping stone, stretched in his mind. "*You betrayed us both by slipping back into your mediocrity. Though I suppose I should thank you. That final act of plunging the sword into the dirt released the Green Falls water and saved me.*"

Mateo surged to his feet. "*You twisted me! The pendant twisted me!*" he hollered in his mind.

A slow, dangerous chuckle echoed inside Mateo.

"*You know that is not entirely true. You tasted what it meant to be truly powerful, Mateo Stromm. You loved it. Craved it. More than Avalynn. More than the Only One.*"

"I do not acknowledge the name Stromm." His heart pounded against his ribs. "*And I will NEVER serve you again.*"

Silence stretched, then a cold whisper slid down his spine. "*You already do.*"

Mateo froze. Was he still acting for *Teyocel*? Against his will? Was it possible? "*No,*" he gritted.

"*I own more than half your soul,*" *Teyocel* murmured, savoring the word. "*Serve me, and I will let you live. Deny me, and I will take the rest.*"

Rage flared so hot Mateo thought his skin would melt. "*I will take it back,*" he snarled. "*Every last piece of it.*"

Another laugh—quiet, delighted, utterly sure. "*Come try.*"

The connection snapped, leaving Mateo shaking with fury at *Teyocel*, at himself, at the cruel truth that thrummed beneath his ribs. *Teyocel* still lurked inside him, still had influence. He was a fool to have thought otherwise.

"*Mijo*, you're already up."

Mateo jerked around. Manny stood in the doorway, fully dressed for travel, a steaming cup of tea cradled between his palms. In the thin morning light, he looked smaller somehow, more fragile.

Mateo quickly processed his next words. He could not tell his father about *Teyocel*. Not after last night. Not after losing Gareth. Not when Manny's heart was already buckling under fresh grief. The truth would break him. Worse, it might make him fear his son. Mateo already feared enough for both of them.

There was also Avalynn. He couldn't tell her either. What would she think if she knew the dragon was still in his mind? Still whispering? Still twisting shadows into shapes meant to break him? After everything they had clawed their way through, he couldn't put that on her again. No. This was a burden he would carry alone at least until he understood it and could rid himself of it once and for all.

Mateo straightened, forcing the tremor from his voice as he stepped into the light. "Yes, Father. I'm up. I couldn't sleep." He pushed the remnants of darkness behind him, sealing every crack he could.

Manny lifted the cup slightly. "Some tea will help. There's breakfast too."

He offered his father a nod. "Good idea."

Mateo moved toward the cookroom. The steam rising from the kettle wrapped the room in the scent of herbs and warmth, a stark contrast to the cold dread lodged in his chest. He poured himself a cup and forced himself to sip. The heat steadied him, barely.

He tore off a piece of bread and chewed, though it tasted like dust. He nodded along to Manny's quiet morning motions—packing the last satchels and checking the bedrolls. He mimicked the calm, keeping his breaths even, his hands busy, his thoughts caged.

"Hey," Avalynn whispered out of earshot of the others, her brows raised. "You okay?"

He painted a smile on his face. "Just focused. Ready to get going."

She rubbed his arm. "Me too." If only she knew.

When everything was ready, they gathered in the front room for their goodbyes. The fire had burned low, reduced to embers, but the warmth lingered, heavy and bittersweet. Camilla's and Floriana's eyes were rimmed red, fighting fresh tears. Camilla hugged Avalynn first, then Manny, before wrapping her arms around Mateo with a fierceness that nearly pulled him apart. Floriana pressed her body against his legs, demanding he be careful and come back.

Mateo crouched to her eye level. "We'll be back," he promised, kissing the top of her head. "All of us."

Outside, the morning light washed the Sublands in pale gold. Two saddled horses waited, shifting and snorting softly, breath fogging the air. Then Mateo saw the third. He stopped short. The horse stood apart from the others, tall and luminous, its coat a smooth sweep of silver that caught the sun like living metal. Its mane stirred though the air was still, pale strands gleaming as if threaded with starlight. Power rolled off the creature in quiet waves—ancient, patient, watchful.

His chest tightened as he looked at Avalynn in wonder. It was her Enbarr. The one that had belonged to her father. He hadn't seen her since before entering the Wild North, before everything shattered.

Avalynn squeezed Mateo's hand. "Silverhoof."

The horse lifted its head at the sound of her voice, ears pricking forward. Her hoof struck the ground, answering a call that had never truly faded.

"Well, well," Manny said with a smile, stepping forward. "It is a blessing."

Avalynn approached Silverhoof without hesitation. The Enbarr lowered its great head, breath huffing softly against her chest as if greeting something it had never forgotten. She rested her palm against its neck.

She turned back to them. "A blessing indeed," she said quietly.

Mateo agreed, even though his heart ached at the weight of it. A sign didn't mean forgiveness. It didn't mean redemption. But he had to believe it meant the road ahead hadn't closed its doors to them, not yet.

Manny mounted first with surprising ease for his age. Avalynn climbed onto Silverhoof next, her posture steady, her presence a quiet anchor. Mateo swung up last, settling into the saddle with one last look at the home he'd lost and found once more. Would he really see it again? He wasn't so sure. But having the Enbarr with them gave him hope.

The morning sun lightened the reddish earth as they set off. The village receded behind them, a cluster of familiar rooftops and smoke trails fading into the rugged horizon. Ahead lay the jagged ridges of the northern path and beyond that, the Wild North.

Mateo tightened his grip on the reins. He inhaled the desert air and nudged his horse forward. "*Okay, Teyocel. I'm coming for you.*"

The longest pause stretched out. "*Good.*"

CHAPTER TWENTY-THREE

L ysandra's fingers closed around the nearest vase. She hurled it against the stone wall. It shattered on impact, shards skittering across the stone floor like startled insects.

"What do you mean!?" she hollered, her voice cracking through the war room. "Mateo no longer wears the necklace!?" The news stripped away her composure like flesh from bone, leaving raw fury beneath.

Raelor stood perfectly still on the other side of the round table, hands folded neatly before him, diamond eyes fixed. "The magic has been severed, my queen. Completely." His jaw tightened. "I can no longer track it. Which means..." He hesitated only a fraction. "He no longer wears it."

The king slammed both fists onto the wooden table, the force rattling maps and goblets alike. "How?!" he barked.

Raelor inclined his head, as if choosing his words

with care. "After the attack by the Oathriders, and the ambush at Sand Bluff manor, Prince Mateo took matters into his own hands and flew north with *Teyocel* to go after Avalynn. He left with the pendant on, so it either came off on the way or while there."

Lysandra turned on him in a flash. "Do you at least know its location?"

Raelor's silence stretched too long. "I do not," he admitted at last.

A sharp, humorless laugh escaped her mouth. "Some witch you are," she sneered. "You bind a relic to my son, tether it with magic, and now you tell me you do not know where it is?" She stepped closer, her voice dropping to a deadly whisper. "Can you do anything at all?"

Raelor met her gaze, unflinching. "The severing changes nothing about our ultimate goal," he said evenly. "Find the girl. Find the sword. Reassert control. But now there is another matter that demands our attention."

Lysandra lowered herself back into her chair, her movements precise and controlled. "And what," she asked coolly, "would that be?"

"Lady Sonia."

Lady Sonia? The elusive and powerful witch had not been seen in years. Was she involved somehow? Her fingers tightened on the armrest. "What about her?"

"As you know, Verona has been unable to cross the boundary into the North and has been staying in a village on the southern edge of the border. They have been watching things closely and have spotted Lady Sonia."

Lysandra's eyes narrowed. "And?"

"They claim Lady Sonia has crossed through."

The king leaned forward, his chair scraping loudly across the stone. "Why would she go there?"

"Unclear," Raelor said. "But there's more."

A slow, terrible heat began coiling in Lysandra's chest. Lady Sonia was a powerful witch, older than possibly even the Wild North boundary itself. Always meddling. "Go on."

"This same village has ties to the Oathriders," Raelor said, slower now, almost in a whisper. "They study the prophecy." He edged closer to the table, as if sharing a deadly secret. "They claim Lady Sonia was responsible for the switch at birth."

The room quieted. The world narrowed to a single, blinding point of rage. *Sonia.* That witch. The architect of everything stolen from her—her son, her bloodline, her legacy. The reason she had raised another child while her own had been taken, hidden, molded.

Her hands shook, not with weakness but with the force of restraint. Lysandra exhaled slowly, the rage settling into something colder, deadlier. "I no longer want explanations. I no longer want penance." Her eyes blazed with calculating certainty. "I want results."

"Of course, my queen," Raelor said.

She lowered her voice until it cut like a blade. "Bring me the girl's head. Bring me the witch's head." Her gaze sharpened. "And bring me the sword." She straightened, power radiating from her in suffocating waves. "Do this, and the prophecy dies with them."

Raelor placed his fingers on the edge of the table. "What of Mateo, my queen? What if the prince stands in the way?"

She glanced at the king before locking her gaze back on Raelor. "Then he is no longer our son."

She rose and turned away from Raelor, wrath simmering beneath her composed exterior. Mateo had been given everything—power, protection, glory. But if he dared to defy her, if despite everything he chose weakness, then he deserved to be damned. If her will would not shape him, then he would be destroyed by it.

"Go!" the king hollered. "Do not come back until you have what we want!"

Raelor scrambled away, and the room fell silent again. For the first time since taking the throne, Lysandra felt the unmistakable fear of losing her power and her destiny.

CHAPTER TWENTY-FOUR

M ateo, Avalynn, and Manny galloped north, Stormshroud meeting them on the journey and keeping pace. With each stride, Mateo kept one eye on his father. His old body was crouched low, his chin tucked tight to his chest, his eyes squinted, his long white hair flowing behind him. His father hated horseback riding and had told Mateo so many times before.

Once, his father spent an evening with him, Gareth, and Lirien, telling them how he had crossed Faevenly in the dead of night on an Enbarr. He had been with his best friend, Julio, and Princess Celyse—Avalynn's grand-sires—saving the realm as he put it. When the ride was over, he had slid off in a boneless heap, then wretched the contents of his stomach for a solid hour.

He believed his father's stories, though he'd always assumed time had expanded them into something larger than actual life. Now, he understood all too well. If Manny and the others had endured anything close to what he and Avalynn were facing, then the danger had never been overstated, only survived. Would they survive this, too?

With each hoofbeat, Mateo imagined the perils waiting for them in the Wild North, when a sharp pain detonated behind his eyes. He sucked in a breath as the world tilted. White heat split his skull, fierce and sudden, and his vision swam. He clenched his jaw and tightened his grip on the reins, forcing himself to stay upright as a warm trickle slid down his nose. *No. Not now.* He wiped it away with the back of his hand, smearing red across his knuckles. The horse snorted beneath him, sensing something was wrong. Stormy growled. Mateo leaned forward, anchoring himself and shielding his pain from the others.

He had felt this before, on the road to Sand Bluff and at the Sand Bluff manor house. He'd thought it was exhaustion. Now he knew better. Mateo held on, pushing through the pain. He refused to give the dragon the satisfaction of seeing him break.

"*Is that all you got?*" Mateo snarled in his mind.

Teyocel's menacing laugh echoed between his ears. "*For now, little prince. For now.*"

They rode for two days. As they closed the distance to the Wild North, Mateo's stomach wound tighter and tighter. He had no idea what *Teyocel* had planned for him, but he fully expected the worst.

"I think I see it," Avalynn called out, pointing ahead.

The animals reacted too. Stormshroud slowed to a trot. The horses followed suit, hooves faltering as they reduced their pace. Mateo peered ahead until, finally, he saw it. It rose from the ground like a living thing, a curtain of shimmering light that rippled like a pale ocean.

Mateo frowned. "This doesn't look the same."

The last time he'd stood here, the veil had been nearly invisible—a whisper in the air, easy to miss. This was loud, and wrong. Stormshroud growled low in her chest, hackles rising. The horses skittered.

"It's Sonia." Avalynn moved closer to Mateo. "She's doing this for us."

As the words escaped her lips, Sonia came into view. Her form wavered, edges blurring, as though she were caught between dueling sunrays. Pale light threaded through her cloak, her hands, and her skin. She shimmered the way heat distorts air. Even though Avalynn had explained what Sonia had done, seeing her in that state still left Mateo speechless.

Manny sucked in a sharp breath, then quickly dismounted. "Sonia!" His voice cracked like a brittle branch. He stumbled forward, boots crunching on frost. He stopped short of the glowing boundary. "What have you done?"

Her smile came softly. "Oh, Manny," she said gently. "My dear friend. Do not be afraid. I am okay."

"You're—" His voice failed him. "Not okay."

"I am exactly where I need to be." Her gaze flicked briefly to Mateo and Avalynn, sharp and knowing, before returning to Manny. "I will be fine. Truly."

Mateo didn't believe her. It was clear his father didn't either.

"I can't let you stay like this," Manny said, shaking his

head. He turned toward Mateo and Avalynn. "She can't stay like this!"

Sonia shifted, her hand moving as if to touch Manny. "Someone has to hold the boundary while the realm decides what it wants to become."

A chill slid down Mateo's spine. The realm, not just the Wild North. Every road he had walked converged here at this magical wall, at this moment. From competing in the hunt, to being betrayed at the finish line, finding out he was a Stromm, and giving half his soul to a monster like *Teyocel*. Everything hinged on his actions, *Teyocel's* next move, and even Avalynn's choices. Would he be capable of doing the right thing? With *Teyocel* still in his mind?

If Mateo stayed, if he listened, there would be no such thing as secrecy. Every word spoken, every decision made would bleed through him, straight into the dragon's grasp. Mateo swallowed hard. He couldn't let that happen. Mateo forced his hands to unclench. He had only one move left that *Teyocel* couldn't twist.

"I can't be here," he said quietly.

"What?" Manny's gaze snapped to Mateo.

Avalynn's mouth fell open with a gasp. "What do you mean?"

He didn't look at her, not because he didn't want to, but because if he did, he might falter. Faltering now could doom them all and hurt her all over again. He refused to do that.

He let out a breath. "I mean that *Teyocel* is still with me."

"No, *Mijo!*" His father's face fell. "Why didn't you tell us?"

"Because I heard him only a few days ago." He stepped back away from them, as if the distance could protect them, feeling like a fool for thinking *Teyocel's* injury and being rid of the pendant meant the dragon would leave him alone. "I must go."

"Wait, Prince Mateo," Lady Sonia said. "There is information needed that only you can provide." Her gaze fixed on him. "Cross into the Wild North. Meet with the others and say what you know. Leave only then."

"Yes." Avalynn squeezed his hand as if she'd never let go. "We'll cross over. When it's time for strategy..." She paused as if not wanting to say the words. "You can leave."

A sharp pain worked through his heart. Could he protect her if he couldn't even protect himself? He searched the shimmery boundary. Somewhere on the other side, Gareth had died because of him. But Lirien and Keeth were still alive. If he had information that could turn the tide and help them defeat *Teyocel*, then he had to risk it. If his father and Avalynn trusted Lady Sonia, he could too. There was also the matter of telling Keeth about his brother, Karl.

He squeezed Avalynn's hand back. "Okay. I'll cross over." He searched the magical boundary for the annoying faun, Bramble. "Will we need seeds?"

"No, you will not." Sonia held out her hand, revealing a pearlized dragon scale on her palm. "This is *Izel's*. As long as it is in my possession, the boundary will not take anything from you or others."

"See?" Manny placed a reassuring hand on Mateo's shoulder. "Things are going our way, now." He rubbed. "You'll see."

Manny never ran out of faith. He carried it the way warriors carried weapons, steady, unquestioning, ready when everything else failed. Mateo had always envied that. Now, he needed to learn from it.

With one last look at Lady Sonia, he stepped forward with Manny and Avalynn, the Enbarr and the other horses trailing behind, Stormshroud close at their heels. The cold struck first. It cut through skin and muscle, stealing his breath in a sharp gasp. Light flashed behind his eyes, then vanished, leaving him standing on frost-hardened ground beneath a wintry blue sky.

He drew a shaky breath, waiting to see if he'd feel any different, but he was still himself. Movement from the thin trees caught his eye as figures emerged. Mateo's heart stuttered. Lirien. His best friend strode out with his sharp eyes glaring, his hand hovering over the dagger slung at his waist. Mateo's chest tightened painfully. He deserved the hateful glares, and more.

Mateo advanced slowly, cautiously. "Lirien, it's me." The words tore out of him before he could stop them. "It's—"

Lirien froze. For one terrible second, Mateo thought he'd miscalculated everything. Then Lirien hurried forward. He slammed into Mateo with a force that nearly knocked him from his feet, arms locking around him, breath hitching hard against his shoulder.

"You fool," Lirien rasped, voice breaking. "You absolute fool."

Mateo closed his eyes, the weight of the embrace crushing something fragile inside his chest. He clutched Lirien back, breathing him in and grounding himself in the solid proof that some things still existed.

Manny joined in, wrapping his arms around the two of them. "My boys," he muttered. "*Gracias a Dios.*"

They stayed like that for a long while before slowly parting. "I heard about Gareth," Mateo finally said. "I'm so sorry."

Lirien shook Mateo's shoulders. "It's not your fault. It's *Teyocel's* and Raelor's and that mad king and queen."

His anger flared. Lirien was right. Gareth hadn't been lost to chance or weakness, but to deliberate cruelty. Mateo would carry that truth with him to the end. Every name spoken, every hand that had shaped this outcome, would be answered—*for Gareth*, for what he had done to Avalynn, and for everything they had taken. They would pay.

They sat around the fire, close to the magical boundary. With Sonia holding *Izel's* scale, the memories that had been taken returned—not just to Lirien, but to all of them. Dorn was Engrendorn again. Axe was Keeth.

"So, I called myself Axe because it was my last thought?" Keeth stared down at his weapon. He gave a slight shrug. "Seems like an okay name to me."

"I almost died, and I was given back to myself here," Engrendorn said quietly. He stayed close to Zalarae, threading his fingers through hers. "This is my home now. I am Valian. I will stand for the Wild North—for all of Faevenly—against any king or queen or creature who would see it burned."

Good. They would need Engrendorn, along with every Valian willing to stand for the Wild North. Nothing less would be enough to face a dragon who had already taken half his soul.

Now, to tell Keeth about his brother. "There is something you must know, Master Keeth."

Keeth angled toward Mateo, his brow lifting. "Why do I not like the tone of your voice?"

Mateo drew a slow breath. Say it clean. Don't hide. "Upon your absence, your brother, Karl, was appointed Master of the Blade. He accepted in hopes of finding you." The fire cracked, sparks leaping skyward. "Our duties took us to Sand Bluff Manor. We were ambushed." His jaw tightened. "He did not survive."

Keeth didn't move. He didn't blink. The world seemed to pause around him. Then his hand tightened around the axe, a controlled, almost imperceptible flex. "Karl," he said quietly.

Mateo felt the wave of silence press down on his ribs. He waited for a judgment he deserved.

Keeth's gaze lifted—cold, focused—but it didn't settle on Mateo. It drifted past him, southward. "The king and queen," Keeth said, voice low and deadly calm. "My brother's blood is on them."

"I'm sorry, Keeth," Mateo said.

Keeth nodded once, a warrior's acknowledgment. "So am I." He exhaled through his nose, sharp and controlled. "This ends where it belongs."

Lirien clasped Keeth's shoulder. "We will make sure of it."

A sudden rush of wind tore through the clearing. The

fire flared as a massive shape descended from the sky, wings beating with thunderous force. Frost and snow scattered as *Izel* landed, the ground shuddering beneath her weight. Her brood followed, circling before settling nearby, watchful and alert.

Izel lifted her great head, eyes blazing as she fixed them on him. "*Teyocel* is in the Wild North, but not in his den."

"Can you sense where he is?" Zalarae asked.

"I cannot." She sat, her tail curling around her. She faced Mateo. "If we are to face the great dragon, the prince must speak it all. Every word. Every promise. Every truth exchanged when he gave *Teyocel* half his soul."

As if summoned by the thought, a familiar pressure coiled behind Mateo's eyes. Somewhere out there, *Teyocel* stirred. Mateo kept his expression neutral, but his pulse quickened.

"It's okay, *Mijo*," Manny said.

Murmuring from the others joined in Manny's reassurance, but fell far short of making him feel any better. How could he when he had brought so much ruin?

"We're here with you," Avalynn reassured him.

His thoughts took him back to that cave—the stench of mud and metal thick in the air. *Teyocel* had perched atop black obsidian stone while Mateo stood before him, the ground trembling beneath his boots.

"I was in his den, on his perch," Mateo said quietly. "In a cave within a dark mountain. I asked him to fight alongside me against the other provinces."

The fire popped sharply, sending a spray of sparks

into the cool air. Someone sucked in a breath. The wind stirred, low and uneasy, threading through the clearing.

Mateo remembered *Teyocel's* cruel laugh, the sound echoing in his mind even now. "He said his soul was bound to the Wild North, tethered by ancient magic. But if I shared half my soul with him, he could leave and fight by my side." His jaw tightened. "He said that when I was finished with him—when my enemies were slain—he would return my soul to me."

The fire crackled louder, logs shifting as if unsettled by the words. Silence pressed in around them, heavy and disbelieving, while a constant aching pain pulsed behind his eyes.

Mateo shook his head. "I knew I'd be at his mercy. I told him I was no fool. But he said he had no interest in keeping what wasn't his." Mateo swallowed. "He said the bond would break the moment he returned here."

"Has it?" his father asked. "Has it broken?"

"No," he admitted. "*Teyocel* is still with me."

The words barely left his mouth when pain detonated behind his eyes. Mateo gasped, vision blurring as white heat tore through his skull. He squeezed his eyes shut, fingers curling into fists as something dark and amused brushed the edge of his thoughts.

"*A pity*," *Teyocel* murmured, his laugh sharp and cruel, like stone grinding against bone.

"Mateo." Avalynn grabbed his hand.

He loosened her hold, staggering to his feet and putting distance between himself and her, between himself and all of them. His pulse roared in his ears as he backed away, every instinct screaming that he was a storm about to unleash.

"I have to go," he said hoarsely. "I am putting everyone here in jeopardy."

"*Mijo—*" Manny started.

"No, father." Mateo shook his head sharply. "*Es mejor así.*" He couldn't risk staying. He felt poisonous, like rot spreading through living things.

Lirien jumped to his feet. "I'm coming with you."

Mateo didn't argue. He only nodded. He knew Lirien would come no matter what. He would do the same thing. The boundary sparked as they approached, light brushing his skin like a farewell, and he crossed without looking back.

The cold bit deep, then released, leaving him and Lirien standing on the other side of the magic. Lirien exhaled. "Now what?"

Mateo stared up at the sky, feeling the dragon coil tighter in his mind, patient as a blade at his throat. "Now, we wait."

CHAPTER TWENTY-FIVE

A valynn's chest ached as she stared at the magical boundary. One moment, Mateo was there. The next, the boundary swallowed him and Lirien whole. The pain inside of her moved slowly, pressing inward with every breath as if her heart were folding in on itself. She wrapped her arms around herself, nails digging into her sleeves. He had done the right thing. She knew that. *Teyocel* was still inside him, watching, listening, waiting for weakness. Every plan spoken near Mateo would have been a risk, every hope a weapon the dragon could use against them. Understanding those truths didn't make it hurt any less.

Silverhoof shifted behind her, releasing a low, uneasy huff. One hoof struck the frozen ground, then another. The Enbarr's ears pinned forward toward the sealed boundary as if she expected it to open again. Avalynn swallowed hard. Even the horse felt the loss.

She moved closer to Silverhoof and stroked her soft

muzzle. "It's okay, girl. We'll see him again." She prayed to the Sun, Moon, and Stars she was right.

She turned away from the boundary at last, forcing herself back into the circle of firelight. She sat beside Manny, and he squeezed her tight. She hugged him back, drawing in a steadying inhale. The fear was still there, sharp and cold. Yet beneath it, something more substantial now sparked. Resolve. They would find a way to sever the bond. They had to. But they had to act before *Teyocel* returned and claimed what he believed was already his.

Stormshroud padded closer, her body brushing her legs as she circled before settling at her feet. Her weight was solid, warm, real. She turned to Manny, searching his face for some sort of wisdom. He had lived a long time with the help of Sonia's magic. He had seen what came after fear and loss. He loved Mateo with his whole heart, and her mother and father and grandsires had trusted him. Surely, he'd have some ideas.

"What do we do now?" she asked.

"Easy," he said, mustering his best attempt at optimism. "We work the problem." He glanced at the others. "Every word from a dragon means something, right?"

"That is true," Zalarae said. "We will pick apart everything that was said between *Teyocel* and Mateo. There we will find the answer for our next move."

Engrendorn rubbed his chin. "*Teyocel* said he would return Mateo's soul when his enemies were slain, which is folly. A prince's enemies will never be slain. Let alone a Stromm prince."

"Wait a minute," Manny added quickly. "Do dragons lie?"

"Never," *Izel* puffed from where she sat.

"Okay, so let's focus on that." Manny pinched the space between his eyes. "*Teyocel* told Mateo the bond would break when he returned here." He pointed around. "Well, we're here, and it hasn't broken."

"So *Teyocel* lied then?" Keeth asked.

"No," Manny said with a shake of his head. "He doesn't have to lie."

"What does that mean?" Keeth asked. "You speak in riddles, human."

"*Teyocel* speaks in riddles, Master Dwarf." A hopeful look sparked in Manny's eyes. "My friend Leto, a wise fae, used to say fae didn't need to lie because they were masters at twisting the truth."

"*Teyocel* is most definitely cunning and devious," Avalynn added. "But where is the lie?"

Manny rose to his feet. He folded his arms and began pacing the fire's edge, boots crunching softly over frost-hardened ground. He murmured Mateo's words, turning them over like stones. "The bond would break when he returned here... When he returned here... When he returned here... When he returned—"

"Here," Avalynn blurted. Her pulse kicked hard. "When he returned *here*."

"He returned here and nothing changed," Keeth said, his bushy brows pulled together.

"Not here," Avalynn said. "Not the Vale, or even the Wild North." She turned to Manny as the truth snapped into place, cold and sharp.

"His den." They spoke the words together.

Manny's eyes brightened as he faced the others. "Their conversation was in the den, his perch to be exact, so when *Teyocel* said here, he meant..." He pointed toward the mountain tops. "There."

Izel's great head lifted, eyes narrowing as her gaze snapped upward. "That is why he is not in his den," she said. "*Teyocel* never moves without purpose."

Keeth straightened. "All we need to do is get the mad dragon back there?"

Zalarae let out a quiet, humorless laugh. "If that's true, then he may never return willingly. He knows what he bargained."

"Unless..." Avalynn's hand drifted to the sword at her side. "He has a reason he can't resist."

The hilt settled into her palm. The blade hummed faintly, the aquoise stone along its black onyx core glowing with restrained power. This sword had been forged for her, tempered with magic created by her human bloodline. It wasn't just metal and spell—it was choice, defiance, inheritance. *Teyocel* would want its power. Stormshroud's ears flattened. A low warning rumbled in her chest, not at her, but at the blade.

"The sword?" Engrendorn asked.

"We plant it there," Avalynn said.

"Have you lost your mind?" Keeth's eyes widened. "We cannot give him the sword of the Only One!"

"We won't." Avalynn's grip tightened as resolve locked into place. "We will lie in wait. We draw him in and take it back before he ever touches it."

Silence fell heavy around the fire, the kind that whispered of death and loss. "The danger would be great," Zalarae said. "If we fail, the realm will never be the same."

"It will never be the same if he fully takes Mateo's soul either," Avalynn said. Her hand moved to her stomach. She knew what Mateo was capable of when consumed by dark magic. What would he be like if *Teyocel* owned him entirely? A prince with the full backing of House Stromm, wholly consumed by a dark dragon, would turn the fae realm to ashy ruins.

"We must save Mateo, my boy, no matter the cost," Manny urged with a shake of his fist.

"I know," Avalynn said. Her heart hammered, fear threading through her confidence. She could see the risk, could feel the cost pressing in on her ribs. "I don't see any other way. If *Teyocel* won't return to his den on his own, then we'll have to give him something he can't ignore."

The fire popped, sparks leaping into the sky like warning signs no one could afford to heed. They all understood the truth now. It was reckless, terrifying, and the only option left.

Keeth rose to his feet and slapped his hands together. "Well, how do we pull this off?"

Izel's gaze swept the circle. "My brood and I will carry Avalynn to *Teyocel's* den. She will place the sword upon his perch. There, he will feel it," she continued. "The aquoise stone and the human magic bound within it will call to him. He will return at once." A low rumble vibrated through her chest. "When he enters the den, my brood and I will give Avalynn time before we collapse the main passage. Stone and fire will seal it behind him. It will be up to Avalynn to get him onto the perch."

Avalynn's pulse quickened. *Teyocel's den. His perch.* She shuddered. She could almost feel the darkness all around her. The sword at her side stirred, as if it, too, recognized the danger.

"Avalynn will snatch the sword the moment he reaches for it," *Izel* said, her eyes locking onto her. "Then she will flee through a narrow crevice at the rear of the cave—one too small for a dragon to follow. With swift steps, she will make it through before the den collapses."

"And you know it's there?" Manny asked. "This crevice?"

"Yes," *Izel* said. "It has always been there."

"What if he reaches the sword first?" Keeth asked.

Izel's voice darkened. "Then Avalynn will run. Or she will die."

Cold settled in Avalynn's chest—not fear, more like acceptance. She had lived her life being told her destiny. This was the first time the danger felt honest and chosen. If this was the cost of saving Mateo and the entire realm, then she would pay it.

"I can do it," she said, her voice sounding smaller than intended.

"The plan is sound," Manny said at last. "But it needs one minor adjustment. I'm going too."

"As am I," Keeth blurted. He flashed Avalynn a rough grin. "Someone has to keep this spoiled princess alive."

Avalynn smiled despite herself, the tension easing

just a fraction. "Not a chance. If I need to grab and run, having others around will only slow me down."

"The Only One speaks the truth," *Izel* said. "An escape for one is the easiest to execute."

And just like that, the plan was settled.

They rose slowly, the circle breaking apart as boots shifted and cloaks were gathered. The fire popped low, settling into embers. Avalynn stood, rolling her shoulders, trying to steady the tremor moving through her muscles.

Manny caught her arms before she could step away. He held her steady, his hands firm but gentle. His eyes searched her face, serious and unguarded.

"You can do this, *mija*," he said quietly. "Be calm. Keep your mind clear. Act fast." His grip tightened just a fraction. "The dragon won't even know what's happening until it's too late."

Her throat burned. She nodded, afraid that if she spoke, the sound might break.

His gaze dropped to her chest. "Where's your cross?"

The question landed like a stone. Avalynn's hand lifted instinctively to her neck—and met bare skin. A gasp escaped her lips. The cross. Her mother's. Gabriela's. The one Lady Sonia had tucked inside the box with the note. She searched herself, panic flaring sharp and sudden.

"I don't know," she whispered. "I must have lost it. Maybe when I fell. Maybe when I—" She swallowed. "I don't have it."

Manny shook his head gently, cutting off the spiral before it could take hold. He pulled her forward, drawing her into his embrace.

"No matter," he murmured into her hair. "Your faith is inside you. It always has been. Same with Mateo. It doesn't disappear because you lose the symbol."

She breathed him in; the warm, familiar scents of his Sublands home steadied her. Woodsmoke and old leather, steeped herbs drying near the hearth, earth after rain, and the faint sweetness of bread always lingering in his cottage. His arms were solid around her, anchoring her to the ground and to herself. She clung to that smell, to the quiet certainty in his voice, and to the hope that she would make it back to feel it again with Mateo at her side.

"Thank you, Manny." She straightened, then stepped away with a smile. "I will see you soon."

"Yes, soon."

Avalynn leaned into the wind, keeping close to *Izel's* warmth. The world rushed past beneath them as they flew in a loose formation. *Izel* took the lead while her brood skimmed over ice and stone below her. They passed Skywatcher Mountain in silence, its familiar peaks swallowed quickly by distance, then crossed a vast, frozen clearing where the snow lay untouched and blindingly white.

Several wing beats later, the land began to change. Another mountain range rose ahead, this one sharper, darker, its slopes cut with jagged lines like scattered daggers. The mountain did not gleam or glitter. It burned, its peak piercing the clouds like a black bolt.

Avalynn's stomach clenched, fear tearing through her in a cold, steady wave. The task ahead felt impossibly large and crushing in its scale. She whispered a silent prayer to the Sun, Moon, and Stars for strength. Mateo had been in that mountain alone, facing the darkness without her when he'd needed her most. She would be alone too.

As they drew closer, the air thickened, warming in a way that had nothing to do with fire. Each breath felt heavier than the last, as though the mountain were pressing down on her chest and stealing her air. Magic crowded in from every direction—ancient, layered, and restless. It wasn't the clean pull of the Vale or the steady hum of *Izel's* power. This magic was coiled and patient, watching with deadly stealth.

"*I feel something,*" she said to *Izel.*

"*It is the mountain. It knows you are coming. The same way I knew when you arrived in the Wild North. Soon, Teyocel will sense you too.*"

Great. She was some beacon now. Would she even be able to pull off her plan before *Teyocel* arrived?

Izel descended sharply, landing on a wide shelf of obsidian stone. Behind them, the brood circled, then settled into position along the mountain face, watchful and tense. Avalynn hopped off. The den snarled open before her. Inside was where the bond had been forged. Where Mateo had given half his soul away. Fear curled tight in her chest, cold and sharp, but beneath it burned something as fierce. If this was where it began, then this was where it would end.

Izel lowered her head, her gaze locking onto Avalynn.

"Once you step inside, you are no longer under my protection."

"I know. Thank you for everything, *Izel*," she said. The words almost sounded like a goodbye, and she regretted it the second she uttered them. "Just make sure you collapse the opening after he enters." She placed her hand on the hilt. "I'll do the rest."

Avalynn didn't hesitate. If she did, she might never move again. With a final glance at *Izel* and the others, she stepped through the cave opening. The darkness swallowed her. The sound dulled first. Then the light was erased. She stayed still, waiting for her eyes to adjust, when gray shimmers appeared. The den opened into a vast chamber, its obsidian walls catching faint reflections that distorted her shape as she passed. Each step echoed too loudly, the stone beneath her boots warm, thrumming faintly as if the mountain itself had a pulse.

At the center stood the perch. Around it piled coins, weapons, and gemstones nestled amidst mounds of ash and dirt. Avalynn climbed. She took slow steps, trying her best not to disturb the treasure.

Her fingers loosened as she reached the top. She paused, her gaze sweeping the chamber, searching for the exit. Where was it? Panic clawed at her. Was it somehow removed? But then she spotted it and exhaled. To her left, the obsidian wall separated into a narrow crevice, its edges sharp and uneven, slanting downward into darkness. Could she fit in that? It was barely wide enough for a body. One wrong step, one stumble on the ash-slick stone, and it would become a trap instead of an escape. She'd have to be careful.

She traced the route. From the perch, she'd go down the slope, across the piles, then into the crevice before *Teyocel* claimed the sword and torched her or chomped her to bits. Her stomach tightened. The margin for error was thinner than a blade's edge. She repeated the path in her mind. She could do this. But for one suspended heartbeat, she hesitated. This choice would not end well for her. She knew that. But, it would end well for Mateo, for the Sublands where he was raised, for the family that loved him no matter his bloodline. The lowborn would finally win. The once-Stromm princess would get what she deserved.

She crouched low. She held her breath. She placed the sword upon the perch. The moment it left her hand, pain flared sharp and sudden through her chest. The air shuddered. The mountain groaned low, like a warning dragged from deep stone. Outside, the sky split with a roar. Wind tore through the den's mouth as ancient magic surged and the walls trembled.

Avalynn pressed her body against the stone and waited, her heart hammering. Somewhere beyond the mountain, something vast and furious answered the call.

Teyocel was coming.

CHAPTER TWENTY-SIX

The ground shuddered beneath Mateo's boots. It wasn't a tremor, not the distant roll of thunder. This was deeper, older, something that reached up through Faevenly's bones and settled hard in his chest like a striking anvil. Birds burst from the tree line, black shapes spiraling into the sky in a frantic scatter.

Mateo stilled. The air thickened, magic scraping against his skin like a warning. Pain lanced through his head and pulled, not inward, but away. He gasped as something tore loose inside him, a violent wrench that left him reeling. The pressure that had coiled around his thoughts for days altered in an instant, yanked in another direction, not gone. Redirected.

"Avalynn..." Mateo muttered, already turning and facing the Wild North. "She's pulled *Teyocel* away. I can feel it."

Lirien was beside him before he knew it, hand tightening around his dagger as the rumble deepened. "Sun,

Moon, and Stars," Lirien said, scanning the sky. "I know I haven't been here long, but I've never seen the land react like this."

The ground shook again, harder this time. The pull inside Mateo surged, like a tide dragging him toward disaster. "I'm going," Mateo said. It wasn't a decision. It was a fact. "She needs me."

Lirien never questioned Mateo when he sounded like this. "Then let's move."

They broke into a sprint, boots tearing over frosted ground as they raced for the magical boundary. The air screamed as they crossed it. Mateo skidded to a halt.

Scaled muscle and searing heat towered before him. *Izel.* Massive. Waiting. Her golden eyes locked on to him as the mountains beyond the Wild North groaned like a waking giant, the sound rolling through his bones, deep and wrong.

Why was she here?

"You are too late," the dragon said quietly.

Mateo's blood iced over. *Izel* would be the one to stand in his way? Not *Teyocel?* He raised his sword. "What do you mean?" The blade felt small in his grip, laughably light beneath the dragon's weight bearing down on him.

Izel did not blink. "You cannot help Avalynn."

The words struck harder than any blow. "You don't know that," he snarled.

"I do," *Izel* said. "His attention may no longer rest on you, but your link remains."

The truth landed like a blade between his ribs, his chest tightening. He could feel it now, the bond stretched thin, taut as wire, screaming in the same direction his instincts had already chosen. Toward her.

Mateo's jaw locked. "Your plan is already in motion. I'm no risk now."

"You are always a risk." A low, solemn growl rolled from her chest. "You gave him part of yourself. Not flesh. Not blood. Soul. That bond does not loosen because you wish it to."

Lirien shifted beside him, stance widening, weapon lifting. Mateo felt the unspoken question between them. *What do we do?*

"You are not enough," *Izel* said, her voice hard as rock. "Not against a dragon who carries part of your soul. Not against power that answers him before it answers you. You would play right into his hand, breaking any chance she has of besting him." She stretched her neck. "To protect Avalynn's success, I must end you."

The words settled with terrible finality, understanding hitting hard and fast. He wasn't part of the plan at all. He was the thing that had to be removed. Permanently. He refused to play along. Always a lowborn, always a fighter, he stepped forward, sword rising. If this was where it ended, then so be it. He would not turn back. Lirien moved with him, silent and resolute at his side.

Mateo bared his teeth, every instinct screaming for battle. "Then I'll go down fighting."

"As will I," Lirien said.

The mountain groaned again, deeper this time. And *Izel* moved.

Her wings unfurled in a thunderous sweep,

stretching wide and blotting out the sky. Her golden eyes burned brighter. Then, with a sickening inevitability, they darkened to red. Her lips peeled back, revealing rows of gleaming, heat-slick teeth. Fire bubbled low in her throat, the sound wet and terrible, like the earth itself beginning to melt.

Mateo reacted. "Move!" He slammed into Lirien with his shoulder, sending him stumbling back as *Izel's* maw opened and the world burned.

Dragon flame tore across the ground, white-hot and screaming. Mateo flung his arms in front of him as the inferno hit full on. Pain exploded. The air ripped from his lungs, the force hurling him backward across the frozen ground. He skidded through ice and ash, everything spinning violently before he crashed to a stop.

He landed on his side, then rolled onto his hands and knees. Heat radiated through his skin. Smoke curled around him, thick and choking. Mateo gasped, dragging in air that barely reached his lungs.

He forced his head up. *Izel* advanced. Her footfalls struck the ground like hammer blows. She unleashed another blast. The flames tore through Mateo's body. Bone stretched with a sickening crack, lengthening and reshaping. His spine arched violently. Muscles seized. Something ancient and feral ripped its way to the surface. He screamed, hoarse and raw, heat surging through his veins.

What is she doing to me?!

Agony detonated. His skin prickled, then split. Pressure built beneath it, enormous and unrelenting, as something vast pushed outward from within. Scales rippled in waves, swallowing his skin, red and molten like freshly forged steel pulled from fire. His hands twisted. Fingers fused and reformed. Claws tore free. The ground quaked beneath him. His weight shifted, his body no longer bound to the shape he had been born into.

Then the world snapped into terrifying clarity. He felt the wind now—the currents, the pull, the vast open space above him calling like instinct made flesh. His wings jerked wide—too wide. He staggered, his balance vanished completely, his weight yanking him sideways. One wing slammed into the ground with a thunderous crack, spraying ice and dirt. The other swept out blindly, missing Lirien by a hair.

"Mateo!" Lirien shouted, ducking low, shock written plainly across his face.

Heat gathered in Mateo's throat, and he heaved, spewing a torrent of fire that scorched the air itself.

No, no, no. Panic flared hot and sharp. *Stop blasting!* Mateo clamped his jaw tight, then tried to step away from Lirien, nearly collapsing under himself. His body was unable to respond the way it should. Every movement was too large, too powerful, too slow.

But then instinct clawed through the chaos.

He spread his wings again, fighting for balance. This time, the ground dropped away in a sickening lurch as he half leaped into the air. Wind tore past his scales, not resisting him but yielding, bending to the sheer force of his ascent. The world shrank beneath him. Trees were reduced to dark bristles against the snow, stone and ice rendered small and distant. His wings caught the currents at last, strength surging through unfamiliar muscles that answered him now without hesitation.

He hovered, power thrumming through every part of him, vast and undeniable. The air belonged to him. The open sky beckoned. It stretched endlessly above, bright and unclaimed, and for one impossible heartbeat, he felt unstoppable. Fear still burned, but it was braided now with awe, with fury, with a fierce, reckless joy that tasted like freedom.

"Everything is on fire," Mateo rumbled. "And so am I."

Across the scorched clearing, *Izel* launched, joining him in the air. His dark-red scales reflected against her pearlized ones—the same desert-red hues as the Sublands that had shaped him.

"*Now*," she said, her voice resonating through bone and flame alike. "*Now you are ready to face him. But know this. Dragons do not relinquish soul bonds. They end them. Or are ended by them.*"

Mateo's wings beat effortlessly, every movement innate. This was never a punishment. It was preparation. There would be no undoing what came next. One of them was going down. It sure as hell wouldn't be him.

Izel soared northward. Mateo hesitated for only a heartbeat, long enough to think of Avalynn alone in the dark, facing a monster who had taken half his soul.

A roar tore free, vast and furious. Fire followed, ripping into the sky. Time to end it. He surged after *Izel*, red scales glinting as they flew toward the mountain where everything would be decided.

Toward *Teyocel*.

Toward her.

CHAPTER TWENTY-SEVEN

T he stone beneath Avalynn's body vibrated, a low pulse that crawled up her arms and into her chest. Dust sifted from above in fine gray threads, clinging to her forehead and lashes. The air thickened, growing hot and heavy, each breath harder to pull than the last.

She didn't move. She counted instead. *One. Two. Three.* Her stomach tightened. She pressed herself flatter against the stone. *Four. Five. Six.* If she ran too soon, the plan would shatter. If she waited too long, *Teyocel* would incinerate her. *Seven. Eight. Nine.* A sound rolled through the den, deep and thunderous. Not a roar. Not yet. Wings. *Ten. Eleven. Twelve.* The wind rushed in hard, ripping through the chamber, scattering ash and rock. *Thirteen. Fourteen. Fifteen.* The ground shuddered beneath her. Heat surged through the walls like blood through a vein.

He was here.

Every instinct screamed to grab the sword and flee into the crevice while she still could. But she stayed still. *Sixteen. Seventeen. Eighteen.* She needed to see him, needed him to get closer. He had to touch the perch. *Nineteen. Twenty. Twenty-one.* She kept her arm out, fingers stretched toward the hilt. Footfalls thudded. *Twenty-two. Twenty-three. Twenty-four.* Her gaze moved from the den opening to the sword, flicking back and forth, until she saw him.

Her heart stuttered. The numbers scattered from her brain, blown apart by the sheer size of him. His scales blended with the rock, shades of black and gray glinting with menace. His wings were tucked in tight. He lifted his neck and inhaled through flared nostrils, the sound gravelly, long, and deep.

"Powerrr," he murmured. "I smell it thick as warm blood on stone. Metal and flesh. Two of my favorite things."

She gulped. He smelled her and the sword. Did that mean he knew where they were? Her thoughts raced. She had two choices. Stay. Or run and pray. Her muscles coiled ready, screaming with urgency.

Teyocel moved deeper into the chamber. His claws scraped against stone, sending tremors through the floor and shivers down her spine.

"You know," he said almost conversationally. "Most creatures try to flee the moment they realize they have been scented."

Avalynn lunged. Her fingers closed around the hilt. She spun and ran, boots slipping on ash-slick stone, heart hammering as she sprinted for the crevice. She reached it, then froze. Stone closed the opening like a shut door. No gap. No room for air. Nothing. She pounded with her fists.

"Sealed," *Teyocel* said.

Izel hadn't known. Now Avalynn was trapped. She frantically scanned for another escape, but there was none.

"There is nowhere to go, Only One," *Teyocel* said, clicking his tongue, amusement curling through his voice. "You are mine now."

She spun and pressed her back to the stone, breath coming fast and shallow. The plan was gone, crushed in a blink. Panic flared, then burned away just as quickly. She needed to do something. But what?

"*Izel*," Avalynn called in her mind, forcing her nerves to steady. "*The crevice is sealed.*"

There was no response, only a rumbling laugh from *Teyocel*. "You. Are. Alone."

He moved forward but steered clear of the perch, avoiding the raised stone. A chill slid down her spine. He knew their plan, or enough of it. Avalynn tightened her grip on the sword and lifted it, the motion snapping her back to the training circle and Engrendorn's voice in her ear, sharp and unforgiving. *Predictability gets you killed.*

What would be more unpredictable than striking a bargain with *Teyocel*? If she was going to survive this, she had to offer him something he believed only she could give. Something that might set her free.

"I have power," she blurted. "Not just from the

sword." She swallowed, her heart pounding. "I will give it to you willingly."

Teyocel stilled, a predator deciding whether the thing before it was prey or something rare.

"Willingly?" he repeated, tasting the word. His head lowered, nostrils flaring as he inhaled again. "What power do you think runs through you that I do not already own?"

Avalynn's pulse thundered in her ears. "Blue power," she said. "The magic from my human bloodline. The power is bound into this sword and into me. It's rare, and I am the only one in Faevenly who has it." If she were wrong, if she couldn't make it answer her now, she would die for the attempt.

He circled half a step, tilting his massive head, one molten eye fixing on her with razor-sharp focus. "Show me."

"Okay." Her mouth went dry. The back of her neck tingled. "Move closer."

For a second, she thought he might laugh. Instead, his lips curled. "Brave," he said. "Or very foolish."

Foolish. Definitely foolish. He advanced. Each step brought him dangerously close to the perch. Close enough that the stone beneath her boots vibrated with his weight. One blast. That's all she needed. Enough to push him forward. Long enough for her to run.

Avalynn lifted her hand. She spread her fingers and shut her eyes. Focus. Not the sword. Not the fear. The power. The warmth beneath her skin, the quiet hum she didn't understand, the power that flared in desperation and vanished before she could grasp it. *Come on. Come out.*

A flicker bloomed in her palm. It came softly at first, like moonlight caught underwater. It pulsed, then brightened, the glow spilling between her fingers as blue energy unfurled, coiling up her wrist and threading her arm in warm, shimmering light.

Teyocel inhaled sharply. His head lowered further, eyes burning now, his voice dropping to a reverent whisper. "There it is."

So close to the perch. One more step. But her power faltered. The magic wavered. It slipped from her grasp like water through open fingers. Avalynn's stomach dropped. *Oh no.*

Teyocel smiled. "Time to end this game, Only One."

A scream tore through the den. Avalynn's head snapped up as a blur of red scales smashed through the chamber. Wings slammed into walls. Talons gouged through stone. Treasure and ash exploded into the air. She staggered back, shielding her face as heat and wind ripped past her.

A red dragon. She had never seen this one before. It wasn't sleek like *Izel* or ancient like *Teyocel*. It was feral. The dragon threw itself forward, slamming into *Teyocel's* side with a sound like a mountain breaking.

Teyocel roared, the force shaking the den as the red dragon clawed up his back, teeth sinking into scaled flesh. Blood, dark and smoking, splashed across the obsidian floor.

Avalynn stared. The red dragon clung to *Teyocel* like

rage made solid. Neither graceful nor controlled, it was desperate and savage.

Teyocel bucked violently, trying to throw the attacker off. "What are you?!" he thundered.

The red dragon lifted its head. "I AM FIRE!"

Avalynn gulped. That voice. Those eyes, not molten, not draconic. Steely gray. Her heart lurched. She knew them. She had known them in every way that mattered.

Her voice came out broken, disbelieving. "Mateo?"

He screamed again, raw and furious, this time at her. "GO!"

Mateo dove back in, teeth bared, wings thrashing *Teyocel* with reckless violence. All at once, Avalynn understood. The Frost-Forged Trials. The transformation. While she, Manny, and the others were making their plan, *Izel* had her own. Now, she needed to run.

She darted as a sweep of wings tore straight for her. She dropped and rolled as stone and ash rained down. She scrambled up, then slammed herself flat again as an onyx slab careened past, missing her by inches. The impact shattered against the cavern wall, the boom rattling her teeth.

She stayed down, hands locked over her head, panting in sharp, panicked bursts. She lifted her gaze. A storm of smoke and ash filled the den as *Teyocel* and Mateo tangled together, claws raking and teeth snapping.

"Off!" *Teyocel* roared. He pulled and twisted beneath Mateo, wrenching free. With a ferocious thrust, his jaws clamped around Mateo's shoulder.

Mateo screamed, the sound tearing straight through her heart. He slashed at *Teyocel*, battering him with wild wing strikes, but it wasn't enough. *Teyocel* hurled Mateo into the cavern wall. Stone split and rubble burst outward in all directions. Mateo scrambled to hold on to something, anything, but he couldn't. A massive talon pinned his chest, another raked deep across his flank, blood spilling across the floor.

"No," Avalynn whispered.

She saw it with cold, awful clarity. This wasn't a fight anymore. This was an ending. Her heart slammed against her ribs. She couldn't run, not now, not when Mateo was fighting for her. If she fled, he'd die. If she stayed, she could help him.

The sword pulsed at her side, the blue etchings burning brighter now, answering the chaos. Her mind raced. She couldn't fight a dragon, but she could break things.

Her gaze snapped to the perch, the prophecy whispering through her mind. *Transformation ... sword of blue...* Manny's voice rose over it, steady and sure. *Your faith is inside you. It always has been.* Abigail's words followed, quiet but unyielding. *Some prophecies are meant to be broken.*

She had broken the prophecy back at the Green Falls. Time to do it again, but this time permanently. Avalynn eyed the blade. She didn't need it at all. It was not the source. It had never been. The blue power lived in her blood, in her bones, in every choice she'd ever made without understanding why. The blade had been a vessel, a bridge, a gift meant to carry her this far. The rest was up to her.

Avalynn's fingers tightened around the hilt, and she

bolted. The ground quaked beneath her boots as she ran, dodging falling stones. The perch loomed ahead, ancient and black. She didn't slow. She didn't think. She leaped the final step and drove the sword down. The blade slid into the slab without resistance—smooth, effortless, as if the sword had been waiting for it.

For one suspended heartbeat, nothing happened. Then the mountain reared.

A concussive force tore through the chamber, hurling Avalynn backward as blue light erupted. The den convulsed. Cracks split across the obsidian walls, racing toward the ceiling as the mountain groaned in protest. The perch collapsed inward, dragging light and stone with it, and the ground began to fall as the mountain folded into its own heart.

Avalynn scrambled up and ran for the far den opening. She skidded over jagged slate and jumped over fractured stone as the floor split beneath her. The den was coming apart now—walls tearing, ceiling collapsing.

Teyocel roared, his fury sharpening as the ground beneath him and Mateo gave way, and the dragons fell.

"Mateo!" she hollered.

She staggered, heart clawing at her throat. She forced her legs to keep moving. He'd be okay. He had to be. But she needed to clear the chamber before it took her with it. She pumped her arms. The exit loomed ahead. Closer now. Then a shadow swallowed her.

Izel tore through the smoke and falling rock, her wings pounding the air. Talons closed around Avalynn's waist as the den collapsed, stone shearing past where she'd stood a blink before.

Across the way, another dragon dove—one of *Izel's* brood—vanishing into dust and fire. A breath later, it burst free with Mateo in its grasp—no scales, no fire, only his broken body as the mountain imploded into blinding blue behind them.

Teyocel's roar thundered once more from the depths —furious, defiant—then the mountain answered. Stone and fire crashed inward, sealing the den in final, crushing silence.

CHAPTER TWENTY-EIGHT

Cool wind brushed across Mateo's skin, tugging at the scorched tatters wrapped around his body. He was moving, lifted away, though his body barely registered it. His limbs felt distant and weightless. Pain should have been there and wasn't. His chest ached instead, hollow and bruised, as though something had been torn out rather than healed.

The pressure was gone. The pain behind his eyes had vanished. The voice that had never truly been quiet was silenced. For the first time since the bargain was struck, his thoughts were his own. The sudden freedom left him shaking.

Teyocel?

Nothing answered.

Wetness streaked his cheeks. The tears came silently, pulled loose by the absence rather than pain. Or maybe by both. Mateo didn't move. He couldn't. It was as if he'd forgotten how. Then, slowly, steadily, sensation began to creep back in.

The sky stretched wide and pale above him, the air thinning as they climbed away from *Teyocel's* dark mountain range. Ahead, *Izel* flew, vast and radiant, a beacon of hope. Avalynn was with her, a small figure against the sweep of pearlized wings. Relief washed through him in a dizzying wave, sharp enough to hurt. Avalynn was alive. The Wild North still stood. Faevenly still breathed.

He was free.

And yet—Mateo didn't know what to do with the feelings that followed. The space where rage had lived. The place where a voice had shaped his thoughts. Without it, everything felt too wide, too quiet. For the first time in days, maybe longer, there was no command waiting for him.

Only the sky. And her.

Izel and her brood touched down back where they had started, by the magical boundary. Mateo was set down, his legs shaky when they finally bore weight. He brought his hands up to his face. The red scales were gone, yet the marks remained. Like the Valians.

Avalynn called his name and rushed toward him, and something in his chest finally cracked open. He scooped her up and held her tight. They stayed like that for the longest minute until Avalynn pulled away.

She cupped his face in her hands. "Are you okay?"

He nodded. "Yes."

"Is he gone?" She searched his eyes.

He didn't have to check. The silence remained. "He is."

She took his hands and squeezed. "We did it," she choked out. "We really and truly did it." Her fingers traced the dragon markings along his arms. "And you're a ... dragon shifter."

"I am." Mateo turned his hands, studying the faint red etchings along his skin. "*Izel* did it when I thought she meant to kill me. She couldn't let *Teyocel* sense what she was really doing."

Movement burst from the trees. Manny, Lirien, Keeth, and Stormshroud charged out, racing toward them.

Tears streaked Manny's face as he wrapped his arms around Mateo and Avalynn, pulling them close. Lirien joined without hesitation. Manny didn't say a word, then he laughed, a broken, breathless sound. Somehow, they all laughed, relief pouring out of them, the fear and pain finally spilling free.

"It's finally over," Manny said, pulling back. His gaze lingered on the markings along Mateo's hands, arms, and neck. "And you, *Mijo*, are changed," he said, awe threading through the worry in his voice.

"I am, Father." Mateo placed a steady hand on Manny's frail shoulder. "No one will ever hurt us again."

"Where are the others?" Avalynn asked.

"At the village," Lirien said.

"We've been waiting for you," Keeth said.

"We saw *Teyocel's* mountain collapse," Manny added. "The blue light. Then we saw you being carried this way. We came as fast as we could." His gaze drifted to the magical boundary, still shimmering. Still standing. "Now that everything is done, we need to get Sonia out."

Something in Avalynn shifted. Mateo caught it in her eyes—the doubt, the fear. He felt it too. Could they really bring Sonia back? They hurried toward the boundary, toward the place where Sonia blended so thoroughly into the magic, she was almost impossible to see.

"Sonia," Manny said. His voice cracked with desperate hope. "You can come out now. It's over."

Mateo barely had time to register the relief flickering across his father's face before steel pierced the shimmer. A blade pushed through the boundary, its tip pressing against Manny's jugular.

Mateo froze. Raelor stepped through next, smooth as poison, Lady Verona at his side, her sword the one at Manny's throat. The boundary warped to allow them passage, bending enough to let the threat through.

"Well, well," Raelor said lightly. "This is a most fortunate gathering."

Stormshroud growled low, hackles raised. Avalynn sucked in a sharp breath beside her. Lirien's hand went to his daggers and Keeth's to his axe.

Mateo caught Lirien's arm and swept his other hand in front of Keeth. "No." His voice stayed steady, but his pulse thundered. One wrong move and his father would be dead. He couldn't risk that. Not now. Not after everything.

Raelor's eyes left Manny's throat and met Mateo's stare. "This is what will happen," he said calmly. "If you wish the human to live, then you, Mateo—along with Avalynn, Lady Sonia, and the sword—will come with us. Peacefully."

"The sword is gone," Avalynn snapped. "Destroyed. You're too late."

Raelor didn't blink. His diamond eyes didn't even flicker. "Then I suppose we only need what remains." His gaze slid past them. "Now. Where is Lady Sonia?"

"I am here. I have been waiting for you, Raelor." Sonia's voice came from everywhere at once. It rang calm, resolute, unbearably close. "I allowed your passage so that we might finish this."

Mateo felt it before he saw it. The air around them tightened, the magic drawing taut like a storm about to break. The boundary sparked as light gathered, dense and luminous. Two beams shot forward, swooping around Raelor's chest like spectral arms before anyone could move.

Raelor gasped. "No—"

The magic gagged him, yanking him backward in a blinding flash. It sealed around him like closing water, locking him fast.

"Stars," Avalynn uttered.

Sonia stepped forward. Not out of the boundary, but with it. The magic had shaped itself around her form, light clinging to her skin like a second covering. It was as if the magic had never been a prison at all but an extension of her being.

The blade at Manny's throat lowered as Verona stood transfixed.

"Sonia," Manny whispered.

She turned to him, and she smiled. "My dear friend," she said gently. "It is time for me to fulfill my life's purpose."

"You can't," Avalynn said, her voice breaking. "We were supposed to get you out."

Sonia's smile didn't fade; it deepened—luminous, and full of love. "I am where I need to be, dear one."

Her hand emerged from the shimmer and pressed something into Manny's palm. Mateo watched his father's face collapse.

"Sonia," Manny breathed. "No. Please don't do this."

"I will see you again," she said softly. "When the realm is ready."

Mateo had never seen his father look so small, so helpless. And there was nothing he could do. Sonia was already stepping back. The boundary began to glow, not violently, not in alarm, but in recognition. Light lifted from the ground in slow, graceful ribbons, drifting upward like stars freed from a net. The shimmery magic unraveled, dissolving into the sky, the magical boundary disappearing like a soft wind.

Verona's sword slipped from her fingers and struck the dirt. She staggered, hands shaking. "The spell," she whispered. "Raelor's hold on me. It is gone." Her knees buckled, and she collapsed.

"How?" Avalynn asked, disbelief sharp in her voice as she looked around. "The boundary. How is it gone without destroying Faevenly?"

The air shifted. *Izel* stepped forward, her form settling behind the last fading traces of light.

"Because she was a maker," she said. Her golden eyes met Avalynn's, then Mateo's. "Together, she and I forged the boundary. And she carried my blessing, my scale." A low rumble echoed in her chest. "Only a maker may unmake what was made."

Manny helped Verona to her feet, the group standing in utter disbelief. Mateo moved closer to Avalynn, taking in the scene. The Wild North stood open. Lady Sonia and Raelor were gone. But there were two who still needed to pay.

Verona snatched her sword from the dirt. "My brother is being held in the Stromm dungeon."

Mateo's gaze burned past the empty sky where the veil had vanished and locked onto Verona. "Your brother? That is what they held over you?"

"Yes," she said, voice shaking. "They made me poison the Sublands' waters. They are responsible for the Dragon's Bellow."

Something in Mateo clicked into place. The Stromm pendant. The spells. The whispers woven so deep he'd worn them like his own skin. The way his body had obeyed commands he hadn't chosen. The souls ended because of him. The bruises on Avalynn's wrists. The way the king had looked at her, like she was mere property. The dungeon doors he'd passed without question. The screams he hadn't listened for, and the ones he had caused.

They hadn't only used him. They had built him into a weapon.

He stepped forward, the scorched, red-scaled fabric still clinging to his body like the shed skin of something dead. It hung across his shoulders and chest, half-cloak, half-armor, dragon fire fused into thread.

Mateo drew a slow breath, the fire stirring within

him. "It's time for the king and queen to get what they deserve."

Lirien spun his daggers in his hands. "What's the plan?"

Mateo's eyes lifted, hard and unflinching. "We go there. Now. We end their treacherous rule."

A low growl of approval came from Stormshroud. "The Stromm Palace will be heavily guarded," Avalynn said.

Mateo's eyes searched the horizon. "So will we. We go fast and focused. Me, Avalynn, Verona, and Lirien."

"And me," Keeth said, axe in hand. "The guards may yield when they see me."

Engrendorn, Zalarae, and the other Valians emerged from the trees. "We will supply the swords," Zalarae added.

"For the Wild North," Engrendorn said. "And the retribution that is due."

A flicker of light flashed where the boundary had been, and out spilled Bramble. "Where is my boundary? My home?" His eyes were wide, his hair standing on end as he took in the weapons and the dragons. "And what in all the frostbitten roots is this?"

"It looks like you do not need a boundary to be tied to this place," Engrendorn said with a raised brow.

Mateo turned to him. "We are taking down a tyrant."

Bramble blinked. "Ah." He nodded once. "Right. I will stay here." His gaze swept over Mateo, lingering on the scorched fabric and exposed skin. "You look like death had an argument with a dragon and lost."

Mateo almost smiled. "Something like that."

Bramble sniffed. "You are not marching off to overthrow a tyrant dressed like a half-burnt omen, are you? Honestly. No sense of presentation." He waved a hoof and huffed. "Terrifying is one thing. Distracting is another."

"The annoying faun has a point," Keeth added.

"I always do." He twirled, then bowed. "So long, you fools!" And he disappeared.

Keeth shook his axe at the spot. "Next time he won't be so lucky."

A quiet step sounded behind them. Engrendorn moved forward and held out a small bag. "We thought you might need fresh clothing," he said.

Mateo took it with a tip of his head. "Thank you."

He turned toward the trees, and Avalynn fell into step beside him, as if it had never been a question. They stopped where the branches thickened, the sounds of wings and voices fading. For a moment, neither of them spoke. Then Avalynn reached for him and buried herself in his chest. He wrapped his arms around her and held her like he wasn't letting go.

She tilted her face up, her deep blue eyes steady on his. Their foreheads brushed in an unspoken check before his mouth found hers. The kiss deepened gently, not with urgency but with certainty, a shared exhale after too much fear. Her hands slid into his long, dark hair; his hands settled at her waist, steady and sure, anchoring them both.

It wasn't fire this time. It was warmth. It was relief. It was love that had survived the fall.

When she drew back, her hands didn't leave him.

They traced the lines of his arms, the scaled markings left behind by fire and magic. Her fingers lingered over the markings on his hands and wrists, followed them up his forearms and across his chest, stopping where they ended at his neck.

"You're still you," she murmured, more to herself than to him.

Mateo swallowed. "I am."

She helped him out of the ruined garments. Each touch felt like reclamation, like she was reminding his body who it belonged to—not a dragon or a crown, but to himself, to her. He dressed, pulling on the dark trousers and matching tunic that felt almost strange against his skin. When he turned back to her, she was smiling softly.

He leaned in, resting his forehead against hers. "Thank you."

"For what?"

"For not letting me disappear."

She kissed him again, briefly this time, then stepped back. She laced her fingers with his. "Come on," she said. "Let's finish this."

Together, they walked back toward the others.

Izel lowered her head. "I will take Mateo and Avalynn." The three remaining dragons shifted, wings unfurling. "My brood will carry the others."

Manny stepped closer, gripping Mateo's forearm. "Be careful, *Mijo*," he said. "Please do not forget who you are."

"I will be careful, Father." He drew his father in for a hug. "I will never forget who I am. Never again."

When their embrace ended, Manny opened his

palm. Resting there was the object Sonia had given him—a necklace with an opal pendant. "The pendant is a portal. The last remaining one in all of Faevenly." He placed it in Mateo's hands. "You pinch it and pull it out. Sonia used it to take her home. It will take you wherever you want if you concentrate hard enough." He ran his fingertips over it before letting go. "Sonia gave this to me for a reason, and something tells me it's for you."

A portal. Mateo had no idea what he would do with it, but he trusted his father. He slipped the necklace over his head. "I will keep it well."

Manny smiled. "I will head to the Sublands from here. Come home when you finish the job."

"I will." He turned to Avalynn. His fire met the storm in her eyes, his love for her brimming within him. "Ready to end this?"

She nodded. "I'm with you. Always."

They mounted quickly. Avalynn and Mateo climbed onto *Izel's* back, while *Izel's* brood took up Verona, Lirien, and Keeth.

Wings beat the air into submission as the dragons lifted, angling south toward Stromm Palace. Mateo's gaze fixed on the horizon. He forged a promise he would not break.

No more chains. No more crowns built on manipulation and deceit. Stromm Palace would burn, not in chaos, but in judgment long overdue.

CHAPTER TWENTY-NINE

A million thoughts raced through Avalynn's mind. They flew south toward the palace where she had been raised, toward the ones who had shaped her childhood and raised her. The queen she had called Mother. The king she had called Father. The little princess she had called Sister.

She touched her wrists without thinking. The bruises were gone, erased by healing and time, but the memory of being a Stromm princess stayed with her. The way the queen had never looked at her, the way the king had laid hands on her. She wanted their reign to end, wanted them to answer for every cruelty dressed up as duty. But beneath that desire, something steadier began to rise, something quiet and insistent—the need to be nothing like them.

The dragons descended beneath a sky choked with clouds, the sunlight dim and colorless as they touched down in a field hidden from the palace walls. The stone spires loomed in the distance. Avalynn's stomach churned. This was where she had been forced to be someone she wasn't. Now, back here again, she would decide who she would become.

They dismounted quickly, and Verona didn't hesitate. She turned toward the palace with fire in her eyes, her long, dark braid snapping around her. "The dungeon." She pointed. "Do whatever you will. I am going there."

Keeth was already nodding. "I know the way. I can get us in and out."

Avalynn studied Verona. She could see the fury barely contained beneath her composure. If she were Verona, she'd be doing the same thing.

"Go," Mateo said with no argument. "You and Keeth. Release all the prisoners and be careful."

Verona met his gaze, gratitude flickering once before hardening into resolve. She turned and was gone with Keeth at her side, disappearing into the tree line that bordered the palace grounds.

As they vanished, Avalynn's chest tightened. The dungeon remained a wound in this place. She prayed Verona's brother would still be there, and that he'd be okay.

"We will leave you now," *Izel* said. She lowered her head and held it there for a moment. "We wish you well."

"Thank you, *Izel*," Mateo said. He lowered his head too.

"Yes, thank you," Avalynn added. "For everything."

The dragons launched up and away, blending so quickly into the thick clouds they were near impossible to spot. And probably why their arrival had gone unnoticed.

Mateo faced Avalynn and Lirien. "That leaves the three of us." His gaze landed on Avalynn. "Where would the king and queen be this time of day?"

She looked up, shielding her eyes from the glare. The sun shone from the highest point in the sky. High noon. "They'll be at tea. In the garden."

Lirien's jaw tightened. "What if we are met with resistance?"

Mateo's answer came without hesitation. "I'll show them my fire," he said, his words harsh and bitter.

"I hope it doesn't come to that," Avalynn said.

"Wait a minute." Mateo's brow furrowed. "What exactly are you expecting to happen here, Avalynn?" His scale markings seemed to flare.

"I don't know." She shook her head. "I just don't want to be like them. We are better than that."

The thought settled heavy in her chest. She wasn't a Stromm. She had never been. But Mateo was. Even if he rejected the name, even if he called himself Vela and was raised by a different family, blood was blood. Would he listen to her?

"They will be met with the same consideration they gave you, me, and every soul in that dungeon," Mateo said, his words coming out tight. "Their fate is on them. Not on us."

She searched his eyes. If he burned the palace to the ground, what would that make him? What would that make them after everything they'd fought to undo? Not just for themselves, but for all of Faevenly?

Manny had said faith was a warrior. But could it also be tempered?

She placed her hand on Mateo's chest. "I want them to answer for what they have done. I do. But please, Mateo, we cannot become them."

He covered her hand with his and lowered it gently. "I can make no promises."

Her heart lurched. It wasn't the answer she wanted, but it also wasn't an outright rejection. What would he do when pushed to the brink?

"We need to move," Lirien hissed. "Before we are discovered."

Lirien ... Rien. Back in the Vale, she had grown to know him. They were close. Keeth too. What kind of choices would Lirien make standing beside his childhood friend? A lowborn with everything reason to want blood? She already knew the answer.

They darted quickly through the field, keeping low, grass brushing their legs as clouds dragged shadows across the ground. Avalynn led without thinking, memory guiding her feet. They skirted the palace walls until the scent of clipped hedges and blooming roses reached her.

They turned the corner and stopped short. A massive shape loomed ahead, broad shoulders filling the path. Greenish gray skin. Thick arms. Marina, the queen's personal guard. Avalynn swallowed. One swing from her could crush bone like kindling.

Mateo lifted both hands slowly. "Marina," he said, voice calm and steady. "It's me."

The troll blinked. "Prince Mateo?" she rumbled, confusion in her eyes. When her gaze landed on Avalynn, she drew in her chin. "Princess—uh, I mean, Avalynn?"

"Yes. It's me. It's a long story," Avalynn said. "But we need to—"

"Take down the king and queen," Mateo finished.

"This is an overthrow," Lirien added.

The troll studied them, her eyes lingering on their weapons. She stepped aside. "Tea's already been poured," she said flatly. "The queen is in a foul mood."

Avalynn nodded once. *Good.* She was letting them go by. Maybe there'd be no violence.

Lirien moved first, silent and fluid, already angling to the side. Mateo stepped half a pace ahead of Avalynn as they rounded the hedge.

The garden opened wide. A carved wooden table sat beneath a flowering arbor, porcelain cups steaming gently. The king lounged back in his chair, dressed in his casual silver, one leg crossed over the other. The queen sat perfectly straight, in royal purple, fingers curled around her teacup. Lily leaned forward, wearing a sparkling pink dress. She was laughing at something Avalynn couldn't hear. Two maidservants hovered nearby, platters in hand. There were no guards in sight.

The world stalled. The picture came into perfect view. This was where power lived, not in armor or battle-ments, but in the audacity to believe no one would dare challenge them. Avalynn had lived like that, not even realizing it.

Lily saw them first. Her smile dropped. Her eyes went wide. She screamed, sharp and piercing, like glass shattering in an empty ballroom.

The queen froze, teacup hovering inches from her red lips. The king lurched to his feet, chair scraping against stone.

"Avalynn!" Lily shrieked, pointing. "She's here! She's here!"

The king reached beneath the table and came up with his sword. "Traitor!" He charged, fury twisting his face into something ugly and unrecognizable. "I should have killed you when I had the chance!"

Mateo stepped forward to meet him. Fire rolled off him, not flame, not yet, but a dense, deliberate heat that pressed against her skin. Steel met steel as the king swung wildly, his strikes fueled by rage rather than skill. Mateo parried once, twice, boots grinding into stone as he easily held his ground.

A guard lunged from the hedges, blade flashing for Mateo's unguarded side. Lirien was already moving. He intercepted in a blur of motion, his daggers ringing as he turned the strike aside. He drove the guard back, pulling the fight away from Mateo in a flurry of sharp, efficient blows.

Guards poured in from the far archway, boots pounding, blades flashing as they sprinted toward the king.

Avalynn spun. Her sword came up. "Stand down!" Her voice cracked across the garden like a bell struck hard. "This is a Stromm matter!" she hollered, each word deliberate. "The king and prince alone!"

The guards slowed. Heads turned, eyes narrowed, a few of them faltered outright, expressions flickering. "Princess Avalynn," one of them uttered. "The Only One."

The king and queen might have discarded her, but these guards remembered. She had trained beside them, shedding blood, sweat, and tears under their watchful eye. And they knew the prophecy.

An older guard at the front lowered his blade. "Hold," he said roughly, not looking away from her. He had helped her hold her first sword when she was young.

The king snarled amidst the clashing steel. "Cowards! She is no princess!"

"She is," the older guard said, more to Avalynn than to the king. He shouted at the others. "Fall back! Let the king and prince settle this!"

Swords lowered, and Avalynn exhaled. It worked. They didn't want this anymore than she did.

She turned as Lirien disarmed the guard. Mateo struck next—one sharp kick to the king's chest. He stumbled, and Mateo's blade was already at his throat. They had him, and so easily. A chill crept over her. Too easily.

"Well, now, King Sylrick." Mateo smiled. "Are you ready to answer for what you have done?"

The king laughed, breath ragged. "Answer for what I have done?" He laughed again. "This is what ruling looks like. But you would not know." His eyes burned. "You are no Stromm."

"Pretender!" Lily screamed, her voice shrill.

The queen finally stood. Slowly. Carefully. Her gaze locked on Avalynn, cold and assessing. "So," she said. "You keep surviving, like rot that refuses to die."

Rot? Avalynn fumed but kept herself calm. "I keep surviving so I can end this."

The queen smiled, a smile Avalynn knew all too well. What was she up to?

Mateo glanced back, meeting Avalynn's eyes. The tip of his sword pressed against the king's throat. "Say the word." He was holding back for her.

Avalynn's hand gripped her sword's hilt. "Not yet."

The queen tilted her head. "Not yet?" She stepped forward, her movement both deliberate and terrifying.

Avalynn drew a steadying breath. She needed to choose her words carefully. "Mateo is prepared to incinerate you, the king, and this entire palace unless you relinquish the throne."

The queen raised a brow. "Ah, I understand. The once prince is now a dragon shifter. I see the scales." She stepped closer. "Before you proceed with this grand plan, do you and my son wish to know why I am not concerned?"

"I am not your son," Mateo snarled.

"Allow me to explain my relationship with Raelor," she offered, ignoring Mateo.

Raelor? The name hit Avalynn like an ice-cold splash of water. "There is no need," she said sharply. "He no longer exists."

"I know. But please, indulge me." She held her hands together in front of her. "My arrangement with him was quite simple. He did my will. He protected

Stromm Palace." She drew Lily close, fingers tightening around her shoulder. "In exchange, the king and I ensured his coffers overflowed, and they overflowed well."

"It does not matter!" Mateo shouted. Heat rolled off him in waves; Avalynn could feel it from where she stood. "He is gone, and I am here. Ready to burn this place to the ground!"

The queen barely spared him a glance. "Raelor and I also made arrangements for what would happen upon his untimely demise, should that come to pass."

The king laughed again, and a chill slid down Avalynn's spine. "What do you mean?"

"I mean a transfer of power," she said.

The queen flung out her hand. Her fingers curled. Binding magic snapped tight around Avalynn's throat, yanking her from the ground. Air vanished. Her feet kicked uselessly as everything narrowed to pressure and pain.

"Avalynn!" Mateo roared.

Fire erupted. Scarlet scales tore through skin in a rush of heat and fury. Wings burst wide, shredding trellises and stone alike. Mateo's mighty red dragon surged into the garden, the ground cracking beneath his weight as he reared back, flames gathering in his chest and exploding up into the air.

The king scrambled away. The queen didn't flinch. Her power grip on Avalynn only tightened. "The fire touches me, the king, or Lily, and Avalynn dies."

Silence fell. Fire bubbled in Mateo's throat but stayed trapped, held back by the one thing that had ever truly bound him. *Her.* Now, they were all doomed because of it.

Avalynn clawed at the invisible hold around her neck. Raelor's power might have passed to the queen, but she had her own power. She needed to use it. Now.

"Ava, get her!" Lirien hollered. "I know you can!"

Avalynn Stromm. Avalynn Strong. Ava of the Vale.

The names rose and fell through her mind like echoes in a long hall, each one carrying a piece of her. The infant girl switched at birth. The princess raised in a palace of cruelty and control. The hunter thrown into the Summit Range Hunt to prove her worth. The Valian trained in the Wild North. The girl who had loved Mateo fiercely enough to lose him and strong enough to find him again.

Everything she was, everything she had endured, led her here.

She had been raised a Stromm, shaped by their rules and punishments. Still, they had never owned her. In the Passing Place, when she had met her mother and father, the truth of that had settled in her bones. The love she felt there had not been sharp or demanding. It had not asked her to earn it or prove it. It had washed over her like warm rain after a long drought—quiet, steady, undeniable, and purely unconditional.

She pushed her anger and fear aside. She reached for that love. She needed it now more than ever.

Avalynn closed her eyes. The pressure at her throat still burned, but she no longer fought it. She let it pass through her, like a whisper. Then she reached inward, not for the memory of the sword, not for rage or even survival. She reached for the warmth she had always carried without understanding it, the hum beneath her skin, the steady pulse that had flared in moments of desperation and vanished before she could name it.

She reached for love.

The power unfurled, answering her at last. It spread through her like sunlight through water, gentle and radiant. Avalynn opened her eyes. She was no longer standing on the ground. She hovered, weightless, suspended in a space that felt both vast and intimate—neither here nor gone, but between.

Before her appeared Lady Sonia. Her edges were soft and luminous, as though the magic boundary itself still clung to her. Were they somehow back there? Or was this Sonia's spirit form? Did it even matter? Lady Sonia's presence felt like standing at the heart of a blessing.

"What is happening?" Avalynn whispered.

Sonia smiled. "Look."

The garden snapped into view, not moving but frozen, like a moment caught between heartbeats. Mateo's dragon held his position, scarlet scales gleaming, fire roiling in his chest. Lirien was poised to strike, daggers raised. The king reached for his fallen blade. Lily's mouth was open in a silent scream. The queen stood unmoving, her grip locked around Avalynn's throat. And there, at the center of it all, blazed Avalynn's body. Blue light erupted from her skin, pouring outward in waves.

"I'm doing it," Avalynn uttered, awe threading her voice. "I'm finally using my power."

"Yes," Sonia said softly. "You are." Sonia stepped

closer, her gaze steady and unflinching. "Now is the moment to finish it."

Avalynn drew in a long, steady breath and held it. Warmth flooded her, spreading through her like sunlight on the brightest day, and her magic flowed. It aligned every fractured piece of her—fae and human, past and present, storm and stillness.

Finish it. She exhaled. She fell back into herself, and time roared into motion.

Pain crushed her throat as the queen's hold tightened —cold, invasive, furious at being challenged. It burned with borrowed will, with Raelor's hunger still clinging to it.

Avalynn answered. Blue light gathered in her chest, steady and deliberate, drawing inward instead of flaring out. It wrapped around the spell and held.

You do not belong to her, Avalynn hissed in her mind.

The queen's magic resisted, tightening, biting deeper, trying to force obedience through pain. Avalynn's magic refused. It unraveled the spell strand by corrupted strand, tearing Raelor's power from the queen until the spell collapsed.

The magic severed. The queen gasped. Avalynn dropped to the ground, air tearing back into her lungs as the blue power streamed home, the radiant threads curling back into her blood and bones where they belonged.

Above her, Mateo reared, wings flaring wide, fire boiling in his chest. A deafening roar ripped from him— rage, terror, and restraint all bound together. Avalynn held out her hand. "I'm okay," she said to him.

The queen stared dumbstruck, flinging her fingers.

"No more, Lysandra," Avalynn said, rising to her feet. "That power was never yours."

The queen staggered. She clutched Lily in front of her, like a shield now. Lily's face had paled. Her chin trembled, but her eyes still burned, sharp and furious, as if hatred were the only thing she had ever been taught to hold.

The king scrambled backward. He reached for his fallen blade and found a ring of steel closing in, the guards holding steady.

Avalynn raised her chin. "You built a crown on fear and called it destiny." Her gaze never left the queen's. "You called obedience love. You used violence as a shield." Her voice hardened. "No longer."

Mateo's dragon lowered his massive head. Scarlet scales gleamed beneath the gray sky, fire pulsing behind his teeth.

"You don't have to anymore," she said into his mind.

The fire guttered. With a sound like dying wind, the dragon folded into himself, heat collapsing inward as scales receded. Wings vanished. Mateo dropped to one knee, breath tearing from his lungs, scorched red-scaled tatters clinging to his body. He stayed there for a moment, himself again.

"We're not killing them?" Lirien asked.

"No." Avalynn shook her head. "We are not."

Mateo rose, chest heaving. His hand drifted to the opal necklace at his throat, the one Sonia had pressed into Manny's hand. Avalynn met his gaze, and in it, she saw the same decision taking shape.

The gem caught the light as if waking. "We banish them," Mateo said.

The king let out a brittle laugh. "You would not—"

"To the human realm," Mateo continued, voice steady as stone. "Where they will be ordinary." He shot a look at the queen. "No power. No throne. Nothing but their own hands to survive with."

The queen's lips pressed into a thin line. She did not beg. She never would. But Lily stuck out her tongue at Mateo and then Avalynn, eyes bright with venom. "I would rather go there than kneel to either of you."

Avalynn nodded. "Then go. All of you."

Mateo's fingers brushed against the necklace. With a sharp tug, the opalescent gem slipped free of its chain and lifted, hovering midair as light gathered inside it.

"The shimmer portal," Avalynn whispered. She knew the story. Her great grandsires, Princess Celyse Strong of Strong Haven and the human witch Julio Avila from the human realm, met through a portal—one like this.

Mateo's hands brushed the portal edges and pulled. The hazy, glowing light stretched. It grew wider, its edges alive with a radiant sheen. Beyond the glow sprawled not darkness, but a pale, endless horizon.

"No!" the king bellowed.

"Stop!" Lily screeched, grasping at the queen's dress skirt.

Avalynn's power answered, warming at her fingertips. They would not go willingly; she could see that. She needed to send them. Blue light surged through her hands, warm and bright. It wrapped around her wrists, her arms, her chest, humming with recognition.

The guards shuffled out of the way. Avalynn moved in. She lifted her hand, and with a single, sweeping motion, she released her magic. It flowed outward like a tide, lifting the king, the queen, and Lily from the ground in a rush of wind and force. The queen reached out, face contorted with anger and agony. A glowing burst of blue light ignited, then they were gone.

The shimmer shuddered, edges shrinking, as the opal dimmed and returned to the necklace. Avalynn lowered her hand. The blue light faded. And for the first time, everything felt balanced.

CHAPTER THIRTY

M ateo glanced around, his body trembling all over. Shattered teacups and broken stone littered the ground. Burn marks charred the hedges and walls; the arbor and trellises were torn apart, splintered and ruined. He strode to Avalynn's side and held her close. She had done it. Everything was finally over, but Mateo's work repairing what he had done, both physically and emotionally, was only beginning.

Keeth emerged from the far end of the garden. Verona came next, her arm wrapped around someone who shared her same features. He stood tall, his face gaunt and his body rail thin. Close behind them trailed Selene Baffin. Red hair matted, dress soiled. His stomach clenched. She did not deserve what he had done to her and her family. None of them did. Could he ever make amends? Or would some things have to be carried?

"You missed the show," Lirien said lightly.

"Nope," Keeth replied with a whistle. "We saw it."

Verona's brother swallowed, then bowed his head to Avalynn. She returned the gesture.

Keeth raised a brow at Mateo. "Where did you send them?"

An image had risen in Mateo's mind the moment the portal opened. A place in the human realm his father had told him about when he was young. Red sand stretching to the horizon. Jagged stone. Wind howling through barren crags. A land stripped of beauty and comfort. A place where survival demanded humility. Mateo would have loved it there, but the Stromms would hate it. Each day, the barren landscape would remind them of who they no longer were.

"The human realm," Mateo said at last. "To a place much like the Sublands."

Silence followed, and then Keeth laughed. "Poetic and fitting."

Whisperings rippled through the garden. The freed prisoners gathered in small knots, voices low and disbelieving. Guards stood uncertainly, some with their swords still drawn, others lowering them.

Avalynn took Mateo's hand. "You need to say something to them."

He exhaled slowly. He had never wanted the Stromm name, or the crown, or the palace, or the weight of blood-soaked history. Yet this was his legacy to answer for since he was the only remaining one. But not just him. He had been born a Stromm. Avalynn had been raised as one.

He squeezed her hand. "Not me. Us. Let's use this moment to forge a new legacy."

Her grip tightened, grounding him. "We don't patch what was broken," she said quietly. "We build something that never needed the Stromm crown at all."

His mouth curved. "Good," he said. "I don't intend to leave their shadow standing."

He met her hardened gaze. "Together," she said, and this time it was a vow, not an agreement.

They stepped forward. The movement drew attention. Murmurs faded. Even the guards straightened, attention snapping to them.

"I stand here before you a Stromm by blood," Mateo said, his voice clear and steady, "but a Vela by choice, a lowborn from the Sublands." His gaze moved through the crowd—prisoners, guards, faces marked by fear and hope alike. "And I stand with Avalynn by my side. Raised a Stromm, but the last surviving member of House Strong of Strong Haven—the Only One."

"We saw the power," someone said.

"We did," others murmured.

Avalynn swallowed. "Power isn't who I am." She looked up at Mateo. "I am a daughter of Strong Haven, of Faevenly, wanting to do right by the land we share, and by the people who live on it."

Mateo drew a breath. "I know I have a great deal of work ahead of me. To answer for what was done by this crown." His voice didn't falter. "And by me."

A few heads dipped. Others watched him carefully. Listening.

"The Stromms taught me that power meant control," Mateo went on. "That fear was obedience. That silence was loyalty." He paused, then turned to Avalynn. "But what I learned from my human father, from the Sublands, and from Avalynn ... is that real power protects. It does not take. It does not break. It stands between harm and those who cannot protect themselves. It chooses what is right—even when it costs."

Avalynn's fingers tightened around his. "This realm does not need another crown built on fear," Mateo said. "It needs caretakers. Builders. Those willing to choose differently." He lowered his head, not in submission, but in promise. "That is the legacy we intend to forge. Together."

The garden did not erupt. It shifted. Shoulders eased, stances relaxed. Mateo's gaze moved through the crowd, drawn to a familiar face near the edge of the garden. Maid Penny stood frozen in place, tears tracking down her cheeks. Her hands were clasped beneath her chin as if in prayer. Mateo met her eyes and inclined his head. Penny's lips trembled. Then she nodded back, pressing her hands together tighter, hope written plain across her face.

"What happens now?" one of the guards asked. "What becomes of Stromm Palace?"

Mateo didn't answer right away. He looked at the palace—the towers, the banners, the stone that had watched the Stromms rule through fear. "No new crown," he whispered under his breath to Avalynn, the idea striking him in his heart as the right move. This was their moment to make a real change.

She tilted her head, then smiled and nodded. "Yes," she said in a low voice, tightening her hand around his.

"There will be no new crown," he announced loudly.

The words settled slowly, like the first winter snow. "Faevenly does not need a high throne deciding the fate of every province." His gaze swept across the crowd. "Power will return to the provinces, including the Sublands."

"And Stromm Palace?" the guard pressed.

Mateo's jaw set. He itched to burn the place to the ground, but was that the right move? He didn't want to destroy anymore. "It will no longer be a seat of rule," he finally said. "Let it become something else. A place of peace and gathering. A record of what was. A reminder of what we chose to leave behind."

A servant in the back raised a fist. "No more high kings! No more high queens!"

This time, the crowd cheered. Then a voice cut through the din. "What of the sins of the dark prince?"

The dark prince. He gulped. That was him, a title he had earned while consumed by shadow magic. Mateo exchanged a glance with Avalynn as someone from the back moved forward. Dark hair, dark eyes. Isabelle, the Soltec girl. The young Oathrider.

"Who will exact punishment on the dark prince?" she asked.

His first thought spilled from his lips. "You will."

Gasps rang out. Mateo stepped forward before Avalynn could stop him. The garden seemed to lean inward as he crossed the broken stone, each step measured with purpose. When he reached Isabelle, he lowered himself to one knee.

"I accept whatever judgment you deem just," Mateo said.

"No!" Avalynn cut in sharply, stepping forward. "He was under the influence of dark magic—bound to him by Raelor at the order of the king and queen. I saw it. I lived it. I was a victim of it." Her voice steadied. "That magic is gone now. Forever. I swear it."

Mateo did not turn, did not look at her. His jaw tightened as he stared at the stone beneath Isabelle's boots. He was ready for whatever fate the Sun, Moon, and Stars had written for him. Perhaps his luck—if it had ever been luck—had finally run out.

Isabelle lifted her blade. Several voices cried out. Keeth's. Lirien's. Someone sobbed. Then Isabelle let the weapon fall. Steel struck stone and stayed there.

"I saw the Only One's power," she said evenly. "The blue light. I trust it." Isabelle's gaze shifted to Avalynn. "I trust *her*."

Avalynn placed her hand over her heart and exhaled. "Thank you."

Mateo rose to his feet.

Isabelle retrieved her blade and turned away, walking out of the garden without another word. The crowd began to breathe again. Lirien and Keeth moved in close at Mateo's sides.

Then a shriek rang out. Selene charged for Mateo, a guard's sword held high. Mateo didn't move. He deserved this. She swung the blade wildly, her aim veering at the last second. She couldn't do it.

"You will pay for what you have done, dark prince! Someday, somehow!" She dropped the blade. "But not by me." She wiped the tears from her face, spun, and walked away.

Mateo's beating heart calmed. The dark prince would have ended her on the spot. But he wasn't the dark prince anymore.

Keeth moved his axe to his shoulder. "Want me to have a word with her?"

"No," he said with a wave of his hand, watching her disappear through the crowd. "Let my fate be whatever it will be."

He avoided Avalynn's probing eyes. She didn't know what he had done to the stewards, to Selene's sister, and how he had banished Selene to the dungeon. He added it to the long list of things he needed to tell her, later.

"A terrifying dragon shifter," Lirien muttered, clapping him on the shoulder, "I think your fate will be just fine."

Mateo huffed a soft laugh. "Maybe." *Hopefully*.

Soft light from the cloudy day filtered through the tall windows. Mateo, Avalynn, Keeth, and Lirien gathered with Marina and Penny in the Great Hall. The air felt fresh and light, like the palace recognized the shadows were gone.

Mateo and Avalynn sat together on one side of the long table. Across from them sat Marina, broad hands folded carefully on top, and Penny, spine straight and eyes bright. Keeth and Lirien stayed standing.

Mateo's voice carried boldly in the open hall. "I think

our first order of business should be giving this place a new name."

Penny blinked. "A name, my lord?"

"Not *lord*," Mateo said gently. "Just Mateo." He glanced around the room. "Yes. A new name. The palace was built to intimidate. To rule. To remind everyone who held the power." His jaw tightened, then loosened. "That power is gone."

Marina shifted. "Names matter," she rumbled. "They tell folk what a place expects of them."

Avalynn smiled at her. "Exactly."

Penny hesitated, then lifted her chin. "What about something that remembers what was lost but doesn't glorify it?" Her fingers twisted together. "Something honest and real."

Keeth leaned back against a pillar. "The Palace of Reckoning?"

Lirien winced. "That sounds like somewhere you go to die."

Mateo's eyes drifted to the S carved into the far wall. It would need to be removed, along with a host of other things. "I don't want fear living here at all. Or death."

Avalynn's hand brushed his. "What about something that speaks to repair?"

"Or hope," Penny added softly, surprising herself. "Or light."

Mateo considered the young maiden. She had always been so kind to him, even when he did not deserve it. "Light," he repeated. The word settled into the air as if it belonged there.

Marina nodded. "Light leads people away from the darkness."

A smile spread across Penny's face. "First Light," she said. "The dawn after darkness."

Keeth nodded. "Has a certain ring to it."

"Sounds good to me," Lirien added.

"First Light," Avalynn repeated. "I love it."

"First Light, it is," Mateo said. The name felt solid and right. "Keeth, will you send ravens? Let every province know what transpired here today. Let them know First Light will be a safe haven for any who need one."

"I will do it," he said.

Mateo straightened. "Which brings me to the second matter." He turned fully to Marina and Penny. "This place is still mine. But I'm trusting the two of you to keep it while I am gone."

They froze. "Us?" Marina echoed.

"And Keeth," Mateo added, glancing at his stocky friend. "As protector and blade. First Light will serve as a place open to all as a reminder of what we chose not to repeat."

Penny pressed a hand to her mouth. "Thank you, my lor—I mean, Mateo. And you too, Avalynn. Thank you both so much."

Marina stood and bowed. "We won't fail you," she said.

Keeth clapped his hands. "I accept! And with that settled, where are you two going?"

Mateo took Avalynn's hand. "The Sublands." A statement and a question. He held his breath, waiting for her answer.

She smiled, slow and sure. "Home," she agreed.

He squeezed her hand, then turned back to the others. "We will visit," he continued. "Help where we can. Listen when needed." He glanced around the hall one last time. "But we won't live here."

"I won't live here either," Lirien added. "But I think I'll stay a while, to help get things settled."

"And to be a thorn in my side," Keeth grumbled.

Mateo had no doubt about that.

Mateo and Avalynn emerged from the double doors of First Light dressed for the road. Gone were the scorched, tattered clothes and the muck and grime of battle. Mateo wore dark traveling leathers, worn-in and practical, the kind he'd trusted long before the Summit Range Hunt and crowns and dragons had ever entered his life. Avalynn stood beside him in a similar style, wearing deep blue and gray riding clothes. They each wore swords at their hips, not as a threat, but as a promise to defend those who needed defending.

Silverhoof pranced into the courtyard, hooves striking stone with bright, eager rhythm, silver mane catching the light. At her heels bounded Stormshroud. She launched herself forward in great, joyous arcs, paws skidding, tail whipping, the sheer force of her happiness nearly sending her tumbling end over end before she corrected and sprang again. Did she know that battles were over?

Avalynn laughed and dropped to one knee in time for

the wolfbeast to barrel into her, nearly knocking her flat. "Well, there you are," she said breathlessly. Stormshroud huffed, licking her cheek. Avalynn rose and leaned her forehead against Silverhoof's warm neck. "You too," she murmured.

Mateo watched from a step back. Would Stormy ever greet him that way again? As if sensing his thoughts, her ears twitched. Then she bounded toward him. She launched herself up, paws landing heavy against his chest as he laughed and staggered back half a step, catching her instinctively.

He wrapped his arms around her thick neck as fur, warmth, and familiar weight pressed into him. "Thank you, Stormy," he murmured. "For not forgetting me this time."

Stormshroud huffed and butted her head beneath his chin as if to say she never would.

They rode home together. Avalynn settled easily behind Mateo on Silverhoof's back, arms wrapped around his waist. Stormshroud paced alongside them for a time, disappearing and reappearing like a living shadow.

The land changed as it always had. Green fields gave way to red dirt. Stone rose where trees thinned. The air grew drier, sharper. *Home.*

They didn't announce their arrival. They didn't need to. Manny was already running when Silverhoof crested the ridge.

"Mateo!" His voice broke on the name as he crossed the distance with surprising speed, arms open wide.

Mateo barely had time to dismount before he was

pulled into a fierce embrace, Manny's hands gripping the back of his coat as if letting go were no longer an option.

"Father," Mateo choked out.

He squeezed tight. "You're back," Manny whispered, pressing his forehead to Mateo's shoulder. Then he pulled Avalynn in as well. "You're both back."

Camilla and Floriana were there too, laughing and crying as they rushed forward. The embrace widened until all of them were pressed together, breathless, warm, and genuine.

Camilla scrubbed at her eyes and gave Mateo a crooked smile. "You look awful," she said affectionately. "Which means you lived." Her gaze flicked to the dragon markings along his neck. "I kind of like those."

Mateo huffed a quiet laugh, the tightness in his chest finally loosening. "Thank you," he said. "Yes. I survived." He lifted his eyes to Avalynn, finding her gaze across the small, chaotic circle of warmth and noise and love. "We both did."

He squeezed Avalynn's hand, grounding himself in the truth of it.

He had left this place chasing survival, chasing worth, chasing a prize he thought had to be earned through blood, fire, and victory. He had gone to the Summit Range Hunt to prove himself, to win something tangible for his family, for the Sublands.

But this ... this was the reward he had never known to ask for.

Home. Family. Love.

CHAPTER THIRTY-ONE

Manny's home smelled like savory spices, warm bread, and something sweet. Avalynn sat at the small table beside Mateo, her knees brushing against his beneath the wood. The conversation drifted in and out between Sublands news of Lady Verona's return with her brother, Adrius, and debates over whether the delicious soup Manny called *caldo* could even contain too much spice.

For once, there was no urgency. No prophecy humming in Avalynn's bones. No sword waiting to be claimed or destroyed. No looking over her shoulder. Only warmth and laughter existed in the space, like bright sunshine after the darkest storm.

When the plates were cleared and the fire burned low, Manny rose from his chair and clapped his hands. "Come on," he said, eyeing her and Mateo and nodding toward the door. "Let's take a walk."

"Have fun," Camilla said with a chuckle.

Avalynn exchanged a look with Mateo, amused and curious, before pulling on her cloak. The night air was cool and clean, the deep dark sky scattered with stars. Manny led them down the path and beyond the cluster of homes, boots crunching softly against the crushed red dirt as they walked.

He stopped in front of a small house set slightly apart from the others. It stood sturdy with a low roof and red brick. Light-colored smoke drifted skyward from the single chimney. Soft light glowed from within through the square-shaped windows.

Mateo tilted his head. "Who lives here?"

With a smile, Manny clasped his hands behind his back. "You and Avalynn."

Mateo blinked. "What?"

"Yes," Manny said, grinning now. "I was hoping you'd both come back here after everything." He shrugged. "So, I secured it. The girls and I have been fixing it up for you. I hope you both like it."

Avalynn's chest tightened. Was this really happening? "Manny..."

He pulled her into a hug before she could finish. Then Mateo, too. "You belong here," Manny said. "Both of you." He released them and stepped back. "Now go on in and get settled. I will see you both tomorrow."

Warmth swirled inside the home. The small sitting room oozed with cozy comfort. Firelight flickered low in the hearth, casting soft shadows across the thick clay walls. Handwoven rugs covered the stone floor, soft beneath her boots, their patterns simple yet elegant. A deep sofa sat across from the fire with a folded blanket draped over one arm.

Avalynn's chest tightened. "This is so beautiful."

"It really is," Mateo said, eyeing the place with wonder.

A narrow doorway led into the bedchamber. Avalynn stepped through. The bed was wide and solid, built low, layered with thick blankets and pale-yellow sheets that smelled of clean linen and open air. Moonlight spilled through a single cracked window, painting the quilt in silver and shadow. A small wooden table nestled beside the bed with a lantern already lit, its flame turned low.

Her fingers brushed the edge of the soft bed. "I can't believe all this."

He smiled. "Me either."

She took Mateo's hand and wandered past the bedchamber into a modest washroom. Towels were neatly folded beside the basin, with water already waiting. At the rear of the house, the cookroom was stocked. Bread was wrapped in cloth on the small table, butter set close by.

Everything here felt intentional, thoughtful, like someone had believed they would come home. She turned toward Mateo, emotion rising too quickly to contain. "Everything is so perfect."

He swallowed, his gaze lingering on the space before looking at her with something heavier in his eyes. "There's something I need to say."

He took her hand and led her back to the sitting room. He drew her close, settling her in front of him. She tipped her face up to meet his gaze.

"What is it?" she asked.

His thumbs brushed slow circles along her hips. "I never really thought I had much of a future," he admitted softly. "Then, I met you."

Her hands slid up his chest, over the familiar rise of muscle and heat. "We hated each other," she said with a laugh. "And then we didn't."

For a long moment, neither of them moved. The fire crackled. The house settled around them, holding their silence like a promise. Mateo drew back enough to look at her, and Avalynn saw something different in his eyes now. It wasn't fire or fury, but a deep, aching vulnerability that made her pulse flutter, her heart reaching for him the way it always had.

He took one of her hands in both of his, turning it palm-up. His lips pressed gently into the center, a kiss so intimate a flurry of butterflies unleashed in her stomach. Slowly, he lowered himself to one knee on the rug.

Her breath caught in her throat.

"Avalynn," he said, his voice steady but threaded with emotion he wasn't trying to hide. "I have done terrible things. I have hurt people." His gaze never left hers. "I have hurt you." His voice faltered. "I know I don't deserve you," he went on quietly. "I know I am not worthy." He held her hand over his racing heart. "But I cannot breathe without you."

Her knees nearly gave way, emotion stealing their strength. She tightened her grip on his fingers, anchoring herself in the truth of him, the truth of this moment.

His eyes were fierce and unflinching. "I choose you, Avalynn Strong, every day, for as long as I exist. I am asking you to please choose me." His voice softened, raw and bare. "Will you walk this life with me? Will you stay with me forever?"

Tears slipped free as she dropped to her knees before him. She cupped his face in her hands, thumbs brushing his cheeks.

"Yes," she whispered. "Forever, and even longer. I will always stay with you."

He kissed her, slow and reverent. The world narrowed to the space between their breaths, to the quiet certainty of love found and chosen. When they finally pulled apart, neither of them spoke. They didn't need to.

"Come here," he murmured.

Mateo led her toward the bedchamber. He stopped inside the doorway and drew her close again. They kissed once more, slower this time, deeper, the kind of kiss that carried burning desire. Avalynn felt it everywhere, in the way his hands trembled slightly at her waist, in the way he exhaled against her mouth like a prayer finally answered.

Her fingers slipped beneath the hem of his tunic, warm skin meeting warm skin, and Mateo stilled—only for a heartbeat—before his hands came up to mirror hers. They moved together naturally, without hesitation, easing layers away as if there were no past, no wounds, no fear left between them, only trust.

Fabric pooled at their feet. His mouth traced her jaw, her throat, each kiss unhurried, lingering, as though he was learning her again in this new life they had chosen, with this new body he had been given. Avalynn's hands roamed over his shoulders, his chest, over familiar muscle and heat, marveling at his dragon markings and grounding herself in the reality of him—here, alive, hers.

He guided her back toward the bed, never breaking the connection between them. They fell onto the soft linens together, laughter mingling with breath, kisses deepening as the world outside the little house slipped quietly away.

Mateo braced himself over her, forehead pressed to hers. "I love you," he whispered, the words spilling free as if they had always been waiting, had always belonged to her.

"I love you," she answered, her hands framing his face, her body fitting to his as if it had been made for him.

The night held them close. Wrapped in warmth and softly spoken promises, they finally let themselves rest.

Together.

CONCLUSION OF BOOK THREE

The veil has fallen.
The bloodlines have been forged.

Discover the beginning of the legend in *Fae Away*.
Because every prophecy starts with a single choice.

Start reading *Fae Away* now.

NOTE FOR THE READER

(Only read AFTER you've finished the book!)

Thank you so much for reading *A Legacy Forged*, the epic conclusion to the *Bloodlines Legacy Series*! I hope this ending felt as rich and satisfying to you as it did to me! *cue the tears*

So what can I say about this series and its conclusion? LOTS! But first, let me begin by explaining a few things about how I write. I'm two things in equal measure—a discovery writer and an intuitive writer. I have big ideas and concepts for my characters; but mostly, they tell me what they want to do. More often than not, things fall into place without huge amounts of planning.

Let me give you an example.

When we first met Mateo in *A Storm Rises*, he was sitting atop Spirit Butte, looking out at the red landscape and thinking, *"Everything is on fire, and so am I."* That one line became his theme throughout the series—a theme that happened organically, as I didn't even know when I wrote the first book what would ultimately happen to Mateo. And then, when he shifted into a red-scaled dragon in *A Legacy Forged*, his theme came full circle with, *"I AM FIRE!"* Shivers raced across my skin when he said that. I mean... WOW!

When we first met Avalynn in *A Storm Rises*, she was doing her best to be a loyal daughter, but she never truly fit in with the Stromm family. And when her memory was taken by the veil magic, she had to figure out who she really was—not just her name, but herself. Did I even know she wouldn't need the sword to step into her power? Not exactly. But Manny knew!

Okay, deep breath—let's talk about Manny. *cue even more tears* Traeliorn Letormis, aka Leto, said in *A Shadow Falls* that Manny was the best person he knew. He wasn't kidding. Manny is first introduced in the *Fae Bloodlines Series* as Julio's faithful best friend, and he went through A LOT with Julio. In this trilogy, he goes through even more with Avalynn and Mateo. But through it all, he never loses his faith or his belief in the power of love and family. He truly represents the best of us. I had no idea he would become such an important presence in my stories—and I love him dearly.

Another person I need to mention is Lady Sonia. *wipes eyes* I did not even know how important she would be to my characters and to Faevenly as a whole. I was so sad when she met her end, but her sacrifice was the only way to take out Raelor. And she knew it all along. But she is not gone gone, she is a part of Faevenly now. Will we see her again? Maybe! But don't quote me on that, lol.

So what's in store for Faevenly next? I've left many doors open for new stories to be told. Every province in the realm will need to be rebuilt, including the Wild North and the Soltierra South. Not to mention, Lirien, Keeth, Marina, and Penny now have First Light to run. And let's not forget those awesome Oathriders. There's so much richness in these characters and places, and I can't wait to discover where the story leads next.

If you loved this series, please consider recommending it to your family and friends—word of mouth truly goes a long way. And if you're able, I'd be so grateful if you'd leave a review on your favorite e-retailer site. It means more to authors than you might imagine.

Lastly, I'd love for you to stay in touch. You can sign up for my newsletter at www.RoseGarciaBooks.com/newsletter to receive updates, news, and behind-the-scenes extras.

Again, thank you so much for reading my stories!

With all my love and gratitude,

Rose

ALSO BY ROSE GARCIA

BLOODLINES LEGACY SERIES

(sequel series to Fae Bloodlines)

A Storm Rises, book 1

A Shadow Falls, book 2

A Legacy Forged, book 3

FAE BLOODLINES SERIES

(prequel series to Bloodlines Legacy)

Fae Away, book 1

Fae Fractured, book 2

Fae Hunted, book 3

Fae Rising, book 4

FINAL LIFE SERIES

Final Life, book 1

Final Stand, book 2

Final Death, book 3

First Life, book 4

ABOUT THE AUTHOR

Rose Garcia is a USA Today bestselling author and screenwriter known for crafting heart-stopping fantasy stories where belief is power, love defies all, and hope burns brightest. Magic is real in her world—and the only thing more dangerous than a broken heart... is a hopeful one.

A lawyer turned writer, Rose weaves stories of complicated romance, powerful families, deep-rooted friendships, and ancestral magic drawn from her Mexican American heritage. Her Latinx heroes are driven by bold hearts, forced to confront tangled destinies and make impossible choices.

When she's not writing, you can find her designing escape rooms for her husband, obsessing over fantasy shows, traveling, or hanging out with her needy and precious rescue dogs.

Rose lives in Houston, Texas, and believes tacos are a core food group—because well, they are.

Welcome to the Garciaverse!
For more on Rose, visit www.rosegarciabooks.com.

Join Rose's FB Group!
www.facebook.com/groups/TheRoseBudSociety
Subscribe to Rose's newsletter!
www.rosegarciabooks.com/newsletter

facebook.com/AuthorRoseGarcia

instagram.com/rosegarciabooks

tiktok.com/@rosegarciabooks

bookbub.com/authors/rose-garcia